RIGHT TO KILL

JOHN BARLOW

ONE PLACE. MANY STORIES

HQ
An imprint of HarperCollins*Publishers* Ltd
1 London Bridge Street
London SE1 9GF

www.harpercollins.co.uk

HarperCollins*Publishers*
1st Floor, Watermarque Building, Ringsend Road
Dublin 4, Ireland

This edition 2021

1
First published in Great Britain by
HQ, an imprint of HarperCollins*Publishers* Ltd 2021

Copyright © John Barlow 2021

John Barlow asserts the moral right to be identified as the author of this work. A catalogue record for this book is available from the British Library.

ISBN: HB: 978-0-00-840885-5
TPB: 978-0-00-840886-2

This boo ᵀᴹ paper

For m⟨ ⟩green

This bo ⟨ ⟩orway

100% Renewable Electricity at CPI Group (UK) Ltd

For Stef

1

It happens so quickly. You've got no idea.

Imagine you're standing somewhere. A bus stop, a quiet road, the park. Somewhere familiar. Then the whole world tilts. There's a massive rush, like the first breathless lunge down a roller-coaster. You're carried forward, careering over yourself, unstoppable, so fast you can hardly think.

A second and it's done. You're back where you started, and everything's the same.

Only everything's different.

It happens so quickly.

Tuesday evening. I've taken a short stretch of road that runs beneath an old railway line just out of town. The high walls are damp, the Victorian brickwork almost black, forming a kind of semi-enclosed underpass.

There's no more than forty or fifty yards of it, including a sharp bend, right beneath where the trains used to go. Not many people come this way. It's obsolete, little more than a nuisance for town planners.

I like it. For the time it takes to go from one end to the other, the world feels empty, a silent snapshot of times gone by, not a soul to break the stillness.

But tonight there's a car. Maroon, a bit tatty. It's parked up on the kerb, just after the bend. I move out and walk in the middle of the road, give it a wide berth. There's a guy at the wheel. He's alone and he's watching me in his mirror. He has a baseball cap pulled down, but I can see his eyes.

He lowers his head as I approach. It looks as if he might be in some sort of trouble. I slow down as I get level with him.

Then he turns his head and looks at me.

Now I know why he's there.

I'm not scared. When you've dealt with enough people like this you stop being afraid. But I'm curious. I want to know what he's going to do now. So I stay where I am, in the middle of the road.

He lets the electric window down, looking straight at me as it opens.

'Are you OK?' I ask, good citizen voice.

He nods very slightly. Nasty eyes. They all have the same eyes. Doesn't matter how old they are. And this one's not old. Mid-twenties, scrawny body, bony face.

'Good!' I say, upbeat, friendly.

I want him to know I'm not scared.

His eyes are small and ugly, animal eyes.

'You need somethin'?' he asks.

I shake my head.

He exhales, looks away, and even his boredom seems evil. It annoys me, that casual gesture. But it's also meant to be threatening. I get ready to go. I've had enough.

'Right, great!' I say. 'I'll be off!'

Screw him. I'll get a photo of his number plate when I'm at the top of the road, up by the entrance to Tesco's car park. The police can have him.

'Yeah, go fuck yourself,' he says, a spasm of irritation running through his angular body.

I freeze.

'I... I'm sorry?'

I feel myself moving towards the car.

'Go on. Leg it, yer nosy twat.'

The world lurches violently. My body floods with something ice-cold and utterly terrifying. I feel myself being carried at unimaginable speed to a place I've never been. It only takes a second.

'I was worried,' I explain, moving closer.

My hand reaches out, fingertips touching the roof of the car.

This can't be right, but it feels right. I don't know why. Everything's changed. That's all I know.

'Worried,' I repeat.

My other hand slips inside my jacket. I lean in until my body touches the driver's door. What am I searching for? What am I doing?

Then I find it. Between my fingers. A pencil. I can feel its smooth hexagonal shaft, its strange steely rigidity. This can't be right. But it must be. My world twists irrevocably on its axis. My roller-coaster moment.

'I... just...' I say, leaning further in to him.

But he's not listening. He's not even looking at me. He's looking straight ahead, like I'm not there.

The point enters just above his eyeball, taking part of the upper eyelid with it. Easily, easily it goes in. Shockingly so. And shockingly fast, although in fact I'm calm, not shocked at all.

His face hardly changes. There's the slightest expression of surprise. But mild surprise, no more than that. It might be that he remains exactly as he is, and the lack of horror is somehow expressive; peaceful, like he knows that this is what needs to be done, that I have no choice.

The pencil slides right in.

There must have been some force. But I can't recall.

When I let go only a couple of inches are sticking out. With the ball of my hand I push it in all the way.

Then I wait, resting against the car.

When his body starts to sag I know it's over.

That's how it happens.

So quickly.

You've got no idea just how quickly it can all change.

Everything.

THURSDAY

2

Joe Romano reached for his mug and took a gulp. The coffee was stone-cold. He put it down on his desk amid a pile of case files. Break-ins mainly. There was another case open on his screen. Just admin for the insurance adjusters at this stage. Fiddly paperwork. Everything's got to be right. This last one must have taken him, what, an hour?

He clicked 'save', logged out of the system and looked across the open-plan operations room. The shift was winding down. People rose from their seats, attending to aching lumbar regions, exchanging friendly words with night-shift officers and support staff, who'd just begun to trickle in.

'Joe! Fancy a drink?'

A young man in a trim grey suit grinned. The question was ironic. Nothing new there. A few people looked over at Joe with a mixture of amusement and pity.

'Or a bit of unpaid overtime? More your style, eh, Joe?'

Detective Constable Gwyn Merchant was one rank lower, and a decade younger. But you'd never have known. Cocksure with a wardrobe to match. The kind of guy who rarely got creases in the trousers of his Paul Smith suits.

He came across and handed Joe a slip of paper.

'*Misper*. Only been gone a couple of days.'

'Adult?'

'Friggin' scag,' Merchant said, laughing, already walking away, thinking about his first pint. 'His mammy rang it in. Worried sick. Bet she's the only one.'

'This is everything?' Joe asked, looking at the paper in his hand.

Merchant stopped, turned, as if the question was slightly impertinent.

'Mum wasn't making much sense when she called, apparently. I was his last arresting officer. So they sent it through to me.'

'Right. I'll look into it.'

'Piece o' shit. He'll be off his tits in a gutter,' Merchant said as he went back to his desk. 'Or *dead* in a gutter. Either way, log it 'n' leave it, unless you've nowt better on.'

He patted his pockets, making sure he'd left nothing on his desk, and followed his mates towards the door. They all looked like they were gagging for a drink, for a laugh. CID officers? More like teenagers.

On the slip of paper there was a phone number and a name: Craig Shaw. One of Merchant's arrests? Joe didn't recognize the name. No surprise there. After a year coordinating missing persons and break-ins, Joe's knowledge of serious crime in Leeds was about as peripheral as it got.

He logged back into the system for a quick look. It wasn't as if anybody was going to be working at his desk tonight. It was an age since he'd handed over a live case to the night shift. At least this was a *known individual*. He could have a quick look for nothing.

Craig Shaw's file summary flicked up on the screen. A dozen entries, mainly arrests and cautions, but also a couple of convictions. Drugs. Such small-time stuff that the very lack of ambition was depressing. Selling blow on a couple of university campuses, amphetamines in a nightclub. One gram of coke. One bloody gram. He got eighteen months for that, suspended. A while later, the same thing. Two years this time. Out in less than one.

Mugshot: face so thin he looked malnourished. An arrogant stare, something self-assured about the way he held his head up. And he was an ugly runt. Ugly and unpleasant. Merchant was probably right: who was going to be bothered that he'd gone missing?

He drummed his fingers on the desk. Mrs Shaw rings the police a couple of days after her drug-dealing son disappears. The twenty-five-year-old son who presumably still lives at home. Now his mum's worried sick. The whole thing was like a Johnny Cash song.

Reining in his prejudice, he reminded himself of the official definition of a missing person: *Anyone whose whereabouts is unknown, whatever the circumstances… obligation to protect the rights of citizens without discriminating on any grounds.* He scrolled up the file, saw the address.

'Really?'

What else was he going to do of a Thursday night?

3

The Brick. Unusual name for a pub. He took his pint and went to stand outside the front doors. The light in the sky was fading fast, and there was an annoying February wind. In Leeds there's always an annoying wind, unless there isn't, then you wish there was. Either way, the weather's always just a little bit shit. On the door was a poster, handwritten in thick black marker pen on bright orange paper: a DJ on Friday, a band on Saturday. What might have been, eh, Joe?

Across the road from the pub was a strip of grass that sloped upwards, long and irregular, too steep to be of any use. Beyond it were half a dozen rows of back-to-back houses running all the way up the hillside, their chimney stacks jet-black against the evening sky. They were larger than average for the area. Good solid stuff. Turn of the century. The previous century.

He sank a third of his pint. IPA? Bitter? He couldn't remember what he'd ordered. It had the reassuring aroma of dusty rags and sweet mould. Real ale, the taste of his youth. Young lads today? Hardly any of 'em drank this stuff. He studied the pint glass in his hand. A young lad? Forty-eight hours he'd been gone. Could you even class that as missing? It was a decent bender, was all. Mum didn't think so, though.

He looked again at the houses. The one at the end had two little attics, a narrow, angled staircase leading up to them. Each room had a fireplace, an original ceramic surround with floral patterns in relief on the tiles, an unexpected touch of elegance. For his entire childhood, a small vase of plastic flowers had sat in each fireplace. Other than that, the rooms had stood bare and unused. They could never persuade their grandma to do anything with the attics. When she died, they sold the house to a mobile hairdresser. Did he still live there? Had he done anything with the top floor?

DS Joe Romano spent the next couple of minutes wondering whether he could use his warrant card to talk his way into the house and have a quick look at the attics. While he was there, he might just pop down into the cellar and see if he could find his grandma's old mangle.

He finished his pint and considered another. It was only as he was walking back to the bar that he remembered why he was here. Mrs Shaw had lost her son and didn't know where to find him.

4

The terraced houses down behind the Brick were a little less impressive than the ones over the way, where his grandparents had lived. Same vintage but not quite as large. Attics with staircases? Lofts more likely. Trapdoor in the ceiling. There were about a dozen streets, hypnotic in their sameness, something majestic in the repetition, age-darkened red brick houses lined up to order, one after the other, street after street, the columns of a Victorian terracotta army, imperious in its discipline.

But as he walked up Claremont Road he noticed that the lintels of many houses had been painted in red or black gloss, and several houses had their entire façades done in sickly, brick-like colours. This wasn't how he remembered the area. What had once been a latticework of neat, identical houses had mutated into something less uniform, dowdier, more random; wheelie bins outside, crappy double glazing, old satellite dishes that nobody'd bothered to take down. The odd nicely maintained one – white sash windows, a decent wooden door, the immediately recognizable patina of ordered living – looked out of place amid the general malaise, like a bloke wearing Harris tweed to go dogging.

Wortley, West Leeds: the Romano family had been based

here since the early 1900s. The area had seen better days. Then again, he thought as he made his way along the street, wishing he'd had that second pint, you could say the same about the Romanos.

As he stood there and knocked he felt the eyes of several people on him. Young, heavy-set adults who seemed to be there for no reason, nothing better to do, their front doors open, and them neither in nor out, just hanging around. He noted the gaudy colours of their casual, loose-fitting clothes, and it occurred to him that he, sporting a mid-grey Burton's two-piece and a tie, was the one who looked out of place.

'Mrs Shaw?'

'Police?' she said, standing well back from the door, which was open less than a foot.

'Detective Sergeant Romano, Leeds CID. I'm here about Craig.'

'You found him?'

'I've only had his name an hour. Can I come in?'

The door opened wider, with her squarely behind it. Joe went inside, and the door closed again quickly.

She stank of smoke. The house did, but it came from her. A stale smell, one he knew well enough. Ex-smokers never forget. But here in the narrow entrance of the hall it was bitter and overpowering.

She was average height, and about fifty, he reckoned, but thin and drawn. You could have added another ten years to that and no one would have argued.

'I've got some questions about your son.'

She lifted a hand. It seemed to shake. Even her arm was unsteady.

'Front room?' he asked.

She nodded, lowering her arm and searching for the wall behind her, palm flat against it. She was pissed. That explained the front door. She hadn't wanted to open it too much because she was off her face.

He stepped into the front room and almost gagged. The stink of cigarettes was overlaid with an acrid stench of food, sweat and farts. He glanced at the windows, wondered how long it was since they'd been opened.

'I don't have anything to tell you, as of yet,' he said, taking a seat on a large white leather sofa, one of two that took up most of the room, along with a huge TV in the corner, which was switched on, the volume turned down.

She made her way to the other sofa and eased herself down onto it, turning the TV off with a remote.

'So, how long's he been gone? Tuesday, is that right?'

'Aye. Tuesday.'

'You've rung around the hospitals?'

She nodded, then reached down to the floor for a can and took a drink. He didn't recognize the brand.

'Want one?'

He smiled.

'Depends what it is.'

She took another gulp, almost grimacing.

'Cider. Cheap stuff. I got a lager in the fridge.'

'I'm all right, thanks.'

She manoeuvred the can back down to the floor with the deliberateness of someone trying to stay on the right side of comatose.

'Sure?' she said, gesturing towards the floor. 'This stuff's cheap as shit.'

You can't argue with that, he thought, scanning the place for evidence of the missing son, and finding none. No photos, no games console, no men's magazines, in fact nothing to read at all. There were the two sofas, the TV, and a boarded-up hearth with a gas fire, shelves on either side stacked with DVDs. There were a few odds and ends, a pile of opened envelopes, a decorative mug from somewhere he couldn't make out, a huge red glass ashtray that looked like it'd been stolen from a pub several decades ago.

'This your house, is it?'

'Yeah, right! I rent it from Mr Azrim. He's all right. Been here a while.'

'How long's a while?'

'Four, five year.'

'Do you work, Jane? Can I call you Jane?'

'You can call me what you want, love. And no. I mean, yes and no.'

Joe sighed.

'I'm not here about your benefit claims. Could I have a straight answer?'

'I'm on the social. I do a bit of cleaning. Cash in hand. Haven't done it for a while. It's not regular.'

He nodded, considered Ms Shaw's lot. Housing benefit for the rent. The cleaning money for cheap cider. Over the last twelve months he'd thought about doing something similar himself. Downsizing.

'Craig's dad? Is he worried?'

She looked for her cigarettes, then took an age getting one to her lips and lighting it.

'Never been a dad,' she said, staring at the tip of her cigarette as it smouldered in her hand.

'No one at all? Anyone Craig might have gone to, or contacted?'

She shook her head.

'Doesn't know who his dad is. Was.'

'Dead?'

She raised her head, keeping it as steady as she could.

'Dunno. I never knew.'

'And there's no one else he might have gone to stay with? Family? Friends? Have there been any arguments recently, with you or anyone else?'

She shook her head.

He sat back, took a few breaths. The stink was getting bearable, and the sofa was pretty comfortable. *Leather's definitely the way to go. Pricey, though. You can't afford it the moment, Joe...*

'Have you lived in Wortley long?'

She took a long draw on her cigarette. He watched as she sucked the smoke in. There was something unnatural about it. Her shoulders actually lifted to expand her lungs, as if to get more smoke into them.

'Leeds. Here and there.'

He didn't press the point. He sensed that Jane Shaw would be on file back at Elland Road.

'I'm from round here as well,' he said. 'My grandma lived across from the Brick 'til the day she died. And my Uncle Frank started out as a clerk at Leeds Fireclay, just after the war.'

He thought about his uncle for a second. Francesco Romano. Dead now. Didn't stay a clerk for long. The Romanos? *We're not clerks.*

When he looked up, she was lost.

'Fireclay?'

'They made ceramics,' he said. 'Bricks, pots, plates, that kind of thing.'

This wasn't getting him very far.

'OK. So, these cases normally resolve themselves. Does he drive? Has he got a vehicle at the moment?'

'He's got mine. He borrows it.'

'Model, registration?'

She coughed. A big loop of phlegm crackled in her throat. She swallowed it back down.

'Toyota something. It's purple.'

'Number plate?'

She came close to a smile, then looked for an ashtray. There was a saucer at her feet halfway under the sofa. She pulled it out and used that.

'Never mind. I'll find it,' he said. 'The car's registered in your name, at this address?'

'Aye.'

'And he uses it to do what? Does he have a job?'

That semi-smile again.

'You know what he does.'

'Full-time, is it? He sells drugs, nothing else?'

'Needs a car.'

He was losing patience.

'So, Jane Shaw, here's the thing. Your son's a grown man. And he's only been gone two days. Tell me, why am I here on a Thursday evening, when I should be at home tucking into a Sainsbury's cottage pie for one and cracking open a nice bottle of Côtes du Rhône?'

She took the can and drank what remained of the cider.

17

''Cos he hasn't paid his rent.'

'That's why you rang the police?'

Her head was unsteady, but she was working to keep it stable. She was drunk, but there was a jumpiness to her, hidden somewhere beneath the languid movement of her body.

'He's not here, is he? I got the right.'

'And does he supply you with anything? To pay his rent?'

'Sometimes.'

'So you're drinking cheap cider as a substitute? What are we talking about? What do you use?'

'*Use?* Owt. Owt I can get.'

He shifted forward in his seat, considering a charge of wasting police time. But her son had been officially reported as missing. Call it a catch twenty-two. Call it bullshit. He had no choice.

'When did he last answer his phone?'

'Tuesday.'

She recited his number from memory with some difficulty. Joe dialled it into his own phone and called. Unavailable.

'Got any recent photos?'

She twisted on the sofa, pulled a phone from her pocket. Juggling her cigarette and the phone, she made an attempt to find the photos.

'Here,' she said, finally passing it across to him.

Android, like he used to have. Easier to find stuff than on his bloody iPhone. He opened the image gallery and flicked through the most recent ones. There he was, Craig Shaw, ugly and unimpressive, a selfie with his mum in Nando's. There were a few other shots taken in similar surroundings, Craig eating a burger, Craig drinking a beer, Craig pulling a stupid face and pointing at it with both index fingers, as if otherwise you might miss it.

Joe flicked through a few dozen others. Mostly mother and son, a few images taken by mistake, blurred and indecipherable. Then a young woman. Just one shot, a portrait, the background dull, unfocused.

'Who's the girl?'

She was young. Pretty, in a devious kind of way, willing the camera to find her unattractive, knowing that it couldn't. Long black hair, single nose piercing, her make-up dark and severe.

'What girl?' she said, fussing with her empty can.

He passed her the phone. She squinted at it briefly, then gave it back to him.

'Dunno. He lost his phone a few weeks ago. Used mine for a while.'

Joe stood up, took the phone from her.

'Can I borrow this? I'll have it back to you in the morning. What's the password?'

'One-nine-nine-six.'

He wrote the code in his notebook. Addresses he could remember, passwords not so much. All his passwords were written down on a slip of paper in his wallet.

'He turned out bad,' she said, sensing that he was ready to go. 'Didn't deserve to.'

'Craig? Why did he turn out bad?'

She looked at him. For the first time her head was steady.

'When he were a kid, his mother were a friggin' junkie. His dad were friggin' nowhere.'

She paused, looked away, embarrassed at the description of

herself, of the world into which she'd brought another human being.

'Are you gonna find him?'

'I'm going to try. If I call around tomorrow at ten o'clock will you be sober? We have to do a formal interview.'

'Could you make it eleven?'

'Half-ten. Get a good night's sleep. I'll find him.'

5

No assumptions should be made about the priority of police action until all the facts are ascertained... If in doubt, think the worst until the contrary is proved.

GUIDANCE ON THE MANAGEMENT, RECORDING
AND INVESTIGATION OF MISSING PERSONS

Joe sat at his desk. It wasn't unusual for him to be in the ops room this late in the evening, and no one on the night shift was surprised to see him there. When he was a young DC he'd been absurdly impressive, working all hours, so dogged and stubborn that cases seemed to get solved simply because he wouldn't give up, always a new line of enquiry, a new way of looking at things. These days he was on *mispers*. Cool respect was about all he got. That plus a touch of schadenfreude, after his return from France, tail between his legs.

He thought about giving Sam a ring. Too late? When did parents get so worried about invading their children's privacy? Sam wasn't a child, though. He was nineteen and in his first year of Medicine at Edinburgh. He was doing fine, that's what he said whenever the two of them spoke. Everything's fine, Dad.

Text instead: **Just checking in. All OK? Dad.** Sam always poked fun at him for signing his messages. But he couldn't help doing it. In fact, he didn't want to stop, just like he didn't want to stop doing lots of things: reading printed newspapers, buying stuff in shops, writing letters... The joys of browsing in a record store? Jeff Bezos deserved a good kicking for putting paid to that little pleasure in life.

He was waiting for technical assistance to become available. Missing persons don't get priority unless they're high risk. Craig Shaw wasn't in that category, not yet. Joe had the risk assessment form in front of him. But until he could get some straight answers from the victim's mother, there was no point in making any kind of assessment.

Remember, if in doubt, think the worst until the contrary is proved.

He was ready to think the absolute worst. He had the rest of the paperwork in front of him too, including a National Missing Persons Database form and a SIRENE European Missing Persons form. But none of this could be done until Jane Shaw decided to sober up. Meanwhile, he'd have to wait his turn for technical assistance, and he was hard pushed to imagine who *wouldn't* get ahead of him in the queue.

Jane Shaw's phone was on the desk, along with a number of print-outs that he'd assembled over the last hour or so. He picked up the phone and found the image gallery. Mother-and-son shots, nothing out of the ordinary. She was smiling in all of them. Her eyes were bright and clear. It made such a difference. Were they happy moments, or just posed? The happiness seemed natural. He saw the humanity in her face, the softness of her soul. It made him ache with sadness.

That's why he was still a DS at forty-four, working the cases no one else wanted. It wasn't that everything had gone wrong in Lyon, the failed leap to greater things, then the humiliation of coming back. And it wasn't because he was too soft for this job. He'd seen his share of horrors, more than a decade in plain clothes, the full gamut of criminal squalor.

No, this was different. Things were out of kilter. He felt it every morning when he woke up. There was a kind of reticence in him. His former boldness was ebbing away, his instincts for a case, the sense that things would always get resolved. And the optimism. He used to have that in bucketloads. Not now.

Whatever was happening to him, it was too late for a career change. He was just getting back on his feet after France, plus he was chipping in as much as he could with Sam's course fees. Edinburgh University was expensive. Everything was bloody expensive. He was stuck in CID, and he couldn't even afford a leather sofa.

He thumbed through the images on the phone. Jane Shaw a junkie? He looked at those clear, bright eyes as he ran the story over in his mind. She reported her son as missing because she needed a fix. It just didn't ring true. She seemed to be doing all right with the cider and the contract cleaning. Nah.

He'd already checked Jane Shaw's Toyota: it was a maroon Corolla, registered in her name. He also had the ANPR data on the car for the last couple of months, all sightings of the number plate traced onto a map of West Yorkshire. By the look of it, Craig didn't work in Leeds. Most of the trips were a few miles south, in and around the old mill towns of Dewsbury, Batley and Cleckheaton.

Cleckheaton. There's a name to conjure with. Next to it on

the map was Heckmondwike. Someone was having a laugh when they named those towns. Domesday Book scribes after a few jars of mead?

He studied the map. The car's journeys were indicated by red lines, the thicker the line the more frequent the trip. Along with the map there was a whole sheaf of print-outs, logs of journey times, plus a summary that flagged up obvious patterns for further investigation. All the analyses had been done with a computer application, of course. No hard-nosed detection necessary, human intelligence rendered obsolete.

The car had been making regular trips to all these towns to the south of Leeds. One stop-off had been highlighted, an old mill in Batley, now converted into a shopping centre. The car never stopped there for more than a few minutes. Every Monday evening at almost exactly the same time, in and out of the car park. The pick-up point, perhaps? If so, it might be used for more pick-ups, more sellers, part of a bigger operation. He'd have to pass that on to Kirklees CID. It was outside the operating area of Leeds District.

Other trips included longer stops, half an hour, an hour, sometimes more. They were logged for frequency and timings. Most were pretty regular. Craig appeared to have a fixed itinerary. Mondays were in and around Batley. Tuesdays were Cleckheaton, and so on, one weirdly named town after another.

Craig Shaw had the mill-town run sewn up. That's how it looked, a regular sales route, which implied regular customers, or a small-scale supply chain. This was a nice lead, a bit of potential, better than investigating some pusher working the streets. Something didn't fit, though. Craig was living with his mum, borrowing her car and her phone. Nah. If you're picking up a week's gear every Monday, same place, somebody trusts you. It's steady trade. You're higher up the ladder. You wouldn't be borrowing your mum's phone. And what does a drug dealer do as soon as he has any cash? Buys a decent motor. He doesn't drive around in his mum's old Corolla. Yet no vehicle had ever been registered in Craig Shaw's name on the DVLA database.

He checked his watch. He'd already phoned Alex, head of Digital Forensics. Ring him again? No, best not rush him. Don't make it sound like a favour. Not for a case like this. If it even was a case.

He looked at the information he already had. Jane Shaw's police record was limited to a few cautions for possession, the last one fifteen years ago. Nothing since then. He'd ordered her DWP file, but that wouldn't be available until the morning. He rifled through the remaining papers. The rest of her story checked out. She had been at that address for nearly six years, and the car was legally hers.

Think: her son went missing for a handful of hours and she rang the police? He repeated it to himself. *She rang the police.* Because Craig hadn't paid his rent, in kind or otherwise? Bullshit. There was something she wasn't telling him.

Alex Ambler walked into the operations room. He was lanky and unshaven, and had the air of someone who'd just dragged himself away from a very long game of *Dungeons and Dragons*. Yet despite the bed-head and a permanent yawn, Dr Ambler was the best-qualified person in Leeds Police HQ. After a PhD in computing, he'd got bored with university life and applied for a job in Forensic IT. A few years later he was a demi-god at Elland Road. A number of high-profile cases had gone to trial thanks to his expert intervention, and he'd even begun to publish articles in academic journals on cybercrime. He may have been a support worker, but Alex outshone the lot of 'em in CID.

He was wearing faded black jeans and a Whitesnake T-shirt with holes in it. The effect was a touch rebellious, bordering disrespectful. But no one dared to mention it. They all needed Alex, right to the top. They needed him more than they needed the Chief Superintendent, who in fact no one needed at all.

'OK,' he said, 'I'm here.'

There was no small talk with the King of Tech.

Joe held up the phone.

'Is it possible to track the movements of this phone for the last couple of months? Also, is there a way to find out where the photos on it were taken?'

Alex shot him a look of derision. Mock-derision? Hard to tell, but he and Joe had an understanding. Alex showed Joe nothing but contempt; Joe showed Alex nothing but subservience. They'd known each other for six or seven years, and Joe Romano was one of the few people that Alex genuinely got on with at Elland Road. The feeling was mutual.

'Are you asking me because you really don't know, or because you want me to do it for you and you're being polite?'

'Both, actually.'

'Is that a witness's phone? Why not just copy the photos across to yours?'

Joe pulled the brand-new iPhone from his pocket.

'Sam told me to get this. I hardly know how to turn the bloody thing on, never mind copy images to it.'

With a massive sigh, Alex took Jane Shaw's phone, flicking

through a few of its features in as many seconds, as if it was a source of minor irritation.

'You want locations for all the photos?'

'No, just one of a young woman, portrait shot, dark hair, nose piercing.'

'OK... Found it. Give me a few minutes,' he said as he left. 'There's software for all this stuff.'

Joe knew. They had software for everything these days. At some point in the future, data would simply be fed into a massive computer program. Vehicle tracking, phone tracking, social security payments, fingerprints, credit card transactions, CCTV face and gait recognition... Crimes would be solved instantly, just as soon as the data was in. The culprits could be taken straight to jail, and coppers would be downgraded to modern-day rat-catchers.

He put his feet up on the desk, lay back in his chair and stared at the ceiling. Sam had made a good choice. Medicine's a safe bet. You can't teach a computer to have a good bedside manner. Or can you? He closed his eyes and tried not to think about what might await his son in ten, twenty, fifty years. It was too terrifying to imagine.

As Sam had got older, the love that Joe felt for him had changed. What had been fond and natural when his son was a child had slowly turned into a constant worry, a light but noticeable discomfort in the stomach whenever Joe thought about him, and about what the world had in store for his beautiful boy.

The password on Jane Shaw's phone: 1996. The year Craig was born. Joe wasn't the only parent who feared for the future. Jane Shaw hadn't rung the police because she'd needed a fix.

She'd rung because she was worried sick about her baby boy. But why? Because he'd taken off somewhere for a few days?

Alex wandered back across the office. It had taken him a staggeringly short amount of time to do a job that Joe couldn't ever have attempted, despite endless training days in dull, over-heated seminar rooms.

'The photo of the girl was taken on the university campus.'

'Really? That's your old territory, isn't it? You reckon they'll let me poke around in their student database without a warrant?'

'Depends on who you ask. There's some techies up there wouldn't lift a finger to help the police if the Home Secretary told 'em to, never mind a warrant.'

'I'd better turn on the charm, then.'

'Charm? You been on a course? Oh,' he added as he prepared to leave, 'I emailed you all the location info I could get off the phone. It didn't take much time, there's…'

'A program, I know.'

Joe expressed his thanks to the empty space where Alex had been, watching as the tatty T-shirt and jeans glided silently away.

He dialled Craig Shaw's number again. Still unavailable. Two days like that, according to his mum. The mobile provider could be asked for the last active locations. But they'd need a warrant for that. A scumbag like Shaw, forty-eight hours on the loose? Not a chance of that getting signed off.

He opened Alex's email and read through the location data from Jane Shaw's phone. It hadn't left Leeds in a year. It hadn't been anywhere near the Batley drop-off or any of the other towns on Craig's professional itinerary. More lies from mum. Craig hadn't borrowed her phone. Not while he was working, at least. But why would his mum lie about that? Meanwhile, the picture of the girl that had been taken up at the uni was time-stamped nearly five months ago.

One thing was certain: Jane Shaw and Joe were going to have a long and detailed interview tomorrow. As long as she'd not had a liquid breakfast.

6

I can normally come and go without anyone seeing me. I'm lucky like that. With some things it's just a matter of luck, isn't it? But you also make your own luck, take advantage of what you've been given. It cuts both ways. Good luck, bad luck. Sometimes you've just got to reset the balance.

It's been two days. Two days since everything changed, under the old railway line in Cleckheaton. It's come back to me in staggering detail, every second of it. Opening the door, his body already slumped against the steering wheel. Hauling him up by the jacket of his nylon jogging suit. His legs looked so skinny through the thin fabric of his trousers.

I was surprised how little he weighed. Even so, it was a struggle, but finally I managed to get him into the footwell on the passenger side, bottom first, so he was sort of sitting on the floor, doubled up. His arms and head were slumped on the seat, his legs somewhere underneath. A phone fell out of his pocket. I picked it up, pulled the back off and took the battery out, tossing it all onto the floor next to him. It was as if I already knew what to do. You don't have time to think. Not in the normal way. It doesn't feel like thought at all. It's automatic, hyper-fast, primal.

I took my jacket off, laid it over him as best I could. Then I got settled in the driver's seat. I grabbed his baseball cap and put it on, pulled it down as far as I could, until the rim was just above my eyes. For an instant I wondered where his stash was, whatever it was he'd been selling. Did it matter? No, it didn't. It didn't matter at all.

I drove away from town. Up past Prospect Mills, then a left onto Whitcliffe Road, avoiding the traffic cameras in town. I had my head down, forcing myself not to look sideways. I took a right, weaving through rows of terraced houses, hoping that no one would recognize the car.

Keeping to the back roads, I crossed the A58 and drove up through East Bierley (small village, probably no cameras). I went on like that until I reached a stretch of dual carriageway that took me to the M62 junction. I was now travelling in completely the wrong direction, and there'd be cameras there for sure. But I had the cap on.

Then more country lanes, winding back the way I'd just come. Tiny old roads that I knew well, every last bend. Most of them didn't even have lights, never mind cameras. It took a while. But finally I was home.

The car's been in the garage since then, its passenger cold and silent. For the last two days I've been on automatic pilot at work. And the nights are long and black. But there's something else. A strange sense of rightness has been bearing down on me, growing stronger, thumping inside my head, smothering my thoughts. What is it? I'm a tight-rope walker, and there's no safety net beneath me. There's a staggering majesty to it. The fear is so intense it's sublime. Someone's put me up here, on my own, and everyone's willing me to succeed, holding their breath, knowing that they can't help me, that there's no net. No one can help me now.

I wait because I have to. Two whole days, so nobody will know exactly when he disappeared, or where. Not easy, having him at home all this time. But who's going to come calling? Who's missing a drug dealer in a beat-up Toyota? Nobody. That's the truth. The world's a better place without him. I didn't mean for this to happen, but it did. And now this is what I have to do.

Nine p.m. and I'm ready to go. I've had time to think about how to get this right. You can do a lot of planning in forty-eight hours, however much your world is spinning. My clothes from Tuesday are long gone, dumped in a rubbish container at work that was emptied by the bin men yesterday morning. I watched them do it. Every stitch I had on is now in a furnace or a landfill.

I've wiped the car for fingerprints until it shines, as well as his mobile phone, which is still in pieces on the floor. Every inch of the driver's seat has been gone over with the Dyson. And yes, I emptied the dust down the toilet, then washed and scrubbed the vacuum inside and out. I removed the pencil using pliers and snapped it into three pieces. It went down a drain a couple of miles away. I washed the pliers in bleach.

There was a ten-litre petrol can in the boot of the Toyota. Red plastic with a black nozzle. It's now full of petrol, syphoned from the tank. The tube I used was then cut into pieces and is now in the can itself.

By nine I'm in dark cycling gear, gloves, all nice and indistinctive. My bike is in the back of his car. I leave a few lights on in the house, ditto the TV. My phone, of course, stays there too.

I get in the Toyota and sit behind the wheel, staring through the windscreen into the darkness. I don't look at him. But I can feel his presence, the bony body, the nasty eyes. I know if I look down and see him there, the person I killed, I won't be able to do this. It will have been for nothing.

So off I go. It's risky. But it doesn't feel like risk now, as I drive. It feels like a challenge, a puzzle that I'm going to put together piece by piece. It feels like I need to do this.

Birstall is a small town just off the motorway. It's not that far, although it will take a bit longer than normal tonight, since I'll be taking the back roads. I drive steadily, head down. My heart's racing. Nothing can go wrong.

Two days ago, and the knowledge that I could not make a single mistake was energizing, terrifying. I'd never felt anything like it. In fact, I'm not sure I was feeling anything at all. Someone was saying: this isn't about you, it's just what you've got to do. But now it's different. As I drive, I can feel things falling within my reach. Under my control. I'm in charge.

Broadyards Country Park is just outside the town itself. It has a large car park at the bottom, surrounded by trees. I remember seeing a burnt-out car here once. That's what made me think of it.

It's deserted when I arrive. I park up in the far corner, close to a line of trees on the perimeter. There are no cameras here. There's nothing much at all, really, just a place for cars at the bottom of a wooded area that people use for walking their dogs. I get the bike out, keeping my head down as much as I can, just in case I've missed a camera. It's almost too dark to see what I'm doing, though, so it's certainly too dark to be seen.

I get the petrol and give the silent passenger a good soaking. I try not to get any on my clothes, but in the end I'm just waving the can about, my body shaking so much that petrol is going everywhere. By the time the can slips from my hand every inch of the car's interior is drenched, front and back.

I open the window in the passenger door for ventilation, then close the door as quietly as I can. My hands are trembling so badly that they knock against the door, as if I'm beating a drum. Then I turn and make sure there's an easy way through the trees and out onto the road, which is practically unlit. It runs up towards the centre of town. I'm going to have to risk it on the main road at some point, but I have a dark brown beanie hat on and I can ditch my cycling gear as soon as I'm done.

Plus, the bike looks completely different. I've covered all the distinctive paintwork with black insulating tape, and there are now yellow bands on all three shafts of the frame.

It takes a few matches before I get one to strike properly. I drop it through the window and throw the box in after it. Then I'm away. I hear a faint whoosh as I scurry through the trees with the bike, a snap of flames as I go over the wall.

I'm halfway up the road before I turn to look. And there it is, a faint yellow glow amid the trees. Vomit courses up my throat and fills my mouth. It's watery, but incredibly acidic. A little bit trickles out through my nose. But I sniff it back up, clamp my mouth shut and swallow. After all this planning, I'm not going to spatter the road with my DNA.

Head down now, racing mode. I get to the main road. The traffic is light, and I don't see any cameras, although I know that there must be some. My legs are pumping like pistons, but I never let up. A couple of miles on the main road, then I turn off, still pumping, full-tilt. I've planned the route carefully, a series of winding country lanes that lead me all the way to safety. I don't stop pedalling, not for a single second.

Home. First thing: I wash my hands for traces of petrol. I drink a glass of water. Then I go outside and peel all the tape off the bike, rolling it into a ball and stuffing it into the kitchen bin. I put all my clothes in the washer on a sixty-degree cycle and have a shower.

Wrapped in a towel, I go through into the living room. I sit on the sofa and check my emails, searching for a flight to Paris, a hotel on Tripadvisor… Could be anywhere, anything. Just to make sure I'm digitally engaged. An old episode of *House* is coming to an end. It started at nine. Luckily I've already seen it. I make a mental note, just in case anyone asks.

Finally, I lay back and close my eyes, feel the cold air on my body.

It's over.

I never asked for this to happen. But it did. And I made it right.

A dead drug dealer?

One down, is what I say.

I can't stop now.

FRIDAY

7

He followed a double-decker as it stop-started its way up towards the Headrow. There were massive, glass-fronted office blocks on both sides of the street, plus an array of older, more ornate buildings, each one pristine, the Victorian brickwork dazzlingly bright. The city of Leeds was resplendent and bustling, a place that managed to be shiny and smart, going about its business with a minimum of fuss.

Not like Manchester, just fifty miles away, with its irritating self-regard, still twatting on about a handful of bands it once had, and a nightclub that's now a block of yuppie flats. If a city could be an aging, loud-mouthed bore, Manchester was it. Quite literally the Liam Gallagher of cities, a pimped-up Subaru of a place, a cronut covered in cream. And don't even mention the football...

He amused himself with the faux-rivalry of Pennine provincialism as the traffic crawled along. Crossing the city centre at nine in the morning? Yes, it had been a little optimistic. Then again, he told himself, optimism always used to be his greatest quality, even when it was completely counter-intuitive. Where would we be without a bit of counter-intuitive optimism, without a misplaced sense of the possible in our back pocket?

Three years ago Joe Romano had been a Detective Sergeant with just over a decade's service. As a late starter, he'd done well. He'd already passed his inspector's exams, and was biding his time, waiting for a DI position to open up. Then an ad in the Federation newsletter: Interpol was recruiting multilingual British police officers for a new unit, based at their headquarters in France.

Several weeks of excited conversations followed with his wife and son. It would be an adventure, an amazing opportunity to try something totally new. Joe had a degree in French and Italian, and Sam had a few years of French under his belt at school. Jackie was also keen, as if she'd simply been waiting for an excuse to leave the life of a primary schoolteacher behind. A fresh start in France for the three of them. They'd buy an old farmhouse, do it up, live the rustic dream. It was perfect, the chance to spread their wings and eat *pains au chocolat.*

A couple of difficult years later and he was back in his old job at Leeds CID. Still a DS, and now working missing persons cases and the low-level stuff that no one else fancied. *Je ne regrette rien?* It wasn't his theme tune, not exactly. On the plus side, his French was amazing.

Ten minutes later he was on the university campus. Having ditched his plan to do battle with the university's Lords of Data, he was going for the personal touch.

He made his way down a long, warm corridor in the Faculty of Arts, Humanities and Cultures. Things didn't seem to have changed much since he was at Nottingham University, a quarter of a century ago. There was the same air of subdued vibrancy, colourful posters announcing everything from a performance of *Death of a Salesman* to karate classes. Perhaps this was where he should have pursued a career. A university. None of the ridiculous alpha-male game-playing that could make CID so tedious.

Student loans clearly hadn't killed off the spirit of youth. Even in the absence of students, who he assumed were either in lectures or still in bed, the building felt naturally and effortlessly optimistic. Would he choose to study French and Italian now? Ten grand a year in tuition fees, plus living expenses? Not a chance. Perhaps kids were simply braver when it came to facing life with a massive debt. Or they just didn't care anymore. At least Sam's degree in Medicine was a step towards a decent salary. But a *Humanities* degree these days?

He knew when he got to the French Department, because everything on the notice board had a tricolour on it.

He cleared his throat.

'*Bonjour, Mademoiselle.*'

She was putting up a poster.

'*Bonjour, Monsieur!*'

She turned slowly, arms held high, still holding the poster. Mid-thirties, or perhaps a little older, she wore faded brown jeans and a black T-shirt. Nothing very out of the ordinary, but if he'd seen her walking down the street he would immediately have known she was French.

Her tone was friendly, but also a touch quizzical, as if Joe's presence was slightly amusing but she wasn't sure exactly why. She looked him up and down in that way he'd become accustomed to in France, part flirt, part accusation, the kind of feminine once-over he hadn't experienced a single time since returning to the British Isles.

'*Pardonnez-moi*,' he began, the best French pronunciation he could muster, '*je suis policier. Crimes graves.*'

He held up his warrant card and gave her time to read it, which she did, frowning with concentration until she was convinced that he was indeed a *policier*.

'*D'accord, sergent.*'

'*Sergent-détective.*'

'I'm sorry, Detective Sergeant,' she said, switching to English for no obvious reason, which he hoped was not a comment on his French. 'There are bilingual police officers in Leeds?'

'Yes. We're few in number, but extremely eloquent.'

She nodded. He couldn't quite tell whether she'd sensed his attempt at humour.

'Are you looking for an interpreter? We sometimes...'

'No, to be honest I'm here for a bit of help. I'm trying to trace a young woman who might be a student. I came to your department first because I wanted to see if I could still speak the lingo.'

'I wish my students had your pronunciation!'

He felt a frisson of adolescent pride.

'I lived in Lyon for a while, couple of years. Anyway, I'm looking for a woman, and all I have is a photo that was taken on the campus. I thought perhaps she might be a student.'

He showed her the image on his phone. She glowered at the screen, allowing her eyes to refocus as she moved her face closer to it.

'OK,' she said. 'I know everyone who's studying French, and I don't recognize her. Is she in danger?'

'No, we don't think so. But we believe she could help us with an ongoing investigation. She's not in any trouble, as far as we know.'

The woman nodded, seemed to consider her options. He watched as she took her time. He liked that in a person. *Observe all, judge nothing.* Who said that? He'd forgotten, but it had always struck him as a sound philosophy. Make no judgement, until you get to the point where you simply have to judge. The skill is knowing when you've got there.

He looked at her eyes. They were brown, almost black, and he wondered if she was already judging him, whether her measured, courteous manner was simply a means of hiding her prejudices. He'd been in and around universities enough as a detective to know that they were full of judgemental types, especially when it came to coppers.

'Perhaps someone else will know who she is.'

'Another department?'

'Yeah, but which one? Which *ones*!' She paused, thought about it. 'You know, I have a better idea. Can I?' she said, gesturing to the phone. 'I'll send it to myself, is that all right?'

No. Not really. The image was not his. He couldn't really copy and disseminate it. On the other hand, this was a missing person case.

'Legally, I mean…' he began.

'I understand. I will ask Brian to look at it, then delete it? Is that good enough?'

'Brian?'

'Brian Summers. He is the Chief Administrator for the Faculty. He'll do what I ask him.'

I bet he bloody will, he managed not to say.

She took the phone, tapped the screen a few times, then reached for her own phone from her back pocket. With a telephone in each hand she made a call.

'Brian? It's Claudette. *Ça va? Oui, oui, merci!* A quick question. We have a photo and we have no idea which student it is. Could you take a look? Then delete the image, y'know, because of Data Protection?'

She listened for a moment. Joe imagined a fifty-something administrator at the other end of the line, running a hand through his thinning hair and dribbling at the thought of doing his favourite French lectrice a favour. The Data Protection Act would never have come into the equation.

'OK, *merci beaucoup*, Brian!' she said, handing Joe his phone and ending the call on hers. 'So, what were you doing in Lyon?'

'Interpol.'

'Now that *is* interesting!'

'It was mainly paperwork.'

He'd never been one for bubbly conversation, but he felt it more acutely now. *Mainly paperwork?* Just how thoroughly could he talk himself down?

She seemed to read his mind.

'But bilingual paperwork, no?'

He nodded, wracking his brain for something witty to say, just to keep her talking.

Her phone rang before anything came to mind.

She answered, listened, then offered the Faculty Administrator the kind of softly spoken gratitude that would give him continental fantasies for the rest of the day.

'He knows who she is,' she said, slipping her phone into the front pocket of her jeans.

'Really? That quick? How many students are in the faculty?'

'Thousands. But he knows her. Some issue with her tuition fees. Anyway, she's called Lisa Cullen, and she's doing

Media and Communications. So, you came to the right faculty. I can show you where her department is. Or you could ring her. Brian has sent me her contact number. Do you want me to forward it to you?'

'Do you have it there?' he asked.

She held up her phone and showed him the number that the drooling Brian Summers had just sent, in contravention of every Data Protection policy that had ever been written. Joe made a note of it in his book.

They stood in silence for a while.

'I'm sorry, I never...'

'Asked my name,' she said, smiling but not extending a hand. 'Claudette. Claudette Lausseur.'

The smile was rich and beguiling, and immediately made him forget what the French manners were at this point. Was it a kiss-on-both-cheeks moment, or not? Shit, he couldn't remember. And which cheek first? He always got that wrong. So many banged heads in Lyon.

He thrust out a hand, and she shook it.

With that he was off, marching down the corridor, his phone already pressed to his ear.

She watched him go, expecting a backwards glance from him. But there wasn't one.

'Pity,' she told herself, weighing the phone in her hand. 'At least I got *his* number.'

He walked across the campus, the wind coursing through the open spaces between buildings, buffeting him slightly more than was pleasant, his open jacket flapping like a set of ineffectual wings. He looked around for somewhere more protected, intending to call Lisa Cullen. But as he did so, his phone rang.

The conversation was short. Lisa would have to wait. He had a murder scene to attend. And Jane Shaw would need to be informed that her son was dead.

8

A small fire engine was pulling out of the entrance to Broadyards Country Park as he arrived. The occupants looked serious, their mouths closed, none of the usual banter after a call-out. There was a police officer at the gate. Joe held up his card and was waved through.

He drove in and headed across the car park, taking care to avoid the potholes in the rough dirt. In the far corner, the crime-scene perimeter had already been set up, half a dozen vehicles parked in a cluster, people coming and going.

He'd been given all the details over the phone on the journey from Leeds. The fire was called in early that morning, by which time there was little to be done. *Smouldering*, the dog-walker had said, before continuing his walk, quite unconcerned. This wasn't the first time a car had been left in flames here, and it was only as the fire fighters were dousing the burnt-out shell of the Toyota that they saw the remains of a body in the passenger footwell.

He parked a few yards from the white-and-blue tape cordon and got out. First impressions: the park was large, a series of open fields rising to a peak in the mid-distance. Good dog-walking country. But here, at the bottom, there was a sizeable car park, and the Toyota was at the very back, close to a swathe of tall, mature sycamores that would have hidden the flames and disguised the rising smoke. The perfect spot.

'Morning, guv,' said the uniformed officer on the cordon, as he took a note of Joe's credentials.

'How you doing, Mark?' Joe asked.

He knew the lad, an athletic-looking young man with a likeable face. He'd joined the Force just before Joe went to Lyon.

'Been on nights all last week. Today was supposed to be my easy day. Now look!'

'Yeah,' Joe said, watching as three SOCOs in white overalls moved around the vehicle, meticulously taking samples, hardly talking as they worked. 'Well, there'll not be much to see here, I reckon.'

'Black on black's what they're saying.'

'We'll see.'

Black on black. The victim was a criminal. Word had already got out. The car had been identified first: registered owner Jane Shaw, the mother of Joe's missing drug dealer. The occupant had been identified not long after that from the remains of his wallet: Craig Shaw, convicted drug dealer. No one was going to be making much of a fuss about this one. He'd get a standard team, but not for long.

Joe surveyed the crime scene. There wasn't even an inner and outer cordon. Just one section of ground had been taped off, big enough for a decent sweep of the immediate area, but nothing more. There were several rectangular patches with white edges where the prints of car tracks had been taken. Two vehicles in, one out? CCTV might help, not much traffic around here late on a Thursday night. Where were the nearest cameras? Out on the main road, possibly. There were none in the park itself, by the look of things. Someone had chosen well.

'Hi, Joe,' said a woman in white overalls and boots as she walked across to meet him.

It was a young assistant crime-scene manager. They'd met a couple of times, although he wasn't sure of her name.

'Hi there. You managing the site?'

She nodded. 'They let me out all on my own! Do you know this place?'

'Never been here before. Is it even on our patch?'

'Right on the edge. Another hundred yards and Kirklees could've had it. Pity, eh?'

He managed the slightest of smiles. 'Why? For the stats? You think I'm not gonna get a result?'

She failed to conceal a momentary flush of embarrassment. It was quite clearly what she thought.

'I mean, it'll be more difficult to get witnesses, won't it?' she said, glancing over at the car.

'Yep, and resources,' he added as he struggled into his own white suit and overshoes. 'Anyway, while we're here let's do the best we can. A life's a life. OK to go in?'

'Yes, but no touching. But I bet you knew that!'

He acknowledged her attempt at humour and turned towards the remains of the Toyota.

'A life's a life,' she whispered to the uniform next to her.

'Yeah, right,' he said.

Joe heard them both over his shoulder and ignored them.

He circled the car. The ground was muddy underfoot where the firefighters had done their work, and the sound of water dripping from the car was just about audible in the calmness of the scene. The maroon paintwork was still visible on one side, but not on the other or at the back, where the tank had blown and burnt itself out. Inside, the fire had destroyed everything. Seats down to the springs, the plastic dashboard bubbled and deformed like a massive block of half-melted chocolate.

There was a bitter, acrid smell, and some residual heat was still coming from the front end. The passenger door was fully open. He paused before looking inside. Was this the moment when you prepared to meet death head-on? It was so long since he'd been directly involved in a murder that he hardly remembered.

Then he looked. There was a body in the footwell, recognizable largely because he was expecting it. Otherwise, he might have assumed it was a sack of rubbish, or an off-cut of carpet, rolled up and burnt. It had a shiny, irregular surface, where the fabric of the clothes had melted in the heat. Only after a minute or so did he make out the position of the body, its head and one arm on the seat, the rest on the floor. The skull, like everything else, was black, but as he looked harder he could make out a filigree of red cracks where the scalp had contracted and split. There was the outline of a cheekbone, an ear, shrivelled to the size of a walnut, and the messy remains of an eye socket.

'Morning, Joe,' came a voice from behind him. 'Like the coffee!'

A SOCO stood there, a transparent evidence bag in each hand, grinning.

'Hi, Mike,' Joe said, looking at the bags. 'Coffee?'

'Morning, Joe. Y'know, coffee?'

'Oh, right, yes. Those the victim's?'

'Craig Shaw's the name. *Was.*'

'Yes, I know. The fire?'

'The interior of the car was doused with petrol. There's what looks like the remains of a plastic fuel container on the back seat. Fairly consistent burn throughout.'

'Someone did a good job?'

'Yeah, pretty thorough, I'd say.' He held up the bag. 'We found what's left of his wallet in his pocket.'

'And those?' Joe asked, gesturing to some keys in the other bag.

'In the glove compartment. They're from a BMW. Fire-resistant key fobs. German engineering, eh!'

Joe nodded. '*Vorsprung durch...* Or is that Audi? Anyway, what else?'

'Some bags under the seat. One of 'em looks like cannabis. But, y'know, what with the heat and everything, difficult to say for sure. Imagine the smell in there, though! At least he'll have died happy.'

So much for respecting the dead. The SOCO moved off as a photographer leant into the opened door and started snapping.

Joe moved out of the way to let him get on with it. What if that was Sam? he asked himself. Charred to death, his motor loaded with drugs. What if Jackie had been an addict, and Joe hadn't been around? What was it Jane Shaw had said? 'Mother was a junkie, dad was nowhere.' Now this. *Black on black.* It shouldn't matter. But it does.

'Anything in particular you want me to get, guv?' the photographer asked.

Joe looked around, still thinking about Sam.

'You done all the usual? Inside the car? Plenty of wide shots of the whole place, different angles, from all corners of the car park?'

'I reckon.'

'OK. Can you do some 360s from here, looking out from the car? Let's try to see what the quickest way out would be.'

'Will do.'

It was always a good idea to get someone to double up on your thinking. Joe took a step back and watched the photographer work. He felt the low branch of a tree brushing his shoulder, and turned. Quick way out? The trees were so close. This was where you'd go, straight under cover. The car had been parked here for a reason, next to the trees.

The photographer seemed to be thinking exactly the same. He walked past Joe and made his way between the branches.

'This is where I'd go,' he said, as Joe followed him. 'If I didn't have any wheels.'

The two of them went through the trees. A matter of a few yards, no more than that. No point looking for footprints. The ground was thick with leaves and wispy undergrowth. After the trees was a wall, the outer limit of the park. Three feet high, and on the other side was a narrow lane, the tarmac old and scarred, no street lighting in sight.

He leant on the wall and took out his phone. Eleven-thirty in the morning? Sam was probably in lectures. He dialled anyway.

Three rings and it clicked to voicemail.

'Sam? It's Dad. Just ringing to see if everything's all right. Speak later.'

He ran his hand against the wall, felt the cold, knobbly surface of the stones against his fingertips. He wondered what Sam was doing now. A month in Edinburgh, that's all it had been. Freshers' Week. Some intense socialising, everyone out to impress. Then down to work. Had he found a girlfriend? New mates? Too much beer? He didn't know. He knew nothing about Sam's life anymore.

Then an idea. He called the data desk.

'Hi, it's Joe. Quick one. There's a young woman, name of Lisa Cullen. I'll send you a photo. Can you try to find her on the DVLA database, check for vehicle ownership? We're looking for a BMW.'

9

The white leather sofa didn't feel quite so comfortable this time.

He sat, hands clasped in front of him, and watched her body as it shook.

'Here's your phone. Shall I make some tea?'

She tried to speak. There was a crackle of phlegm in her throat, bubbles of watery snot around her nostrils. She was shaking so badly that when she tried to raise her cigarette to her lips it missed her face.

He got up, left her phone on the arm of her sofa and told her he'd be back in a minute. The pain she was suffering was predictable, but that didn't make it any easier to watch. With each harrowing whelp that echoed around the room, he thought automatically about Sam, and how the loss of his only son would destroy him completely. Yet at the same time, her pain gave him strength. It made him want to find the killer. And that, he admitted to himself in a moment of shame, was a good feeling.

No time for soul-searching, though. Something wasn't right about all this. She reports her son missing, says he hadn't paid his rent, that he'd been using her phone, her car... He had to know more about the victim, and it had to be now. Shaw's death was already being written off as a black on black. There'd be no alarm bells sounding at CID. Or with the general public. Who cares about a dead drug dealer? No, this had to be now.

He made his way along the short passageway to the back of the house, preparing for the worst. The kitchen is where people leave the most obvious clues about themselves, a shiny slug-trail of personality traits, enough for any half-decent detective to form a good idea about the individual in question.

The kitchen was bright and tidy. The fittings were a little worn, but everything looked clean. Matching mugs neatly arranged on hooks, gleaming chrome toaster and kettle. And dominating everything a monster Zanussi fridge freezer. Not a mark on it.

Inside were eggs, bacon, milk, a few yoghurts, a pot of hummus, plenty of veg in the bottom drawer. And at the back were half a dozen cans of cider.

He closed the fridge and stood for a moment. There was no presence of Craig in here, he thought, as he looked for teabags and sugar, running his finger along the worktop surface and finding no dirt there. Craig might have bought the TV, the sofas, the enormous fridge. But there were no signs of *him*. It just didn't feel like a shared house. This was his mum's place.

But exactly who was she? An addict? Alchy? Bullshit. That was an act. Whatever she'd done in the past, her home was… what was the word? Respectable. The sense of normality was unmistakable. Not a luxurious existence, for sure, but an ordered one. What was it the snobbish left-wingers used to say? *The deserving poor.* That was Jane Shaw. The kitchen reeked of a decent person living a decent life. Even her social security record had proved to be unremarkable, give or take a bit of unregistered cleaning work.

As he made the tea, his phone was pinging more or less continuously with updates on the crime scene and the scale-up of the operation back at HQ. He let the messages come, glancing at them, replying briefly whenever necessary.

He caught sight of himself in the chrome toaster. DS Joe Romano: CID's number one under-achiever now investigating a murder. A team was being assembled at Elland Road, twelve officers for the initial push. They'd be out on the streets within a couple of hours, knocking on doors, eliminating persons of interest. But they needed to know which doors, who they were looking for. They were waiting for his orders.

He heard the muted sobs of Jane Shaw from the front room, and wondered whether there was much he could do, however many officers he had. Known associates? Informants? How many CID officers would want to pull in favours from their contacts for a drug dealer? In any case, the investigation would be downgraded as soon as something with a higher priority came in. This had to be quick. He needed info, and he needed it more than Jane Shaw needed sympathy.

'Here,' he said, setting down a steaming mug of tea for her. 'It's got sugar. Is that OK?'

She took it, had a sip, then put it down.

'So,' he continued, 'as soon as you're ready, we have to go through some stuff. I'll just pop upstairs to the bathroom if that's all right.'

At the top of the steep, narrow staircase was a small bedroom. A few items of casual clothing strewn about, the bed unmade, a cheap radio alarm clock on the floor. No wardrobe, no drawers or shelves. Not even a bedside table. He didn't have time to poke around. Somebody would be giving it a thorough going-over later in the day, not that there was much to go over. It did confirm what he already suspected, though: Craig might crash here from time to time, but he didn't live here.

'I'm OK,' she said as he retook his seat on the sofa opposite her. 'I'm all right now.'

He took out his notebook. With as much haste as seemed respectful he went through the standard questions. Form-filling, fact-checking, like a delivery clerk ticking off an order.

'His address, please.'

She dithered, trying to get her eyes to focus.

'Come on. Where does he really live? We need an address.'

Still she hesitated, playing innocent, even now, with her son lying dead in a police morgue. But why?

'Where does Lisa fit into this?' he added. 'Were they…'

He stopped, as Jane Shaw's body jerked forwards and vomit sprayed out onto the carpet. It wasn't much. Bile and a few sips of sweet tea. He waited five… ten seconds as she steadied herself.

'Clean that up later, eh?' he said, handing her a tissue, but meeting her frightened stare with a steely seriousness. 'I need something to go on, Jane. Give me an address. And the rest. Let's have it now. Then I'll go and find who did this. You all right with that?'

It came out of her as fast as the vomit. A babbling gush of relief. The address, the fact that Lisa was his girlfriend, that the BMW was registered in Lisa's name, ditto the flat in the city centre where they lived.

'And they've been threatening him,' she said.

'Who?'

She shook her head until her jowls quivered.

'Phone calls, disgusting letters, telling him to stop.'

Joe was writing it down as fast as he could, notebook balanced on a knee. With his other hand he called the operations room.

'And why didn't you tell me this yesterday?' he asked, waiting for someone to answer.

''Cos they said if he went to the coppers, they'd find out.'

He stood up, moved into the hallway and began relaying short, precise instructions. A team to look at Craig Shaw's flat, his finances, his movements, known associates; another one to focus on Jane Shaw, from every angle, including a house search, a detailed interview, background, finances; meanwhile, a CCTV team was already gearing up to trawl traffic cameras close to the crime scene, and their remit was now broadened to include the BMW and the address of a flat in central Leeds.

Returning to the front room, he found her in a calmer state. Her eyes were clearer, and she hardly trembled at all. The smell from the vomit on the carpet was bearable, and she seemed to have forgotten about it entirely. In fact, she looked almost serene.

He sat down again, tried to think of sensitive words, something kind to say. Nothing came. And meanwhile, he wanted information. More than anything, though, he wanted to be away. He was buzzing for the first time in years, desperate to get the case moving, to feel the urgent, unsettling thrill of going after a murderer.

'These people who were threatening Craig. Any idea who were they?'

'Dunno. They never said. They'd phone here, send stuff. Dog shit in a jiffy bag.'

'You saved any of the envelopes?'

'No. Binned the lot. No idea who they were.'

'Rival dealers?'

She said nothing. But she didn't disagree. Her silence made it all so banal. Craig had been killed, burnt to a cinder, because someone else wanted to sell drugs to teenagers in small northern towns with funny names. Someone wanted to take his sordid, small-time place in the world, and it was worth murdering for.

'He was doing his best,' she said.

Joe stopped, wrote the sentence down. *He was doing his best*. That was one to come back to.

'Lisa Cullen. Yesterday you told me you didn't know her. Why?'

Her face held steady for a second, perhaps two. Then she cried. He watched as the tears raced down her cheeks. He felt a wave of sympathy, a sudden, urgent loathing for the world. Then, immediately afterwards, a sharp sense of satisfaction: it had been the right question.

And at that moment, with the faint whiff of vomit in his nostrils, he knew why he'd become *police*. Because he was tenacious enough to do the right thing by a grieving mother, even if that meant putting her through this.

'I were trying to keep Lisa out of it. Thought they might get her as well.'

'OK. The photo was taken up at the university. Was Craig selling on campus?'

She looked shocked.

'No. I took the photo. I went up there. She were trying to get me to sign up for a foundation course.'

'Lisa?'

'Aye. Helping me. She's like that. She were helping our Craig, an'all.'

'Helping?'

'An angel, she is. A bloody angel.'

There was a knock at the door.

'That'll be victim support. I'll let 'em in on my way out. And I'll be in touch soon. In the meantime, there'll be a team here to search the house and to interview you properly and take a full statement. That OK?'

She nodded.

But Joe had already gone.

10

He drove into Leeds and parked just behind City Square. Years ago he'd busked here with his brother Tony. It had been their first gig. Only just teenagers, perhaps not even that. Two guitars and half an hour's worth of Beatles songs. They hadn't made much money, but it felt like treasure, money for nothing. Their parents hadn't been pleased, though. The Romanos are performers, they'd said, not beggars.

He walked across the Square, looking up at the bare-breasted nymphs on high plinths that circled the pedestrianized central area. Titty Square, his granddad used to call it, and even now it was puzzling that the city's strait-laced Victorian fathers had spiced up the plaza in front of the train station with semi-naked women. A nineteenth-century stab at lap-dancing, perhaps. He wondered what they'd done in Manchester.

His phone was pinging less frequently now. The investigation was already well under way. He'd organized most of it over the phone. The teams were assigned, everyone knew what they were doing. He should have been back at Elland Road, overseeing things as people swung into action. Gwyn Merchant had been named as his deputy. Not ideal, but there were no sergeants available. Merchant was a loudmouth, but a decent copper.

He'd rally the troops, get the case moving. That is, he would normally. But for a black on black? Maybe not.

His newly assembled band of merry men and women would be huddled together in small groups, double-checking addresses, sorting out search warrants, divvying up the jobs as they prepared for an afternoon of legwork. Others would never leave the building, condemned to trawl through a bewildering array of databases and other digital resources, dragging up info from the National Crime Database and seeing where the possible links were. Meanwhile, the unluckiest of all would be limbering up for a long session of staring at CCTV footage. How long before a computer could do most of this stuff? Or all of it?

Lisa and Craig's flat was just off the main square, down behind the station. It was in a converted warehouse next to the old canal, impressive in its way, plenty of balconies, cleaned-up brickwork, floor-to-ceiling windows on the fanciest apartments. Exactly the kind of chic city living that would attract an upwardly mobile drug dealer. Back in the day, this area had been somewhere to avoid, a mix of abandoned factories and open land looking onto a dirty, unloved stretch of the water. Since then, gentrification had been pretty much full on. The drugs and sex had moved out. Ironically, Craig Shaw had moved in.

There'd be a team coming to interview Craig's girlfriend and *helper*. But Joe wanted to talk to her first, get a clearer picture of where she fitted into things. Also, someone had to inform her that her boyfriend was dead. Joe wanted to see how she reacted.

'Lisa Cullen?' he said into the intercom. 'DS Romano.'

She buzzed him in without a word.

The communal lobby smelled of lavender carpet cleaner and had the stern, angular appearance of commercial sophistication.

It was like walking into a business hotel stripped of all but the essentials, comfortable yet bleak, despite the framed watercolour prints on every wall. He'd visited plenty of similar places when he and Sam got back from France and were looking for somewhere to live. But he'd resisted the call of the many bachelor pads on offer, mainly, he now realized, because of their soulless entrances. Plus all the bloody watercolours.

Craig's was the middle flat was on the fourth floor. His earnings didn't run to a split-level attic, or one of the apartments with floor-to-ceiling windows. Still, you'd have to be shifting a fair amount of gear to be paying the rent here.

When the door opened, the face that greeted him was nothing like the one in the photo.

'Lisa? DS Romano.'

She looked straight past him. Seeing that no one else was there, she threw the door wide open and walked back inside.

When they'd spoken on the phone twenty minutes ago, she'd hardly been able to conceal her irritation, asking if Craig had been arrested, where he was, what he'd done... And they weren't nervous questions. It was like a lawyer talking, or a minder, as if she knew that she'd be the one sorting everything out, whatever kind of trouble Craig was in.

'Where is he, then?'

She stood in the middle of the large open-plan living area. She wore tight jeans, faded to an off-white and ripped at both knees. Her loose T-shirt looked like she'd had it on all night, but her longish black hair was brushed. There was none of the dark, severe make-up from the photo. Her face was pale, slightly pasty, and there was an edginess to her, but also something hard and resolute. A toughness that she'd definitely not acquired overnight.

'This your place?'

She shrugged. 'It's in my name.'

'The motor too?'

'Motor?'

'The Beemer Craig hasn't been using for his work of late.'

'It needs repairing,' she said, not a moment's pause. 'We haven't got around to it.'

'Right, right. And you, you're studying Media and Communications up at the uni?'

More nodding.

'OK. You better sit down. I've got some bad news.'

She gave a little snort of derision which, just for a moment, made her sound like a petulant child.

'I'm all right on my feet.'

'Craig was found dead this morning.'

She froze. Eyes wide, her breathing coming momentarily to a halt. Her mouth remained closed, jaw clenched so hard that he could see the balls of taut muscle in her cheeks.

Then she let herself slump down onto a large beanbag, the closest thing to her in the modern, Ikea-heavy surroundings.

'Bastards!' she hiss-growled to herself, cradling her head in her hands.

'Bastards? Who, Lisa?'

She wasn't listening. She'd forgotten he was there.

But the anger drained from her in seconds. She sat, arms around her legs, literally pulling herself together, forcing herself to breathe.

'Lisa? Who are they? You said *bastards*.'

She looked up. 'What? I... No, I meant him. Silly bastard, got himself...'

Her voice fell quickly away. But her eyes were busy. She was thinking, moving past the shock, even now.

'He was found dead in his mother's car. It had been burnt out, over near Birstall. That's where he was selling, right? Last sighting was a couple of days ago, Tuesday, Cleckheaton town centre. When did you last see him?'

'Tuesday.'

'Last time you spoke on the phone? Last WhatsApp, text message?'

'Tuesday.'

She had wilted a little by now, and her answers were automatic. She was staring into space. But she was thinking.

'Does his mum know?' she asked.

'Just been to see her. She thinks the world of you. Called you an angel. You've been helping Craig to sell illegal drugs. How does that make you an angel?'

'Helping him to sell? No. Telling him what not to sell.'

'Go on.'

'Minimizing the risks. I told him to sell cannabis. Spliffs and shit.'

'You mean rather than stronger stuff?'

'It's gonna be legal sooner or later. Look at Portugal. Look at America. California, Oregon, Vermont... Can't stop it. You lot can't, that's for sure.'

'Never said I wanted to,' he said. 'And you missed Massachusetts, by the way. The Puritan State. Legal there, too, I believe.'

She was not impressed by his knowledge of international drug legalization. In fact, she looked entirely wrapped up in her own thoughts, as if she'd already shut him out.

He only had a few minutes. His boss wanted to speak to him back at HQ. He gave it one last try.

'OK. There are a dozen detectives on this case, plus me. If we're gonna find who did this, you'll need to tell me who was threatening Craig and his mum, how they were doing it, when they were doing it. And lastly, Lisa, look at me...' She did. 'Tell me why Craig was using his mum's car to sell drugs. In fact, you can start with that. Go.'

She ran a hand through her hair.

'There's competition. They had his mum's address. He got warned off. But he's a stubborn bastard. *Was.*'

She stopped, a look of intense concentration on her face.

'They threatened him?' Joe asked. 'And what, he ignored them?'

She nodded. Nothing else.

Joe continued.

'He was getting his supply in Batley. Every Monday. Whoever was threatening him must have known that. So why are they going after the guy on the street? Sending dog shit in the post, calling his mum? None of that makes sense.'

'They must have thought he lived at his mum's house.'

He turned this over in his mind. Tried to imagine drug dealers scooping dog poo into jiffy bags to send to a rival. Ringing his *mum*? Nah.

By now there was a trail of tears running all the way from the corner of her eye down to her neck. Her head was held slightly forwards, so that strands of her hair fell across her face.

'You're gonna get 'em?' she said, her voice suddenly a faint croak, her words slow, measured, innocent.

'We'll need a lot more from you. Details, everything you can think of. There'll be an interview team here in half an hour. They'll do a full search of the flat as well. They'll have a warrant with your name on it. You have to tell 'em everything, Lisa. Every last detail.'

She took her time. But finally she looked up at him, making eye contact for the first time. She nodded obediently. A small, frightened girl with big, imploring eyes.

She was still sitting on the beanbag when he let himself out.

A good performance, he told himself as he took the lift back down to the entrance. Good, but not great. There was a hint of calculation, the sense of a person already planning their next move, just seconds after hearing the bad news. With his phone pressed to his ear, he threw open the main door and headed back out into the cold air.

'Gwyn? Change of tack on Lisa Cullen, the victim's girl-friend? I'm outside her flat. The Tannery, it's called. Warehouse conversion behind the station. I reckon she'll be long gone by the time the interview team gets here. Send someone down in an unmarked car now. I'll wait 'til they arrive. A black BMW's gonna be leaving the building. She'll be driving. Just see where she goes. Nothing else. Asap, eh? I've got brass to talk to.'

11

DCI Andy Mills was sitting behind a large desk, looking bored and stressed at the same time. His shirt was blindingly white, with sharp, pristine creases, gold cufflinks. But it only served to accentuate the large, flabby body of the man within.

'One barbecued drug dealer!' he said. 'Congrats. You're the Senior Investigating Officer. Wrap it up nice and quick, eh?'

Joe stood there and looked out beyond his boss. From the window you could see the back of Elland Road football stadium, the white East Stand towering over everything like a massive shrine to Marcelo Bielsa, the genius Argentine coach who'd led the sleeping giants back to the Premiership.

'Investigation's focusing on Cleckheaton and the surrounding towns.'

'Radius?'

'About ten miles. Tracking suggests it's where he was dealing. He was found in…'

'I know, I know,' Mills said, glancing at the preliminary report on his desk. 'Another few yards and Kirklees could've had him. Now he'll be our bad stat. Unless you can get a conviction. Any chance of that?'

'It's not straightforward, Sir.'

Mills stifled a laugh.

'You're calling me *Sir* now?'

'I'm trying to be formal, Andy. This is an odd one. I think we should see where it leads. I mean, properly.'

'Drug dealer gets bumped off in his burnt-out motor, stash under the friggin' seat? Sounds pretty straightforward to me.'

'It was his mum's car.'

'Correction: small-time drug dealer. How much d'you think I can spend on stuff like this?'

'Stuff? It's a murder.'

'Have you seen the cuts we've had to make these last few years?'

'This isn't what it seems. I've just spoken to his mother, and his girlfriend. Something just doesn't feel right.'

'Says who?'

'Says instinct.'

'Aye, well last time you acted on instinct you ended up eating garlic baguettes and singing the bloody *Marseillaise*. Look where that got you!'

Joe couldn't help smiling. He'd met Andy seventeen years ago, the two 'mature' cadets at the West Yorkshire Police Training Centre. They'd been friends ever since. Andy was slightly younger, having joined the police after a couple of tours of Afghanistan with the Yorkshire Regiment. Joe, meanwhile, had done a couple of tours of the comprehensive schools of Leeds before opting for a career in the police.

They'd moved up to CID about the same time, too. It was always assumed that Joe would be the one rising through the ranks. But years later it was Andy's name with DCI in front of it. That, plus all the trappings of success. The dull, functional office, the white shirt and gold cufflinks, and Andy himself growing more haggard by the day, slumped in his chair writing budgets, or dragging himself off to another meeting with other senior officers in pristine white shirts. Interpol had saved Joe from something far worse.

'*Je ne regrette rien!*'

'Quoting me French, yer dickhead? Look at yourself! Copper as good as you should've been a couple of ranks above me by now, easy. Now this? Tryin' to kick-start your career with some crackhead in, where was it?'

'Cleckheaton.'

'Aye, there.'

Andy Mills had a rare talent for speaking the truth in a truly offensive way. But as a DCI he rarely got the chance. Modern policing, as he and Joe occasionally lamented over their fourth or fifth beer, was like being a filing clerk who occasionally arrests somebody then spends the next week worrying that he's filled out all the forms correctly. And when you're a DCI, you also got to worry about everybody else's forms.

Andy glanced at his watch. His head and shoulders sagged, just a touch.

'Sod it. I've got a drinks reception in the Town Hall. I don't even know what it's for.'

'Warm white wine and the company of town councillors. Where did I go wrong, eh? This could all have been mine!'

Andy shook his head, the beginnings of a smile on his face.

'Stick with it. You've got a dozen men 'til Monday.'

'It's Friday afternoon! Do they get overtime?'

'No they bloody don't. A few of 'em'll be on weekends. That's your lot. Let's see where we are on Monday.'

He waited, saw that Joe was going nowhere, hands thrust into his pockets. It was the old Joe, all instinct and determination, when he'd been the most annoying detective on the Force, absurdly optimistic and wilfully stubborn. A right pain in the arse.

'OK, you win. There's a definite local angle, right? I'll try and get you joint ops with Kirklees. Share the love, that sort of thing.'

'Your bounty is endless.'

'Bounty's a chocolate bar as far as I'm concerned.'

Joe nodded and turned to leave. He'd heard that one before. It didn't matter. He'd got what he wanted. Jane Shaw would get justice, whatever her son had done, and however he'd turned out.

12

It was already dark when he parked in Cleckheaton town centre, just behind the Bull's Head. Twenty minutes down the motorway, but the contrast with an evening in Leeds couldn't have been more marked. No groups of smart young people emerging from offices, jackets unbuttoned, ties loosened, back-slapping as they pushed into crowded wine bars; no streets crowded with pedestrians dodging the endless line of buses, each one full, top and bottom, windows misted up, as the city shifted into evening mode.

In Cleckheaton there was traffic. But only on the main road, and only passing through. There was an air of quiet desola-tion at this time of the day, as if those who worked here had all packed up and gone home in a rush, and now its empty Victorian buildings looked down, challenging your right to be here, daring you to stay. There was a faded grandeur, hints of an affluent past peeping out from behind bland, modern shopfronts; old buildings with clocks and classical stonework high up, but on the ground floor hair salons and pound shops. It was reminiscent of a seaside resort in winter, closed up against the cold, expecting nothing, promising nothing. But not threat-ening. Not a mean place. Almost kind, in its way.

Fortunately, the pub was nowhere near as desolate. It was about half-full, a decent Friday night crowd at the bar. Joe got himself a pint and chose a table by the window, in full view of the whole room. Kirklees District had agreed to cooperate on the Shaw murder. His new partner, DS Scannon, was supposed to be here, although he couldn't see an obvious candidate. He checked his texts and nursed his drink for a minute or two.

Cleckheaton. He ran the word around in his mind. He'd only been here once before, ages ago, in search of the perfect pork pie after a tip-off about a butcher's shop. He pulled up Google Maps. A few miles away was Batley. He'd been right about Lisa Cullen. Not long after he left her flat, she was seen driving off in a black BMW. An unmarked car had followed her to a pub in Batley, the registered landlord a Mr Daniel Cullen.

Joe was still thinking about pies when he noticed someone come into the pub. He wasn't the only one. She didn't actually push her way to the bar, it was more a matter of other drinkers making way for her, like the nervous dither of gazelles when a wildebeest stops by a watering hole in the Serengeti. She stood square on and waited to be served, arms out on the counter, head back, not a trace of patience in her substantial frame. And she made no sideways glance, no attempt to see if he was there.

He'd begun to think that perhaps it wasn't her, when she got her drink and turned. Then there was no doubt about it. She walked over, a slight roll of the shoulders, a pint of lager in her hand. If he hadn't been sitting snugly behind a bar table, he might have cowered, just a fraction.

'Joe Romano, right? Gotta be. Rita Scannon.'

She didn't look very CID, and she didn't look much like

a Scannon either. She was about his height, but wider, some-where on the bulky side of buxom. Jet black hair cropped to a quarter of an inch, a full face, dark complexion. Her faded black jeans strained until the studs squeaked, and her cleavage was deep and unashamedly on view beneath a black v-neck T-shirt and a black leather jacket.

'Jesus,' she said, setting her pint on the table and lowering her considerable bulk down onto a stool opposite him, 'is this your Friday night gear? Talk about a sore thumb. You might as well have a warrant card on your friggin' lapel!'

He looked around. Plenty of people in work clothes, or what he supposed went for smart-casual. Thin jerseys tucked into tight ripped jeans. Was *that* still in fashion?

'I did take my tie off,' he said.

'Oh, we're gonna have fun!'

She leant in close, until he could see tiny flecks of olive-green in her large brown eyes.

'That young lad serving at the bar? We think he's spiking drinks to order. What d'you reckon? Is he the spiking type?' She took a sip of lager. 'I read the stuff you sent about the late Mr Shaw. What else've you got?'

He took a drink of his Tetley's Bitter. It was way too cold.

'We're not doing small talk, then? Getting to know each other a bit?'

She did a pantomime roll of those massive, olive-flecked eyes.

'What? Speed-dating for coppers? I've done my homework, partner. DS Joe Romano. Degree in French and Italian, stint as a schoolteacher, then joined the Force when you were twenty-eight. First time you've been SIO on a murder since you came back from France. I guess Interpol didn't work out too well, eh?'

'I didn't send you any of that.'

'No, I'm a detective, *mon brave*. No university degree to my name, either.'

She sat back, downed about a third of her lager.

'Don't tell me,' he said. 'School of hard knocks, university of life. And,' he raised his arm in an exaggerated gesture and pretended to consult his watch, 'let's just see how long it takes her to inform me of her lowly, working-class roots.'

'Tou-friggin'-ché, *Monsieur*. But,' she said, pointing at her face, 'I don't have to play the working-class card. I've got the ethnic ace up my sleeve, or hadn't you noticed.'

'Can't say as I had, to be honest.'

'A colour-blind male! Look at you! The wokeness! Anyway, I'm half Bangladeshi.'

'Which half?'

The slightest flicker of a smile? He thought so.

'The half that means I can't go more than forty-eight hours without a lamb biryani.'

He watched as she took another long drink.

'This,' she said, holding up her glass with one hand and wiping her mouth with the back of the other, 'is the other half. Fourteen stone of Batley-Bengali, that's me. Pure multiculturalism.'

He sat back and tried to savour his own beer. But it was still freezing. The proprietors of the Bull's Head had clearly not read their Orwell.

'Craig Shaw,' he said. 'Looks like Cleckheaton was his regular Tuesday stop-off. That's when he disappeared. Vehicle tracking has him here that evening. Then nothing.'

'Like I said, I've read the file.'

Joe began to wonder whether the line between matter-of-fact and tetchiness was different for DS Scannon than for most people.

'Not quite nothing,' she added. 'His number plate was clocked on the bypass up near the M62. Nine-thirty on Tuesday night if memory serves. That's about the time his stop-offs in Cleckheaton normally finish, isn't it?'

Joe nodded, persevering with his pint, as if it was at this point his best and indeed only friend.

'We know Craig,' she added. '*Knew*, I mean.'

There was a hint of mischief in her voice as she reminded herself of the past tense.

'Selling cannabis, apparently.'

'He's been inside for selling coke. That's what his record says.'

'His girlfriend told me he was focusing on softer stuff. Her idea. Kind of a business model, in the hope that sooner or later it would be decriminalized and he could go legit.'

She listened, her pint held up to her mouth, then sank most of what was left.

'Interesting. Must have got himself a niche. I used to see him parked up in his Beemer, just round the corner, by Tesco's. Y'know?'

'Nope.'

'The road under the old railway bridge. It was always like, shall I even bother? He's been stopped a few times. Only ever had a bit of blow on him. Must have been shifting a fair bit, though. Nice motor.'

'He was driving an old Toyota when he died.'

'He was in a Beemer whenever I saw him. Flash but not too flash. Good choice.'

'Last few weeks he'd been borrowing his mum's car.'

'Yeah, I saw the tracking. Old Corolla? Bit weird.' She stopped, looked him right in the eyes, her hands flat on the table in front of her, and inhaled dramatically. 'Joe, I think that might be a *clue*. What d'ya say, partner?'

'Apparently he was using his mum's car to avoid being seen by rivals.'

'What rivals?'

'Someone was warning him off. Threatening his mum as well. Phone calls, dog shit in the post, the lot. That's why she reported him missing so soon. She was scared stiff. With good reason, as it turns out. Also,' he said, picking up his phone, 'I've got a picture of his girlfriend. She's involved, one way or another.'

Rita tried not to laugh as he slowly navigated the labyrinthine complexities of his new device. Finally, he pushed it across the table.

'The Beemer's registered in her name,' he said. 'Lisa Cullen, she's a student at Leeds Uni. They have a flat in Leeds. Nice city-centre pad, which is also in her name.'

'You found her quick.'

'A very nice *mademoiselle* in the French Department gave me a bit of assistance.'

She chewed on that one a while, seemed to consider a riposte, thought better of it.

'The girlfriend? Was she shocked about her boyfriend dying?'

'Hard to say. I think so. She's smart, though. All kinds of smart.'

'What's her name again?'

'Cullen. Lisa Cullen. She's from a town somewhere around...'

77

'Address?'

'Ryeman Avenue. Batley. A pub called the Brown Cow.'

She looked at him.

'You're shitting me, right?' She waited a whole second. 'You're not shitting me.'

She was on her feet before he had time to think.

'Come on.'

He considered one last mouthful of his Tetley's, but she was already gunning for the door, gazelles scattering left and right.

13

By the time he got outside, she was swinging herself into an old Land Rover, arse first, hands clinging to the top of the doorframe.

'You follow me. Where're you parked?'

'Just round the corner.'

The Land Rover was covered in dents and had a ripped tarpaulin on the back. He made a mental note of the number plate, just in case they got caught up in an unexpected swarm of beaten-up farm vehicles on the way to Batley.

They left Cleckheaton and headed along a series of brightly lit main roads. She drove with a combination of relative caution and suicidal cornering, as if she disliked high speeds but was equally reluctant to touch the brake pedal. It didn't look like the Landy had much in the way of suspension, either. From a safe distance behind, he could see her bouncing around on the driver's seat as she lurched up and down the gears.

On they went, and it wasn't clear to him at what point they'd left Cleckheaton. It was a strange kind of landscape, piecemeal and uncoordinated, neither urban nor rural. Pockets of housing sat alongside industrial buildings, old and new, nothing too large, and nothing very distinctive. Then there were stretches of farmland and open countryside. You came on them unexpectedly, as if you'd suddenly been transported fifty miles north into the Dales, only for another huddle of industrial units or a makeshift lorry park to come into view, shattering the illusion.

It was a ten-minute drive to Batley. He glanced at his messages. The teams had been out all afternoon, and Gwyn Merchant was now busy relaying the results, which were mainly that no one in West Yorkshire knew anything about Craig Shaw. All the individuals even remotely identified as potential suspects had been traced, interviewed and eliminated from the inquiry. Nothing was getting flagged up for further investigation. Gwyn was certainly efficient. No sooner had a new line of enquiry been identified, it seemed, than the lead had been followed up and discounted.

They passed the Batley Variety Club, the most famous cabaret venue in the North. He remembered the stories from when he was a kid. Every local musician that his parents knew claimed to have been in the house band when Louis Armstrong had played at the Varieties, and for Tom Jones, Roy Orbison, Neil Sedaka... Tony and him used to joke that if they'd all really been there when Armstrong came, there'd have been enough musicians to fill the club, never mind the orchestra pit.

He slowed down to see what had become of it.

'A bloody gym!'

A mile or two further and Rita took a sharp left at twenty miles per hour. They entered a housing estate, the main avenue curving gradually up the valley side. It was the kind of council estate where he'd spent many hours as a copper: door-to-doors, domestic disputes, chasing up likely suspects, most of whom lived in places exactly like this. He remembered the sofas on the front lawns, the odd car on bricks, scary young kids with red faces waiting to cheek you off.

There were no cars on bricks here, though. Lots of cars, but good, solid stuff, decent family motors, right up to the odd Merc.

Rita came to an abrupt stop. By the time he'd parked behind her and got out, she was already leaning against the Land Rover, rolling a cigarette.

'Need a quick smoke.'

'Really?' He looked around. 'That bad, is it?'

'This estate? Nah, one of the good ones. And the jewel in the crown,' she added, nodding over her shoulder, then cupping her hands against the wind as she flicked her lighter, 'is the Brown Cow. Ironic, eh?'

'Is it?'

She took a long draw on her cigarette. They both watched as the smoke descended in a loose cloud around them, then disappeared in a single gust of wind.

'The Brown Cow. It's what the Cullens call me.'

'Famous in these parts, are they?'

'You might say that. Hold on.'

She took a long, long drag.

'I dunno about threatening Lisa Cullen's boyfriend, but I wouldn't go round threatening Ma and Pa Cullen without a bloody good reason,' she said, before tossing the cigarette into the gutter with disgust.

With that she turned and marched towards the pub, the movement of her shoulders now just a little exaggerated.

The pub had been built in the sixties, at the same time as the estate. And it was in the same style. Squat and dull, with wooden panels beneath the windows, the rest of the walls prefab concrete. The reinforced glass door boasted a bright green poster announcing the week's entertainment.

Race Nite – Tuesdays
Karaoke – Wednesdays
Bingo – Thursdays

She pulled the door open. Just inside was another sign:

YOU ARE NOW ENTERING
A DRUG-FREE ZONE. RESPECT.

'We're to believe that, are we?' he whispered as they stood there and took in the surroundings.

'You ain't seen nothing. Come on.'

The main lounge was comfortable enough, with a pool table and dart board to one side, tables and chairs on the other side, and a long bar lined with lager pumps at the back. No real ale in sight. It wasn't the kind of place that would have attracted him, but it wasn't unpleasant.

There were a couple of dozen drinkers, well-inked young lads, some older blokes in baggy jogging pants, one or two in work clothes and boots. And every one of them watched, pint in hand, as the odd couple made their way through to the bar.

It was not until they got there that Joe realized: apart from Rita there was only one woman. She was standing on the other side of the counter, and she didn't look happy to see them.

'Evenin',' Rita said.

'She's not here,' the woman said.

'Joe, this is Karen Cullen,' Rita said. 'Pleased to see you too, Karen!'

Karen Cullen was in her fifties, short, trim, with spiky, inch-long dyed-blonde hair. She was not ugly, but her expression was. Joe knew it well. The expression of someone who spends their life on the hardened edges of life, where an air of tight-lipped nastiness is the best way of facing the day-to-day. Over the years he'd developed a kind of sympathy for people like this, especially women; once you got them into the interview room their vulnerabilities poured out of them like water from a tap.

'Who's not here?' he said, pushing his warrant card part-way across the bar as discreetly as he could. 'Joe Romano, Leeds CID.'

'Lisa, who do you think? We heard. Boyfriend's dead. Now you lot're here causing more trouble for her.'

'When did you last see her?'

The woman sighed. She looked at Joe, and just for an instant the hardness receded.

''Bout teatime. She came, told us and went.'

'Did she say anything else?'

'No.'

'Craig Shaw,' said Rita. 'He'd been getting some aggro. That's what we heard.'

'Aye well, comes with the job, you'd've thought.'

'You'd've thought?' Rita said, and got a faceful of silent derision for her trouble. 'OK, we'll have a word later. Is the big man around?'

'League meeting in the back.'

'Right, let's go.'

Joe already knew better than to argue. But then:

'One thing, Mrs Cullen. You've got a regular race night. It's a while since I've seen that. Was there one last Tuesday?'

She nodded.

'Who operates the machine?'

A deep knowledge of the pubs and clubs of northern England had always been a Romano speciality. *Race Night*: randomized simulations of horse races played on a special TV screen, with punters betting on the outcome. Back when Joe and Tony were doing the clubs it had been pretty common, just like bingo and second-rate singers doing their worst with Elvis and Glen Campbell.

'We do. It's not a machine these days. It's all on DVD.'

Joe nodded and looked around for Rita, who was standing close by, waiting for him.

'Very impressive,' she whispered as she led him down a short corridor off the main lounge. 'You've got a certain way with the ladies! French chick at the university. Now Karen? For your information, that was Karen Cullen at her warmest. I can hardly get a word out of her normally.'

'It's the subtle undercurrent of machismo. Anyway, what's the League?'

She stopped, grinned like an idiot, and cleared her throat:

'The EPL. It's Bengali for Bunch of Dickheads. Come on.'

The door was open a couple of inches. On it a hand-written poster:

ENGLISH PATRIOT LEAGUE, MEMBERS' MEETING, PRIVATE.

With what felt like untypical delicacy, Rita edged the door open and they slipped inside.

It was not a very large room. Four rows of chairs, about twenty people of varying ages sitting there. At the front a tall man was standing behind a table, addressing the audience. He was well built and had thick black hair with just a few streaks of grey. He wore a blue-and-white striped shirt and white braces, which gave him the air of an old-fashioned schoolteacher, the kind you wouldn't want to get on the wrong side of.

He paused as the door opened. The room fell silent. But only for a second or two.

'That's the problem,' he continued. 'They call *us* racist, but what kind of company employs one hundred per cent Asians? One hundred per cent *Muslim*?'

'A racist one!' someone shouted.

Murmurs of agreement arose.

'Danny Cullen, I assume?' Joe whispered.

Rita nodded. Her arms were now folded, and she'd assumed a position that was somewhere between arrogance and Suzi Quatro cock-rocker defiance, that pouty look that had sent him delirious as a kid.

Meanwhile, Mr Cullen was looking in their direction. He opened his arms wide.

'Sergeant Aktar. Glad to see you. I wonder what the official police line is on an employer favouring one racial group to the exclusion of all others?'

'Is that really your name?' Joe whispered.

'It's Rita Hridi Scannon-Aktar,' she whispered back. 'He's got Google. He thinks he's clever. Thing is, I've got his full name *and* his knob size.'

'His what!'

But when he turned to her, she'd ignored Cullen's jibe

completely and had gone over to sit down on the low wall by the door. Everyone in the room was now looking at Joe. He wondered whether he should say a few words about employment law. Fortunately, Cullen called for attention and continued his speech, and Joe went to sit next to Rita at the back.

'You see how much help the constabulary are when it comes to enforcing racial fairness?' Cullen said. 'I bet there's a few people here tonight wouldn't mind working as cab drivers. It's still a good living. Steady. Better than Uber, I've heard. But the private cab firms are run by Asian families and they never advertise. Never have any vacancies. All the licences are taken. You get a taxi in Batley tonight, or up in Birstall. Who's gonna be driving you?'

The audience told him exactly who. As the racial epithets grew in number and offensiveness, Joe felt the urge to intervene, if only for Rita's sake. But when he glanced at her, she gave him a wink. She was loving every second of it.

Sensing that her Batley-Bangladeshi skin was thick enough to take anything the English Patriot League could throw at her, Joe relaxed and checked his messages. Gwyn wasn't hanging about. He'd scheduled a pathologist's examination of Craig Shaw's remains for the following morning. The car was already in safe storage, a forensic inspection booked for tomorrow. Things were moving quickly.

He sat back and let the meeting wash over him.

'They've got a website,' Rita said. 'It'll pass the time.'

He found it easily enough on his phone. The English Patriot League. It had a simple but surprisingly professional layout:

1. WHAT IS THE EPL?

2. ENGLISH PATRIOTISM, <u>NOT</u> RACISM

3. FREE MOVEMENT OF LABOUR? A FAIR
   IMMIGRATION POLICY

4. CLEAN UP OUR STREETS: CLEAN UP OUR
   COMMUNITIES

5. DRUGS: THE IRA WERE RIGHT ABOUT
   ONE THING

Were they? he asked himself as his finger was drawn to the final item:

Drugs create a desperate cycle of dependency. They destroy families, wreck careers and turn our streets into no-go areas. Criminal gangs operate right under the noses of the police, who can't – or won't – put a stop to them.

Not long ago police inaction was also widespread in Northern Ireland. The Republican Action Against Drugs (RAAD) decided to do something about it. Operating with the IRA's approval, RAAD offered amnesties to local drug dealers, and if they refused, they were shot in the arms or knees, their houses firebombed. It was extreme. But was it more extreme than letting the cancer of the drug culture grow and overwhelm your own community? Your own children?

The EPL is proud to be 'vigilante'. We seek out drug dealers wherever they are. We pressure the authorities to take action, to safeguard our towns and villages, and to put criminals behind bars. When we believe it is necessary, we also confront dealers ourselves.

Do we have a choice? Perhaps we should do nothing, until every inch of our country has become overrun with dopers, spice zombies, crackheads and the low-life scum who make a fortune out of this misery. The philosopher Edmund Burke said, 'The only thing necessary for the triumph of evil is for good men to do nothing'.

We say: confront the problem. And remember, many drugs networks are controlled by foreign criminals who are here illegally. Just another reason to join the EPL and help us fight for a better England!

Joe swiped the page closed and turned his attention to the man in braces, who was still talking.

'He keeps mentioning Birstall,' he said to Rita, who was busy playing with her phone. 'What is it, two, three miles away? Is there any connection?'

They both knew what he meant. The murder of the local MP by an English nationalist extremist a few years back. It had happened in Birstall. Right up the road. Next town along.

'We don't think so. The bloke who did it was a loner. Mental case. We looked at it from absolutely every angle. We don't think he knew Cullen at all.'

'Were you on the case?'

'Yeah. Mainly background checks, looking at idiots like Cullen. Looking really, really hard. I mean, we went fuckin' ape. Threw everything at it. And let me tell you, there's a lot of racist idiots about.'

88

Joe thought about it.

'This is Cullen's show, right?'

'Yeah. Him and some creep they call the Professor. He writes the stuff for the website. Real name Leo Turner. Fancies himself as a bit of an intellectual.'

'That'll explain the Burke quote. Is he here tonight?'

She raised her head, scanned the heads there for a second.

'Can't see him. Turner runs a group up at Cleckheaton Library that they're always trying to ban. Racism but with fancy words. And sexism. The Lobster Pot. That's the name of the group.'

'I'll check it out.'

They chatted *sotto voce* about local right-wing groups, until Joe couldn't resist it any longer.

'Come on, then. Tell me about his cock.'

She froze, eyes ablaze, looking right at him. Then, with no warning, she exploded into deafening laughter, falling forwards, hands on her knees, snorting until she sounded ready to choke.

By the time she'd got her breath back the entire room had turned to look. The two of them sat there, like naughty school-children, not quite knowing what to do.

The meeting didn't last long after that. The issue of taxi drivers was discussed some more. There were a few calls for action, a spontaneously hatched plan for a patriotic crusade against the local private-cab sector. But these were voiced half-heartedly, and with glances back to the two giggling police officers at the rear, whose presence was still a mystery.

Then people began to stand, ready to leave. Danny Cullen did his best to maintain some kind of authority, shaking people's hands, the odd word of wisdom in someone's ear, an arm around a shoulder. But as he did so, he too was unable to stop himself glancing towards the back of the room.

Finally, only three members of the English Patriotic League remained: the leader himself, and two large men, both as tall as Cullen, but wider. One was in his mid-twenties, the other perhaps touching forty. Both had shaved heads. They wore black trousers and plain white shirts, bouncer style, their shirts straining around their middles and emphasizing the overall bulk of their upper bodies, which managed to be simultaneously muscle-packed and obese.

'Just a few questions, Mr Cullen,' Joe said as he showed Cullen his warrant card. 'I think we can do without the personal security.'

Cullen shook his head.

'Not security, officer. Witnesses.'

'All right Daz, Ranksy? Good to see you!' Rita said in her best West Yorkshire accent, grinning at the two *witnesses*.

The two men gave her the tiniest flicker of acknowledgement, then returned to the serious business of witnessing.

'Fair enough,' Joe said, noticing that Rita was now standing back, looking amused. 'Mr Cullen, you had a visit today from your daughter Lisa. Why was she here?'

Cullen took his time. Even now, deprived of his adoring crowd, he retained a certain charisma. Was it simply his size, his paternal manner, his stripy shirt and braces? Joe couldn't quite work it out.

'Inspector Romano...'

'Detective Sergeant.'

'Beg your pardon. *Sergeant* Romano. We know why she was

here, don't we? Her boyfriend was killed. Craig Shaw. He was a drug dealer.'

'And?'

'And you've no doubt heard about the League's position on drugs. So now we're under suspicion.'

'Did you know him? You know his name.'

'Never met him.'

'You, gents?' Joe asked.

Daz and Ranksy shook their heads.

Rita exhaled so volubly that all four men turned.

'Ranksy!' she said, somewhere between a guffaw and a shriek of exasperation. 'I've bloody *seen* you with him. I drove past, I honked my friggin' horn. Batley town centre, behind the BetFred's? You were standing there, leaning into his Beemer, giving him the whole finger-wagging bit!'

The younger man's blank expression never slipped.

'Skinny kid?'

'That'll be the one!'

Ranksy shrugged. 'We had a little chat, yeah.'

'So now,' she continued, 'you're, like, even *more* of a suspect in a murder investigation! Come on, fellas. We don't think you did it. Just help us out a bit, eh? No one's dragging you down the nick, are they?'

We don't think you did it. Joe logged that one for further discussion. Rita certainly liked to jump in and get her side of things across. Not his style.

'Mr Cullen,' he continued, 'can you tell us what your daughter said today?'

Cullen nodded. 'Nothing much. She told us what had happened.'

'Time?'

'Around four-thirty.'

'What was her frame of mind?'

'She was distressed, obviously. I told her to stay here for the night, longer, if she wanted. But she wouldn't. She left a bit later.'

'Has there been any tension between you? I mean, about her boyfriend?'

Cullen took a deep breath and opened his arms.

'Yes, officer, there has. We are against everything Craig Shaw was doing. Let's get that straight. But she's our daughter. We stand by her. Now and forever.'

'Family first,' Daz whispered, to no one in particular. Everyone ignored him.

'You stand by her? Degree in Media and Communications, isn't it?'

Cullen nodded with pride.

'Tuition fees? Accommodation? Living expenses? Would there be receipts for any of that?'

Joe counted to five while Cullen failed to answer. Then:

'Tuesday evening? Where were you all? Let's start with you, Mr Cullen.'

'You don't need to start with me. We were together, at Cleckheaton Library, the three of us.'

'At the Lobster Pot?'

Cullen was now trying to conceal a frown, and not making a good job of it.

'Yes. *Modern society. A fresh view.* A discussion group. And if there's anything else we can help you with, Sergeant, I can let our solicitor know.'

'Danny, you're shitting me,' said Rita. 'We're having a word, is all!'

Cullen straightened his shoulders, drawing himself up to his full height.

'I'm just being careful. Right-wing extremists, that's what they call us. Anyone who even dares to raise these issues is a racist. Have you seen the rings they ran around Tommy Robinson? You're surprised we want a lawyer here?'

Joe and Rita looked at each other. It was time to go. But Cullen wasn't done.

'Racists. Vigilantes. Extremists. That's the press we get. And why is that?'

'Because,' Joe said, if only so Rita wouldn't have time to say anything, 'that's how things like this are often perceived? Racism hiding behind reason?'

Cullen's eyes widened a fraction.

'Yes, reason. You heard what I said about the taxi firms? It's the truth, the reality for the white working class. Every word I said. *We're* the racists, though, just because we say it.'

With that, Joe and Rita were done.

'Last thing, officers,' Cullen said as they were turning to leave. 'Grooming gangs. Where've the police been on that, in the last few years?'

'Getting convictions, dick,' Rita said. 'Meanwhile your mate Tommy's doing his best to bring trials down, the twat!'

Joe put himself between Rita and Cullen.

'Come on, let's go,' he said, trying to marshal her towards the door without actually touching her.

'It's not blood on the streets,' Cullen called after them. 'It's semen. Asian semen!'

She spun around, slamming into Joe, who took the opportunity to bundle her out through the doorway.

'Keep walking,' he whispered as he shoved her along.

They made their way through to the main bar.

'Are you all right? Fancy a quick one, take the edge off?'

'In this place? You must be joking!' She lowered her voice. 'Shit, we've still got to interview vinegar tits.'

'I can do that.'

'All right. I'll write up the notes for Danny. You do his wonderful spouse, and we'll swap emails later. OK?' It wasn't a question. She was already turning to leave. 'Speak first thing tomorrow, see where we're at.'

With that she was gunning for the door. And there was no roll in her shoulders now.

Joe turned and leant on the bar. He looked down the line of lager pumps, and eventually spotted one for Tetley's Bitter. Keg not barrel, but it was marginally better than nothing. Or lager.

Karen Cullen resolutely avoided eye contact as she served him. He let the awkward silence run on, knowing that she'd have a word or two to impart when she handed him his drink. It was like a little silent drama awaiting its even smaller denouement.

As the beer rose steadily up the side of the glass, an old man shuffled across and stood a few feet away, waiting to be served. He wore a faded duffle coat and a baseball cap, and his beard was grey but streaked with orange tobacco stains around the mouth. He could have been fifty or eighty, it was hard to tell. Whichever, it looked like he'd spent most of that time leaning against bars just like this one.

'Evenin',' Joe said.

The man looked surprised, but only for a second.

'Evenin' to you,' he said, holding up his empty glass as if it was merely a way of greeting someone. 'And a fine one!'

'Pleased to meet you. I'm Joe.'

'Andrew.'

'What you having, Andrew?'

Karen Cullen looked on with sour-faced suspicion as she grabbed another glass. She knew it was bullshit, but what could she do?

'Are we chasing?' Joe asked.

Andrew thought about it, cocking his head to one side as he considered the proposition.

'A small Jameson's? That'd be grand.'

Joe nodded to Karen. The whiskey was served with the same cynical scowl.

'On your own?' Andrew asked, before bringing his pint glass carefully up to his mouth and sinking a couple of inches.

'Well,' Joe said, 'I was supposed to be having a drink with my daughter. But we had a bit of a row. Screaming blue murder she was! They grow up fast, young girls. And they never stop shouting!'

With that he buried his face in his Tetley's and waited.

Andrew's rasping breath developed into a chuckle.

'He's not wrong there, is he, Karen?'

Joe looked at the landlady, who hovered nearby and was doing her best to ignore them both.

'Just like little Lisa! She tore the bloody place down! Hammer and tongs!'

'What, today?' Joe asked.

'Aye, this afternoon!'

Andrew's face was screwed up now, the whole thing wildly amusing to him. But Karen was pinning him with an expression of hardly disguised loathing. He got the message soon enough, took both drinks, nodded his thanks to Joe and shuffled back to his table over by the wall, out of the landlady's range.

'How old is Lisa?' he asked when the old man had gone. 'What, twenty-one, twenty-two?'

'Twenty.'

'Craig Shaw was twenty-five. You ever meet his mum?'

She shook her head.

'Decent woman. The father was never involved. She did it all on her own. Do you know what she's telling herself now?'

She shrugged.

'She's telling herself that it's all her fault,' said Joe, putting his pint down. 'She brought him into the word, raised him on her own, and he turned out to be some second-rate drug pusher who got torched in a bloody Toyota Corolla. Her Toyota Corolla, actually.'

'That's drugs for you, eh?'

'Lisa was living with him. She was involved. What if there'd been two bodies in that car?'

She took her time.

'It'd be the end of my life.'

He gave it a second.

'Help me, then.'

She shook her head. 'It wasn't anybody from here.'

'You sure?'

'Yeah. I know it.'

'Shall I tell his mum that? You just *know* it? Jane, she's called. Jane Shaw.'

'It's none of my business.'

'It could've been. So easily.'

She tried to look away. But he held her stare.

'Give me a mobile number,' he said. 'Somewhere I can reach you, in confidence.'

He struggled to finish his beer, which was so cold that he could have been drinking chilled piss and never noticed. But when he left the pub there was a Tetley's beermat in his pocket, with a number written on it in Biro. Below the number: *Text first.*

14

Craig Shaw. Drug dealer. It's been on the news, his face all over Twitter. Those nasty eyes.

The world did this. Not me. I was just there, under that railway bridge. Now I'm part of it.

I remember sensing him on the floor beside me as I drove away. It felt like everything had just clicked into place. I had the whole thing mapped out in my head in a matter of seconds. It was risky taking his car, but there was no choice. Leaving him there wasn't an option.

I hadn't been *driving* his car. I realize that, now. I'd been carried along, shooting forward to a new, simpler place. And I can't get back. I don't think I could make any of this go away, not now.

There's good and there's bad. It's that simple. All these years, and it was Craig Shaw who showed me the truth. Good people and bad people. Two columns on a ledger. All you can do is take something away from one of the columns. Add something to the other. Make things right.

On Tuesday I got home, parked the Toyota, sat there. Who was he, this ugly young man who'd shown me the way?

Did it matter?

No. It didn't matter two days later either, when I torched the car. I know exactly the kind of person he was. And I *know* that it doesn't matter. I didn't mean this to happen. Ha! That's what they all say, isn't it? An accident, *I never meant to...* Well, I'm going make it mean something.

It doesn't matter *who* Craig Shaw was. But it matters *what* he was. He was a gift, a chance to make things better, a chance that came my way. And now I have no choice but to go on. Who else is going to do it?

The next one was easy, once I started to think about it. I know him this time. It was a few years back and he won't remember me. A lot's happened to him since then. He's a rapist, a thief and a drug dealer. How's that for a CV? And he's young. So young and so bad! He can't change that. None of them can. They can't change who they are.

But I can change something. I can save the world from a great deal of pain.

From Jason Beverage.

You won't remember me, Jason.

But I remember you.

SATURDAY

15

He skirted Cleckheaton town centre and drove up past Tesco, its car park already three-quarters full. Beyond that was a large mill building. It bore down on everything with a kind of natural arrogance, a presumption so casual that its very presence was easy to overlook. Wouldn't be a mill now. Flat conversions and business units, perhaps.

He drove past it as he made his way up the valley side and out of town. What does a mill town do once its heart is ripped out, when the mills have closed down? He had no idea. But the rows of tightly packed terraced houses in the shadows of the mill looked solid enough, in good condition. They were larger than the one in which Jane Shaw now sat alone, wondering why her son was dead.

On he went, and the terraces soon gave way to larger, stone-fronted houses. Then trees began to appear, mature sycamores and chestnuts amid the buildings. Less than a mile out of town and already the neighbourhood had changed entirely. Judging by some of the older houses, this would have been where the mill owners and their managers lived, higher up, away from the smoke and the grime. The natural order of things.

Ahead of him was a double-decker bus. It indicated and

pulled in, coughing out a little puff of blue diesel smoke as it came to a halt by the kerb. Something caught his eye as he braked. *Lobster*. Large clear letters on a white background. *The Lobster Pot*.

The bus was already pulling away by the time he was out of his car and standing in front of the poster, which had been fixed to the end panel of the bus stop, a fresh piece of clear Sellotape in each corner.

The Lobster Pot
Modern society: A fresh view

How many things are you not allowed to do or say anymore?

- Tell a woman she's looking good? Sexist pig!
- Clip a naughty kid behind the ear? Abuser!
- Criticize a racial or religious group? Racist!

'Special interest groups' now dominate the political debate: radical feminism, ethnic minorities, gays and lesbians, transgender, immigrants' rights… It's a wonder there's anyone left.

But a lot of us are left. And we're becoming an endangered species: the Great White Male (GWM) and the Great White Female (GWF).

How did we get here? And who's responsible?

Modern society simply ignores inconvenient truths (ethnic grooming gangs, criminal immigrant networks…), and it's now borderline illegal to

say certain things (kids need a mother <u>and</u>
a father, corporal punishment works…).

The truth can be uncomfortable, but our
discussions are open to everyone and are
a space for free speech and expression.

Let's build an alternative view of society, one based
on decency, honesty and common sense.

All we ask for is an open mind!

Cleckheaton Library, every Tuesday, 7.30 p.m.

He read through it a couple of times. *An open mind*. The phrase
felt out of place, a cliché, almost cute. How long was it since
an open mind had been of use to anyone?

About as long as it was since he'd been in a library, he told
himself as he took the poster down and got back in the Mondeo.
And how many years ago was that? He tried to answer the
question, but soon realized it was the wrong one.

Not years.

Decades.

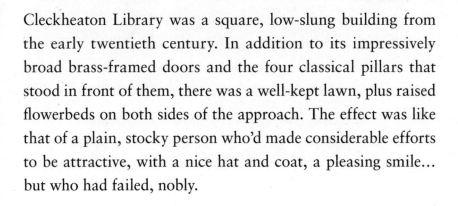

Cleckheaton Library was a square, low-slung building from
the early twentieth century. In addition to its impressively
broad brass-framed doors and the four classical pillars that
stood in front of them, there was a well-kept lawn, plus raised
flowerbeds on both sides of the approach. The effect was like
that of a plain, stocky person who'd made considerable efforts
to be attractive, with a nice hat and coat, a pleasing smile…
but who had failed, nobly.

He pulled open one of the heavy doors and was greeted by laughter. Three men of retired age were taking off their anoraks, rubbing their hands and nudging each other. It looked more like a lively night at the bingo than a place of learning. A moment later they'd disappeared into the main part of the library.

Finding himself alone in the entrance, Joe began reading through the many posters on display: *Mummy Pilates, No Strings Attached Ukulele Group, Kirklees Dementia Hub, Scrabble Club, Get Down and Buggy Pushchair Walkers' Group, War-gaming Club...* It was like a parallel universe in which every possible excuse for seeking out human company had become a reality. The nearest he'd ever got to joining a community group was a monthly neighbourhood *soiree* in France. He'd hated going, whereas Jackie had loved it. The only way he could make it through an entire evening was to drink until he was half-asleep, closing himself off from the bullshit posturing of his French hosts. Meanwhile, Jackie whooped it up, oblivious to the nuances of her neighbours' tedious conversation. Then she'd fallen in love with one of them, as Joe dozed in the corner.

He used his phone to take a picture of each poster, then moved onto a second notice board on the other side of the entrance area: *Creative Writing Circle, Inviting You to a Baby Shower (advice and support for expectant new parents), Living with Bereavement, Building with Lego, Seated Tai Chi, Indoor Curling...* How could you play curling indoors? It sounded as bizarre and improbable as *Race Nite*, an activity done without the main element, like darts without the dartboard. Some sort of in-joke, perhaps.

A young man appeared, easing himself between Joe and the notice board.

'Excuse me,' he said without looking round, as he tore down a large poster, screwed it up, and dropped it into a waste-paper bin in the corner.

He remained there, admiring the empty space on the board between *Cancer Survivors' Circle* and the *Model Aeroplane Club.*

'Lot of groups you've got here,' Joe said, noticing the Kirklees Library Services badge on the breast pocket of the guy's faded denim shirt.

The young man did a *what's it to you?* shrug.

'Actually, the one I'm interested in doesn't seem to be here. Modern society. Open minds. Lobsters?'

The guy turned away from Joe, speaking as he rummaged in the bin.

'There's a bunch of fascists use the meeting room. Can't stop 'em, long as they book it through the proper channels. I can take their posters down, though. Here. He'll be back to put another one up. Little Saturday ritual we've got going.'

He handed the ball of paper to Joe.

'Actually,' Joe asked as he straightened it out, recognizing the same glossy poster from the bus stop, 'I've already got one of these.'

The librarian didn't even dignify that with an answer.

'I'm not a sympathizer,' Joe added, wondering why he'd felt the need to explain himself.

The young man stopped, mid-step, and looked Joe right in the eye.

'I don't care.'

'I think you might, Mark Sugden,' he said, reading the name from the library name tag as he held his warrant card up close to the young man's face.

Sugden was probably around thirty. But he had the pallor of a student who'd been left out in the rain a bit too long, the faint air of crusty radicalism, the whiff of protest marches full of white guys with dreadlocks and bad teeth.

'These lobster people, tell me about them. You know Daniel Cullen? Tall guy, alpha-male type?'

Sugden shook his head.

'You know anyone else in the group?'

Again, a shake of the head.

'I know nothing, officer.'

'They take a vigilante line. Cleaning up the streets, that kind of thing.'

'That's the police's job, isn't it? Cleaning up the streets, keeping everybody in order, nobody stepping out of line?'

He snorted like a sarcastic teenager and looked down at the floor.

'You don't like the police?'

'Got my opinions. It's a free country. *Sergeant.*'

'One last question, Mr Sugden. Indoor curling? Is that really a thing?'

'See for yourself. They're through the library. The meeting room's at the back on the right.'

Joe checked the time on the poster. That was it. The old fellas had been getting ready to go curling. Competitive curling too, judging by the way they'd been ribbing each other a few minutes ago.

With the librarian now making a great show of ignoring him, Joe stepped cautiously into the reading room, saw that there was hardly anyone there and wandered down between the stacks.

The atmosphere was warm and dry, with that subtle but

delicious aroma of paper, the smell of calm, of order, of casual discovery. He hadn't been a particularly dedicated scholar in his youth, but now, so many years later, those evenings in Nottingham University Library came back to him. Lazily reading Giovanni Guareschi's *Don Camillo* stories for the sheer, innocent pleasure, unhindered by any worries about tuition fees, student debt for the rest of his life. It seemed like a distant wonderland that he'd drifted through, and right out of, never to return. He'd chosen a career in teaching, but five years after that he was in the police. Now he was back in a library, looking for the killer of a drug dealer who no one seemed to know or care about. More *Divine Comedy* than *Don Camillo*.

He didn't need to look very hard to find the indoor curling. The raised voices led him right to it. In a long, carpeted room at the back of the library he found a sea of silver hair, muted corduroys and hunched backs. About a dozen men and women were playing, sending small curling stones on wheels across the carpet, each shot accompanied by winces and groans. Yet there was also laughter, a great deal of it, the sound of people having a bloody good time doing something a little bit ridiculous in a location decidedly not intended for it.

'Fancy a go?' asked a ruddy-faced man in a maroon Harvard sweatshirt and brown slacks.

Several others stopped to look.

'Unfair advantage!' shouted one of the ladies. 'Look at him! He's half our age!'

'And able-bodied!' someone added.

'I'll leave it to the experts, if that's all right,' said Joe, sitting down in one of the plastic chairs against the wall.

He watched as a woman sent a wheeled stone along the

carpet, garnering praise from the crowd, several of whom were not only able-bodied but spritely. He hoped he'd be in that kind of shape when he was drawing his police pension.

A large, portly man came across and lowered himself down into the adjacent seat.

'A bit young for this crowd, aren't you?' he asked, wheezing a little as he shifted his weight in an attempt to get comfortable.

'Curling in a library? It's… it's a strange one!'

'That it is!' He paused. 'Looking for anyone in particular, officer?'

Joe thought about it.

'That obvious, is it?'

'A man your age in a suit and tie on a Saturday morning? Few days after a murder just down the road?' He held out a hand. 'Dave Bannister. I was a local councillor for more years than I care to remember. Spent a lot of time with the police. I can spot you lot a mile off!'

'I'm looking into the Lobster Pot,' Joe said, lowering his voice a touch.

Bannister considered the information, nodding appreciatively.

'That the angle, is it? Interesting.'

Joe hated amateur sleuths. And he hated local councillors. It dawned on him that perhaps he hated too many people. Busybodies could be useful sources of information, though.

'No angle, just one of many lines of enquiry.'

'It's all over Twitter,' Bannister said.

Joe had agreed to release the fact that the last sighting of Shaw was in Cleckheaton town centre, expecting a few dozen vague and unhelpful phone calls from the public. As it happened, no one had rung, although plenty of people had taken to social media to offer their theories and opinions.

'Do any of these folk go to the Lobster Pot?' he asked.

Bannister took a moment, glanced around the assembled curlers.

'I think Trevor went once. He's not here today. Having a stent out at Pinderfields.'

'What did he say about them?'

'A bit of anti-Islamic what-not, but mainly traditional values, y'know. A woman's place, smack your kids, that kind of style.'

'He didn't carry on going?'

'Elaine wouldn't let him!'

'Vigilante justice? What's your take on that?'

Bannister shrugged. 'That murdered lad was involved in drugs, I assume. It's *Happy Valley* round here! Could've been anybody. Besides,' he looked at the veterans in front of them, 'a few of this lot smoke cannabis. Or make biscuits. The grand-kids get it for 'em.' He lowered his voice. 'It's better than the stuff they give you for arthritis, now that's a fact. Oh look, it's my turn. Nice speaking to you.'

Back in the entrance a woman was putting up another poster on one of the notice boards. Joe paused, trying to guess: *Advanced Tiddlywinks, Wheelchair Taekwondo…* When she stood back to admire her work, he was a little disappointed. *Job Club: Finance Skills.*

Having perhaps sensed that someone was watching her, she turned. She was about his age, with shortish dark hair and an expression which managed to be both serious and distant. For a moment she seemed not to understand why he was looking at her. Then her expression lightened.

'You'd be very welcome.'

'Job Club?' he said. 'Thanks, but gainfully employed. Well, *employed*.'

She smiled. 'Job satisfaction's overrated.'

'You run it?'

'The club? Yes. We do banking skills, personal finance, some basic accountancy. It's just a hobby of mine.'

'Good hobby.'

'Is it? I'm a teacher, actually.'

'Now that is a job! Local?'

She nodded. 'Whitcliffe Mount School. Just round the corner. I teach Maths.'

'Funny, I used to be a teacher. French and Italian. Not anymore, though.'

She looked him up and down. 'Let me guess. Actually, you still look like a teacher. Y'know, one of the well-dressed ones.'

He held up his card. Best get it out of the way.

'Oh, right. That's...' she searched for the right word '...impressive.'

There was the slightest blush in her cheeks. Surprise? He often got that. He simply didn't look like a copper.

'I'm investigating the murder of a young man. Quite close to here. You might have seen it on the news?'

'I haven't seen the news for a few days. Was it recent?'

'Yes. Craig Shaw. Last seen down near the town centre on Tuesday evening. Perhaps you've seen him around?'

He found a photo on his phone.

She looked at the image of Shaw, took her time.

'Should I have? I don't think I've seen him here in the library. And certainly not at school.'

She returned to the poster. But the poster didn't need her attention. There was a moment's deliberation, for them both. It was silly, Joe told himself, now, in the middle of a murder investigation. He hedged his bets.

'I'd be able to find you at the school? For some background on the town? It's always useful to speak to a teacher, someone who knows the place, the people. I'm from Leeds. Not too familiar with this part of the world.'

She remained there, looking at the poster. Then she turned.

'Chris Saunders.' She took a phone and waved it in front of him. 'I'd be happy to help.'

He knew what Bluetooth was, but not how to do it on his new iPhone. Besides, whenever he tried to use Bluetooth something always went wrong. It was like a digital will-o'-the-wisp, impossible to pin down.

She recognized his helplessness, and recited her number for him. As he wrote it in his notebook she moved closer and watched, as if checking his work for errors. Her perfume reminded him of those first optimistic months in France, when everything had smelled sweet.

'I damn well *can*!'

The raised voice took them both by surprise. They turned to see a middle-aged man holding a poster. Between him and the other notice board was the librarian. The two men were engaged in what looked like a form of non-contact martial arts, moving this way and that, with Mark Sugden trying to stop the poster being pinned up, both of them speaking in aggressive but hushed tones as they did their dance.

'I say what goes up here!'

'We booked the room. We are allowed to advertise the fact!'

'Perhaps you should intervene?' she said, a hint of playfulness in her voice. She was at his side, so close that they were almost touching.

At that point the man with the poster relented, uttered a huge sigh of exasperation, and looked around for moral support.

'England! The land of petty officialdom!'

Sugden laughed out loud.

'Put the poster up, then! See how long it stays there!'

With that he marched back into the library, where he pretended to occupy himself at the main counter, within earshot of the entrance.

'You'll see,' the man said over his shoulder as he finally pinned his large, glossy poster for the Lobster Pot on the board in the space where the previous copy had been, 'it'll be in the bin in two minutes.'

'Are you the coordinator of this group?' Joe asked, stepping towards the irate man.

'I am indeed,' he said, his face lighting up. 'Leo Turner. Pleased to meet you.' He thrust out a hand and gave a hard, enthusiastic shake. 'Always looking for new faces. Are you interested in social justice?'

'Actually,' Joe said, watching the elation drain from Turner's face as he was shown the warrant card, 'I do have a few questions.'

Meanwhile, Chris moved past them and went into the reading room, mouthing a silent goodbye. He watched the smooth, controlled movement of her body as she disappeared, wondering what kind of books she liked to read.

'We generate quite a lot of hostility,' Turner said, lowering his voice and moving towards the main doors, out of the range of the librarian.

He was in his fifties, slim, with thinning hair and an undeniable air of superiority, despite being somewhat flushed after his skirmish with petty officialdom. The Professor, they called him. More like Assistant Lecturer, Joe thought as he scanned the poster, confirming that it appeared to be exactly the same as the others.

'I'm not really interested in fresh views of society at the moment. What I do need from you is a list of everybody that attended the group on Tuesday night.'

'May I ask why? Because if it's more harassment from the authorities...'

'Murder, Mr Turner. I am running a murder inquiry, and we need that list.' He waited. 'Now.'

Turner shook his head. 'I don't carry that sort of information around with me.'

'I'm guessing that it's a small group. Now, you seem to have a laptop there. Perhaps you have a members list saved in a file. Please?'

Turner pursed his lips, thought about it.

'Well, officer. We are very *pro* law enforcement. The rule of law is what distinguishes us from the animals, is it not?'

Joe wasn't answering that one. He waited.

'What I can do,' Turner said, keen to fill the silence, 'is quickly check on the situation vis-à-vis Data Protection, which I can do on the internet here in the library, and I'll be with you presently. Is that acceptable?'

'Daniel Cullen and his two sidekicks, Daz and Ranksy. Yes or no?'

'Like I said…'

'OK, I'm from Leeds CID. Let's do this at Elland Road. That's half an hour there and half an hour back. Plus however long it takes me to find somewhere to do an interview, and a duty solicitor. Or you can phone your own lawyer on the way if you prefer. Off we go.'

He held the door open, gripping it hard to contain his irritation.

Turner took a moment, then nodded. 'Fine. They were here.'

'What time.'

'Seven-thirty 'til nine.'

He was about to ask for Turner's address and phone number. But then he had a better idea.

'OK. Why don't you read up on Data Protection? I'll be wanting a full list. You're also a member of the English Patriot League, correct? I'll need a list of League members too, Data Protection permitting.'

With that he pulled open the door and threw himself out into the refreshingly chill morning air.

'Prick!' he hissed as his fingers jabbed the screen of his phone.

'Rita? It's me. You up at the crime scene? I'll see you there in a few minutes. Oh, and guess who I just bumped into? The Professor himself, Leo Turner. Can you get someone from Kirklees to email me his contact details, plus anything of interest about him? He's kicking up a legal fuss about access to the group info.' He stopped, listening incredulously to Rita's reply. 'A *lawyer*? Shit.'

He ended the call and tried to put Turner out of his mind as he walked back to his car. On the way he noticed a bike chained to a drainpipe at the corner of the building. Judging by the average age and condition of the library users today, it must have belonged to the uncooperative librarian.

'Oh, I bet he bloody loves bragging about how he never pollutes the environment!' he chuntered as he got his car keys out.

16

When he arrived, Rita was poking around in the trees close to where the burnt-out Toyota had been found. Not far off was the Land Rover, driver's door swinging open in the wind, keys still in the ignition.

'They'll nick your motor!' he shouted across to her as he parked and got out.

'They'll friggin' try,' she said without turning around. 'Owt up at the library?'

'Few people of interest. Some of 'em were playing curling on the carpet!'

'Yeah, I've heard of that,' she said, now turning to look at him. 'Sounds fun! Leo Turner?'

'Librarian wasn't happy about him putting up his Lobster Pot posters. Seems like a crank to me. Anyway, I got the email with his info. Thanks for that. One thing: he forgot to mention he was a lawyer when I spoke to him. Strange, eh?'

'They're all bloody strange in the League. Anyway, are you lot all done here?'

He sensed the qualified accusation. *You lot?*

'You've seen the SOC report?' he said. 'There's nothing

obvious with the tyre tracks. Motor comes in. Straight into this corner. There wasn't much in the way of forensics.'

'He was in the passenger footwell. No one bothered to shift him into the driver's seat, to make it look like an accident. Or suicide.'

'Or they were in a rush. Either way, it was a well-planned job. Efficient. Perhaps CCTV'll give us a second car.'

Rita crossed her arms. If she'd tutted it couldn't have been more disparaging.

'There was no second car,' she said. 'Our man drove here in the Toyota.'

'Man? Or men?'

'Man.'

'Care to explain?'

She unfolded her arms as if the effort was considerable and she was doing it just for him. Then she went back towards the trees, speaking over her shoulder.

'You torch the car, then what? You've chosen this spot 'cos it's near the trees, but also 'cos it's close to the road.'

They walked through the trees, and there was the wall, just where it had been yesterday. He let her have her Poirot moment.

'If you wanna be away quick, over the wall you go, and you're off,' she said. 'Which bit would you go over?'

He shrugged. 'It's only three feet high. That's not going to matter, is it?'

'Take a closer look, partner.'

He resented her cockiness, but he knew there'd be a reason, which made him resent it even more. He looked up and down the length of the wall, just like he'd done yesterday.

'Rita, if you don't tell me what I've missed this might end up being a double murder.'

She snorted. 'Don't worry. I'm not gonna *kill* you for incompetence! Just look.'

She pointed to a section of the wall about fifteen feet away. The ground in front of it was slightly risen, and there was a protruding stone a little way up, just enough to serve as a step.

'That's where I'd go over,' she said as they moved towards it. 'Hasn't rained since Thursday, but it rained Wednesday, right? The rock's still damp, never really dried out. But see that? It's still raw.'

He saw it immediately, the lighter hue where a sliver of the old sandstone had been dislodged, right where you'd put your foot.

'Now,' she said, 'if you were carrying something that you had to get over the wall, this stone'd be perfect. You're desperate to be away. In the rush you drag it over, it scrapes against the stone as it goes...'

Shit. *Shit.* Even now, as she extended her index finger he could see scratch marks in the dark, weathered stone. Fresh marks. But that wasn't all. There were the tiniest fragments of something yellow.

'What's that?'

'Scrape marks. And there are minute bits of plastic in them. Something's been dragged over the wall.'

His mind spun.

'Could that be from a bike? Y'know, the tape they have on the frame?'

He sprang over the wall and down onto the road at the other

side, making sure he landed on the tarmac, avoiding the bare earth close to the wall. And there it was, in the still-damp earth. A perfectly formed tyre track. A bicycle tyre.

'Different kind of track, Joe,' she said, looking down at him. 'And it's one set of tracks. One bike. I think we just made some progress.'

He was already on his phone.

17

They'd taken a cast of the tyre track and mud samples themselves. Rita had a kit in the Land Rover. By the time they were back at Elland Road, the CCTV footage of the various routes away from the crime scene had been prioritized, anywhere a bike could have gone, a spider's web on the map, spinning out in all directions from the crime scene. The only thing now was finding someone willing to go through it all.

'You get anywhere with Karen Cullen last night? Your report was a bit vague.'

They were in the pathologist's lab, speaking in hushed tones, as though the dead might resent the sound of raised voices.

'Not sure. I think so. It felt like there was something going on. I reckon she'll tell me. Got her mobile number.'

She smirked. 'You always get their number?'

'I wish.'

'You phoned that French chick up at the university yet?'

'What? No!'

In truth he'd forgotten all about her. No wonder he was single. Then there was the woman from the library. He had managed to get her number. But that was work-related. For the moment, at least.

'You know,' Rita said as they waited for the pathologist to go through the paperwork, 'you've got a good way with folk. All those little silences of yours, the pauses, the patience? I mean, I'm more the jump-in-with-both-feet type.'

'I'd noticed. By the way, what was all that *we-don't-think-you-did-it* stuff yesterday with Cullen and his goons?'

'Well, we don't, do we? Not yet. No point rilin' 'em up 'til we've got a main suspect. Then we can go a-rilin'.'

'I'll look forward to it.'

The pathologist was new. She had a Scottish accent and couldn't have been much more than a teenager. Joe wondered whether Sam might end up doing the same thing, poking around in the singed remains of a scumbag that no one cared about. Was there a more dispiriting way to spend one's Saturday?

'Jesus,' Rita whispered as the white plastic sheet was whipped back.

It was a mound, not a person, so far removed from a discernible cadaver that the dull, depressing sight of a murder victim was replaced by a macabre curiosity. What was it Karen Cullen had said? *It'd be the end of my life.* He wanted to drag her down here now, so she could see what had happened to someone else's child, their only child.

'Death came before the fire,' the pathologist said in a clipped tone, as if her coolness was being assessed for its exact degree of disinterest. 'Around forty-eight hours before, I'd estimate.'

'How precise is that timeframe?' Rita asked, notebook already out.

'Eight hours either way, give or take. Some of the internal blood and organs were more or less intact. Death itself was by means of a pencil.'

She waited. New to the job she may have been, but she certainly had a sense of theatre.

'A pencil?' Joe asked, annoyed by her manner.

'It was inserted through the right eye socket, directly into the brain. All the way in, seven inches to be exact. An entire pencil, pushed in as far as the cerebellum. That's at the back of the head. It caused a *lot* of brain damage. Intracranial haemorrhaging and the associated mass effect caused by the penetrating object. What that means is...'

'We know what it means,' Joe said.

'*OK*... So, massive trauma to the brain parenchyma. You're know what...'

'No, you can explain that one, love,' Rita said.

'Neurons and glial cells, the things that keep the brain going. There was severe damage. Given the assumed trauma, a pencil pushed right through the brain, it was probably sudden and forceful. There might have been some lateral movement too.'

'Evidence of a struggle?'

'Can't tell. The pencil seems to have gone in cleanly, but the lesion certainly fans out a bit. That would have made things worse.'

'How?'

'The brain was so badly damaged that it bled out. Intracranial haemorrhage isn't always fatal, but in this case he clearly didn't receive any treatment.'

'Could he have been immobilized instantly?'

'That depends on many things, but essentially yes, it's possible.'

'No other injuries? Nothing before, or after?'

She shook her head. 'Difficult to see in this state. But nothing

I could find. No broken bones. Nothing showed up on his bloods. No drugs, no meds, no alcohol.'

'Clean-living boy,' Rita said, noting it all down.

Joe didn't quite understand.

'There was nothing about a pencil in the initial report.'

'That's because there was no pencil. But right at the back of his brain there was the tip from a pencil, just a bit of lead. It must have broken off. The lesion fits the dimensions of a pencil. Also, there was a small fragment of paint, again, from a pencil, I assume.'

'And...'

'Forensics have it. I sent everything up an hour ago.'

18

The operations room was quiet. Weekends are rarely busy in CID. And it doesn't matter how long you've been in plain clothes, there's one difference from uniform that always raises a smile: no hung-over troublemakers to process and turf out on a Saturday morning.

'Ah, right,' Joe said as they made their way across to his desk. 'There's Gwyn Merchant over there, he's the deputy on the case.'

Merchant was at the back of the room, leaning against the wall, hands in pockets, the best suit in the department, chatting to a young female clerk at a data terminal. He looked up, squinted for a moment, then broke into a mad grin.

'Rita? Rita, is that you?' he shouted across the room, as if everyone there would be pleased to hear his booming voice.

She stood, hands on hips, and watched as he bounded across to them, laughing as he slalomed between the desks.

'Nah, yer knob 'ead, it's another big Bangladeshi lass with a crew cut.'

'Bloody hell! Good to see yer, mate!'

They did a handshake-cum-shoulder-bump. Joe watched, knowing that the nearest he'd ever come to that kind of home-boy familiarity was a pat on Andy's back when they were both pissed and one of them was struggling into a cab.

'You all right, then?' she asked.

'I'm bloody all right. You?'

'*I'm* all right.'

'Looks like we're both bloody all right!' Merchant said, tapping her forearm with three fingers. 'Getting yer stripes, is what I heard!'

'Passed first time. Sergeant's exam *and* the Board.'

'You're dingin' mi chuffin' dong!'

'Cheeky twat! Anyway, you still like it over here?'

'I friggin' love it. I heard you were sniffin' around.'

'You lot needed a bit of help's what I heard.'

They both looked at Joe.

'He'll do anything for a collar! Druggy scum included. Me? I'm more of a one-sixty-six man!'

'You still going on about that shit?' she said.

'Statistics, not shit.'

'Shit-tistics.'

Merchant shook his head. 'One down, one less to go. That's my motto. One-sixty-six!'

'They'll put that on your grave.'

'Good. I'll stand by it. Or, you know, lie. Anyways...'

'Anyway,' Joe said, 'have you seen the report about the pencil?'

Merchant grinned. 'Yeah. It's on the system. Weird, eh?'

'I'm gonna flag it up as restricted information, just 'til we see where it takes us. Keep it out of the news. What d'you reckon?'

They both nodded.

'OK, I'll clear it with Andy and Comms.'

The three of them stood there for a moment.

'Gotta go,' Merchant said. 'I've got some crimes that really need solving.'

'Anything interesting?' Rita asked.

'Nah, boring old shit. But, y'know, the victims aren't friggin' drug dealers, so we can justify the police time.' He turned to Joe. 'Only pulling yer plonker. I'm all behind the investigation.'

'Good. We need someone to go through a pile of CCTV footage.'

'Sorted. I'm on it. It'll have to be Monday, though. That all right?'

He wasn't waiting for an answer. He winked at Rita, then strode across the office, shoulders rolling, a hand flattening down his silk tie, a kid in his Sunday best.

'Laters, big boy!' she called after him.

He raised his arms, waving into the air as he went: 'That's what they say!'

'You know him, then?' asked Joe when he'd gone.

'Gwyn? Since he was a kid. He's a Batley boy, through and through.'

'Small town, eh?'

'He lived up the road from us. You didn't know?'

'Why should I? He works in Leeds.'

'We were at school together. He was a couple of years below me. I encouraged him to join the Force, as it happens.'

'Well, he was certainly amused that you made sergeant!'

'Yeah, well I wasn't a natural candidate for promotion in my youth. A bit lippy, if you can believe that.'

He nodded.

'He kept that quiet.'

'What, about him being at school with me?'

'No, no. Batley. Forget it. Forensics are waiting. After that, do you fancy looking at a few hours of CCTV footage? I don't want to wait 'til Monday.'

19

'HB,' she said.

'And the flake of paint?'

'Manufacturers all use slightly different colours. Bit like a pencil fingerprint.'

'A pencil-print?' he suggested, trying to lighten the mood.

She didn't laugh. He'd known Bridgette almost as long as he'd been on the Force, but had never really worked out what made her tick.

'We don't have a database on pencil paint, *wouldn't you know*,' she said, speaking more to Rita than to Joe. 'I mean, who uses pencils these days?'

Joe thought about the mug full of pens and pencils on his desk, and the time it always took him to find sharpeners and rubbers.

'Fortunately,' she added, 'there was enough for the spectrometer, so we got an exact colour profile.'

She took a single sheet of printed paper and handed it to him.

'It's a slightly unusual shade of green. I've checked all the manufacturers I could find. A list of all the companies that paint their HB pencils in this colour.'

He took the paper from her. There were three words printed on it, right in the centre in a tiny font. Bridgette's idea of a joke.

'Gaia Office Supplies,' he read out. 'Do we know them?'

She clicked to something more interesting on her computer.

'Not personally, but I believe there's a new computer thing called Goggle or something. It's magic. You just type in whatever you want to know and it tells you. It's like the Deltic Oracles! I bet Gaia Office Supplies have one of those internet page thingies. They're all the rage.'

He watched as she returned to her screen and scrolled down. She'd already lost interest. Forensic scientists never seemed to be very enthusiastic about their work. Yet for him this new information sent a rush of excitement through his body. A single flake of paint extracted from deep within the brain of a dead victim? Never mind the bloody internet, this was the magic.

Meanwhile, Rita was halfway out of the door, already staring down at her phone.

'It was just the smallest bit of a pencil,' he said to Bridgette. 'And it might take us to a killer. Don't you find that even slightly exciting?'

'I'll take dried sperm any day of the week. Sorry, just the way I am.'

He knew. The whole of Elland Road knew. Her divorce last year had briefly been the most talked about in the District. It wasn't sperm that did it, though. It was human hairs. She'd found the same hairs in her husband's underpants on various occasions and had kept them for analysis. They were all from the same person, and it wasn't her. Or him.

'Tell you what, though,' she said, stopping what she was doing, just for a second. 'If my green paint leads to an arrest, there's a drink in it for me.'

'Done.'

He folded the sheet of paper and was about to leave.

'By the way,' she added, a half-decent smile on her face, 'pencils *are* better. Than dried sperm, I mean. And Gaia Office Supplies? It's the sales director you'll want to talk to. I texted you her name and number. A text message? Is that OK?'

He nodded. 'Thanks. Text, yeah, that's good.'

'I would've used WhatsApp, but, y'know.'

'I'm on the WhatsApp! Send me a WhatsApp! I'm a fluent WhatsApper!'

Her smile broadened. 'Joe Romano on WhatsApp? Who knew!'

By the time they were back in the operations room, Bridgette's message had already appeared on his WhatsApp. Her tiny profile photo was an enlargement of a dust mite, the motto below her name: *There's no escape.* She'd re-sent the details for Gaia Office Supplies, no additional message, no gratuitous 'x' or 'lol', or one of those grinning emojis. He replied:

Thanks for that. BTW it's Delphic Oracles.

A moment later, another message appeared: a photo of a woman's hand, the middle finger extended upwards. Fair.

Rita was now going through the various phone numbers on the Gaia Office Supplies website, and getting voicemail each time.

He sat at his desk and stared at the image of Bridgette's hand, her fingers slim and pale, no nail varnish. She had just become his seventh contact on WhatsApp. Three of the other numbers were work-related. His brother Tony the fifth. Then there was a random message from an attractive young woman called Sonya, a smartphone scam from Russia, he'd been told, but for some reason he hadn't deleted it. The final contact was his ex-wife Jackie, who had used WhatsApp a few times recently as their divorce was being finalized. Clipped and painfully cheerful messages to keep him up to date on the progress of various bits of paperwork and arrangements for the sale of the farmhouse in France. It had all been very efficient and cordial; her new partner had bought Joe's share of the property, lock, stock and smoking Jackie.

As a summary of his recent life, the WhatsApp contact list was not what you'd call edifying. But it was accurate. Looking around the office he wondered who he'd like to add, and came up with a shortlist of zero.

'Nearly four on a Saturday afternoon. No one's there,' Rita said, phone in hand. She screwed her mouth up, thought about it. 'This sales director? I'm gonna sniff her out, give her a bell at home. You?'

'Another chat with Jane Shaw. You fancy coming?'

'Nah. I'll make a start on the CCTV if you want. See you back here after you've ministered to the grieving mother.'

He stood up.

'Just one thing. Gwyn Merchant and the one-sixty-six thing? You've heard that from him before?'

'One per cent of the population is responsible for sixty-six per cent of all crimes committed. Yeah, he was always a bit of a hardliner, y'know...'

He waited. She let him wait. The little pauses didn't work on her.

'Well,' he said in the end, 'he's clocked off for the day. That's pretty clear.'

133

'He'll be around if you need him,' she said. 'He's solid.'

'Really?'

'It's all an act with Gwyn. He's a pretty thoughtful lad, as it goes.'

'I'll take your word for it.'

'And he's not had an easy life. But who has, eh?'

'Yep. Anyway, they're getting the footage ready in the AV suite. I'll join you in an hour or so.'

20

He drove past the Brick. There was a van outside, and someone was unloading a large Marshall speaker. A guitar case was leant up against the van, and next to it a microphone stand.

He'd played his fair share of gigs in pubs like this when he was young. The Romanos, they called themselves. Half the audience would come because they thought it was a Ramones tribute band. A few bars into the opening song and people would turn to each other, grimacing in confusion.

But Tony refused to change the name. Too much Sicilian pride, too much love for the old country. Plus, it was Tony's band. A good band too. They were offered a recording contract, on the understanding that they'd change the name. No dice. Tony wouldn't hear of it. They broke up the same day. Joe was eighteen. His big break had come early, only for pride to take a massive Sicilian dump on it. *Che sarà*. He took his guitar down to the River Aire and threw it in. A few months later he was enrolling at Nottingham University.

Jane Shaw had the bearing of someone who'd been drinking steadily all day without getting drunk. The house stank of cigarette smoke. She looked awful. But there was no choice. He was already running out of time. All that stuff about one-sixty-six? No one else cared about small-time drug dealer Craig Shaw. He'd be allowed to slip through the cracks. It had to be now.

'Right,' he said, sitting on the sofa and noting once again how comfortable it was, 'Craig had a BMW. But we have evidence that he'd been using your car for the last few weeks. Tell me why.'

'I…' she said, fumbling for a cigarette. 'His was broken.'

'No. Tell me *now*. He was using your car so that no one would know it was him, right? The people who were threatening him?'

She sighed, nodded.

'These people, they came here, to this house?'

She nodded again.

'Describe them.'

'Two blokes. Heavy, y'know.'

'How old were they?'

'One youngish, twenties? The other one was older. Big, they were. Nasty.'

'What about their hair?'

She thought about it.

'Short. Shaved. Both of them.'

'Did they threaten you directly in any way? Or make threats about Craig?'

She took a while.

'They'd been posting the stuff through the letterbox. And ringing. Said they'd been watching him. Tell him to stop or they'd take care of him.'

'When was this?'

'About three weeks ago. Maybe a bit longer.'

'That was when Craig switched cars?'

'Yeah. I told him to. I was scared. I didn't know what...'

'They said they'd take care of him. Did they make a specific threat to kill anyone? This is important, Jane.'

She took a breath, straining to remember.

'They'd sort him out for good. That's what they said.'

He showed her photos of Cullen's sidekicks. Not surprisingly, Daz and Ranksy both had police records. He'd downloaded the mugshots last night.

As soon as she looked at the phone, tears welled up in her eyes.

'That's them. Did they kill him?'

He stood to leave.

'Ring me if anything else comes to mind. We'll get 'em, Jane. OK?'

As he got to the door his phone pinged. A text message from Rita:

We have lift-off!

21

When he arrived in the AV suite, Rita had her feet up on the desk and was sipping from a can of Dandelion and Burdock.

'Got a main suspect,' he said. 'Two, actually. What about you?'

'This!' She swung her feet off the table and pressed 'play'. 'The old road on the edge of Broadyards Country Park? It runs up towards Birstall, then you can take the B6135 to Drighlington.'

'Jesus, do none of those places have normal names?'

'Cleckheckmondsidge!'

'That's not a real one, is it?'

She shrugged. 'Look. Nine-twenty, Thursday evening.'

He looked. The footage wasn't too bad. It was black-and-white, medium-res, good enough to make out a cyclist in dark clothes and some sort of skull cap going up the hill at a pretty good lick, legs pumping, head down. The bike had three light-coloured strips on the crossbar and three more on each upright.

'This is going away from Birstall?'

'Yes. The back lane goes up towards the town. Then it joins this main road. The bike turned left, away from Birstall, towards Drighlington.'

'And then where?'

She let a massive breath escape from her mouth.

'The options are friggin' endless. Look at the map, it's nuts. And most of the roads have no cameras on 'em. You couldn't have chosen a better escape route.'

He nodded.

'And this is the best image we've got?'

'It's all we've got, so far. The cyclist's about five-ten, I reckon. Lithe, physically fit, owner of a dark-coloured bike.'

'With yellow tape stripes on it.'

'Scuffed yellow tape stripes.' She sat back in the reclining chair. 'How many folk on our radar are gonna fit that description? We'll nail this one. Easy as.' She emptied the last dregs of the Dandelion and Burdock down her throat. 'Anyway, what did you get?'

He sat down, suddenly deflated, despite the progress.

'Your pals from Batley, Daz and Ranksy? They threatened Shaw's mum. Told her that Craig had to stop dealing. But,' he wagged a finger at the screen, 'they're big lads. It's not them, is it? An accomplice? I'm bringing 'em in, whatever.'

'We'll have a job on, tonight.'

'We could at least try.'

'Get 'em first thing tomorrow. I know where they live.' She sprang to her feet, grabbing her leather jacket. 'Oh, I nearly forgot. The pencils!'

'Go on.'

'I got her at home. The Gaia Office Supplies sales director. Hippy-dippy type, based in Dagenham. Fancy acid-free paper, all sorts of ecological…'

'*And?*'

'And they don't supply many places up here. But they do supply Cleckheaton Library. Come on, I need curry.'

'You're hungry after all this?'

'Does the Pope shit in the woods?'

A bhuna it was, then.

22

They drove the six miles down the M621 to Birstall because, according to the more expert of the two, curries in Leeds were 'a friggin' disgrace'.

The short trip gave Joe the chance to phone his deputy and bring him up to speed on the investigation. Gwyn Merchant had clearly taken the evening off, but he listened patiently, the sound of a TV in the background, and agreed to be in the office at six tomorrow morning to get things moving.

Birstall: another small town, but a slightly more picturesque one. There was even a bit of bustle in the town centre, with buses and taxis coming and going around a triangular market square enclosed on all sides by soot-darkened buildings from a century and a half ago, perhaps longer. And in the very centre, a statue of someone or other. Birstall's favourite son. But the town wasn't known for him. Not anymore.

Inside the Bangla Lounge the air was so ridiculously sweet and spicy that Joe was glad he'd let himself be dragged away from Leeds. The smell alone calmed him down, taking the edge off his anxiety. An unidentified main suspect, and two known persons of interest to haul in? The investigation was progressing quickly, but his nerves were raw and jangly. A bit of downtime was exactly what he needed.

As soon as they got a table the manager came across, chatting to Rita in Bengali for what seemed like an unreasonably long time. When they were done talking, everything had apparently been decided.

'I just ordered for the both of us, hope that's all right?' she asked, as the manager disappeared into the kitchen. 'We're going a bit off-menu.'

'That's fine.' He sat back. 'So, Birstall, hotbed of English nationalist rage.'

She cast a glance around the restaurant, which was filling up. 'Not so as you'd notice.'

'Angry white men?'

'It was just off the main square.'

Joe knew. Birstall had been worldwide news. The murder of a Member of Parliament by a deranged English nationalist.

'The bloke that did it,' she said. 'He'd eaten in here a few times. Lived just up the way.'

'Why did he do it? I mean, what leads someone to murder another human being to prove a point? Delusion? Madness?'

'We got him, that's the main thing,' she said. 'You want a beer? It's BYO. Offie's in the square.'

He shook his head. 'Big day tomorrow. Time to decide on a main suspect?'

'Most def,' she said, suddenly sitting up straight as a waiter approached with the first of the starters. 'Stuff about the pencil's good. You'll be off back to the library?'

He nodded as they started eating. But he was tired, almost too tired to think.

'The main courses are Bengali fish, mutton in apricots, some chicken in a minced lamb sauce and…' she twiddled her fingers, trying to remember, 'well, a few other bits and bobs.'

He nodded. There was going to be far too much for the two of them, but it was difficult not to be taken up on the constant wave of Rita's enthusiasm, the way she never took her foot off the gas, even in a restaurant. However, there was something nagging at the back of his mind.

'What?' she said, mid-pakora, noticing his sudden frown.

He glared at her, eyes wide open. He'd just remembered.

'Danny Cullen's cock. Tell me!'

She exploded. A hand flew to her mouth, but too late to contain a spray of pakora bits.

'He was picked up for flashing!' she said, as she dug down into her cleavage to retrieve chicken fragments. 'Near Batley Park, late one night. Mistaken identity, but the description sounded just like him.'

'Flashing?'

'Yeah, yeah,' she said as she inspected her T-shirt for stray food. 'The reports we got were that the flasher had whopped out a massive dong.'

'That was in the report?'

'Plural. Two.'

'He had two penises?'

'Two incidents, yer twat. Both women said the same. Plus, apparently it had some sort of tattoo on it.'

'And you dragged Mr Cullen in because of the description?'

'Look, he was walking along the main road at midnight. A patrol car saw him. He was a perfect fit, height, body type, hair, face…'

'All you needed was the genitalia.'

She could hardly breathe now, her ample chest heaving with laughter as she relived the interrogation of Mr Daniel Cullen.

'We had him brought in, explained things as delicately as we could.'

'I bet.'

'No, no, we just said, y'know, the member in question had several identifying characteristics.' Her face suddenly became serious. 'Do you know what he did? No solicitor, no nothing? He dropped his kecks and pulled it out.'

'And?'

'Not massive. Totally ink-free, though. Respect to him,' she said, piling raw onion onto a poppadum.

He watched her. His hunger was already on the wane.

'What's your thinking on the Patriot League's heavy mob?' he asked.

'Daz and Ranksy? I don't see it.'

'They were over in Leeds visiting Shaw's mum, threatening to sort her son out.'

'That's what she says. She also described herself as a drug addict, and lied to you about the car, about where her son lived, about his girlfriend. You show her photos of a couple of thugs, day after her son dies...'

'Why would she make that up?'

'Dunno, but if they deny it, it's their word against hers. A lying drug addict. It's all in your notes.'

Finally, when she realized that he was staring at her in disbelief, she put her food down.

'Look, Danny Cullen? The Patriot League? No. Not for this. Honestly, Joe, not murder. Danny's a guy looking for a cause.

He's done the usual stuff, dabbling in extreme politics, UKIP, all the Brexit malarkey, now this patriotic shit. He's not dangerous. In some ways I almost admire him.'

'You admire him how?'

'Says what he believes. Not a bad place to start, is it?'

'And the racist stuff? All that about grooming gangs?'

'Like I said. It's what he believes. It's his perspective. And it's all about perspective.'

'Bollocks it is. If it'd been a gang of white men doing the grooming, would you have heard about their colour? Or their religion?'

'Two wrongs don't make a right. But the grooming gangs were all Asians, Joe. Asian men. I don't have an issue with saying so. It's a good place to start.'

Joe was only just managing to believe what he was hearing. 'Tommy Robinson was right, then?'

She shifted her weight, making it look like a massive effort on her part.

'He's a sad wad, and he almost brought a grooming trial down. But I can put myself in Cullen's place. He looks around, sees what's happening to his country. He's an angry white man. I can understand where he's coming from.' She looked at Joe. 'What? You can't?'

'No, I bloody can't, to be honest.'

'Fair enough. We got that out in the open, at least. Oh, I didn't know whether you wanted rice, chapatis or naan, so I got plenty of everything. By the way,' she said, twisting in her seat and pulling a phone from her front pocket, 'have you been following things on Twitter?'

'Not especially.'

145

'The case is getting a lot of attention. Weird stuff, an'all.'

'Like what?'

'Pro-killer, I think you'd call it. Wait, I'll show you.'

But before she had a chance to find Twitter her phone rang.

'I'd better get this.'

She pressed the phone to her ear. Not even uttering a *hello*. She listened, and by degrees her face became sterner. At the other end someone was doing all the talking. Rita's mouth hung open. Then:

'OK. We're on our way.'

She pocketed the phone, set both arms on the table.

'Another kill.'

He let his eyes fall shut. 'Where?'

'A couple of minutes away,' he heard her say as she pushed her chair back and stood up. 'Come on.'

SUNDAY

23

This is me, isn't it?

Or is it?

It's been like this since Tuesday night. I understand, then I don't. I *get* who I am, who I've become. Then I have no idea. Day or night, asleep or awake. It's overwhelming. Confusing. But I've got to do it. I've been driven to it. To Jason.

It was all so easy. I rang him, said I was Detective Peterson from Kirklees Police, did he remember me? No. I told him that I'd questioned him a year or two ago. Surely he remembered me? Nah.

'None taken!' I said with a little chuckle.

I told him we needed some advice. He was confused. Coppers asking him for advice? Yeah, it sounded strange, I said. But there was something in it for him. For his defence, if he ever needed it. Something definite, on paper, signed and stamped by the police. He agreed to meet me. He's not a total idiot.

When I pulled up he was already waiting. A street corner a few blocks from where he lived. I thought I wasn't going to be able to go through with it, but he looked cocky, smirking like he'd just had three bells on a scratch card. It made everything so much simpler.

'Hi there, Jason. Get in!'

He did, but cautiously, a quick glance left and right as he ducked down into the passenger seat.

'You still don't remember me? DS Peterson, Kirklees District?'

Shakes his head, like it makes him cool.

'Well,' I say as we drive off, 'we've got something. An object. Could be evidence. It's still where we found it. There's nobody there. It'll just be you and me. I want you to tell me if you've ever seen it before. You're not a suspect. This is about identifying where the object came from. It's got nothing to do with you. I can't say much more than that.'

His brain is whirring.

'If I've *seen* it?'

'Yes. It's an object. Just tell me if you recognize it. And if you have seen it before, tell us where. It's all anonymous, that's why we're alone. One hundred per cent anonymous, OK?'

He's like a dog, confused but thinks he's done well. Y'know, tail wagging but he's not sure he's getting the bone.

'What's in it for me?'

'A letter,' I say as we take the long way around Cleckheaton town centre, avoiding the cameras, up past the school and down through a housing estate. 'A signed letter explaining your full cooperation with the police. It goes into your file in a sealed envelope. In the event of you being sentenced for any future crime, the envelope will be passed to the judge before sentencing. Tell your brief about it. Make sure it gets to the judge.'

He nods, grinning now. He's on bail for robbery, tells me as much.

'Look,' I say, 'there are no promises. But the information

you give us today could make a big difference. Judges like that sort of thing. They like it a lot. Do you understand, Jason?'

Happy dog now. Tail wagging. I want to pat his head.

We stop under some trees. It's a back road, hardly anyone uses it now, right next to the park, close to the old railway line that used to run into Birstall.

Do it. A voice in my head. No, it's not that. It's my own voice. Only it's new, it's louder, more insistent now. *Do it*, it's saying. Like, *swoosh! Just do it!* What alternative is there, now that I've got this far? I have to.

The sun's just gone down. There's not much light here anyway, and it's already quite dark. I hold a torch.

'There, behind that wall.'

The wall has sunk part-way into the earth, about ten feet from the road. The whole area is neglected and overgrown, disused since Dr Beeching rode into town.

'What is it?' he asks as I make my way through a gap in the wall where the stones have fallen.

I've caught sight of myself in the mirror a couple of times over the last few days. This can't be right, something tells me. But it must be. Why else would I have been there, under the old railway bridge with Craig? That wasn't me. But it *was* me. It's what I've become. I was given this to do, after all these years. And I can't stop. Not now.

The ground is uneven, littered with loose stones. He follows reluctantly. I shine the torch at the base of the wall. We're out of sight from the road now.

'It's down there. Look. All we need to know is whether you've ever seen it before, and if so, where.'

'I can't see nothin'.'

'Get closer, but don't touch anything.'

He follows the light from the torch, crouching slightly, then more, hunkering down and shuffling in towards the base of the wall, still unable to see what he's supposed to be looking for. When his knees are almost at a right angle, I take the hammer from my pocket, get a decent stance, and swing it into the side of his head.

He hardly moves. He doesn't make a sound.

I swing again, harder. The noise of the impact is dull, flat.

I've been driven to this. And now it's my responsibility. No excuses. Not for anyone.

His body sways a little. I wait. Then he falls forwards, head first. His arms do not come out to break his fall. He lands on his head, his body still in a crouched position, but upended.

Then I hear the air escaping from his lungs. His body topples to one side. The dog face is gone. Eyes wide open. Nothing.

Yes, this is how it has to be. How it should have been, all this time. I was brought here to do this. And now it's done.

Another swing at his head. Harder, deeper goes the hammer.

Then I push a pencil in.

Why? Because I can. Because I have to.

There's some resistance as it enters.

I finish it off with my foot.

Two down.

24

There were three patrol cars in attendance when they arrived. Broadyards Country Park was unrecognizable to Joe. He knew that they were close to its perimeter, but on the other side, perhaps half a mile from the car park where Craig Shaw had been left to burn. The new kill, though, was within the Kirklees boundary.

As soon as a pencil had been found in the victim's eye socket, the info had been relayed back to District, and it was immediately confirmed that DS Rita Scannon would be SIO. She'd been informed shortly after she arrived at the scene with Joe. When she got the call, she took a deep breath, looked around, and that was that.

Joe had stayed just long enough to watch her assume control. Suddenly she was everywhere. Calm, smiling, efficient. Rushing nothing, not so much as a raised voice. She knew the name of every officer, and they responded to her orders as if they were glad she was in charge. It didn't feel much like a typical murder scene, he thought as he watched her work. Then again, what was typical about murder?

There hadn't been much for Joe to do. A quick look at the victim: a young lad with his head caved in, a square impression deep into his skull, around the temple area. The pencil had been left this time, pushed all the way in, the eye itself still intact, wide open, a watery grey.

With the gentle chunter of the mobile generator in the background, he'd watched things come to life. Rita was like a circus ringmaster, the way she orchestrated the show but never dominated it, a kind of centre-stage confidence, self-assured but making each player feel like the star.

He'd seen his fair share of circuses, too. Gustavo Romano, his granddad, had been a circus clown. A great one, famous enough in Italy to be offered work at Blackpool's Tower Circus. Not the top job, though. Another Italian got that, and never let go of it. As Joe's grandma used to say: Be careful with clowns, they're the worst.

By one in the morning Joe was back in Leeds. There were no other officers at Elland Road from the Shaw case, not at that time of night, so he did it all himself, manning the phones, sending stuff from the Shaw case file across to Kirklees.

Now, as dawn broke, he was back at the murder scene. Light was just beginning to break through the trees overhead. There were vehicles parked right along the narrow lane, some facing one way, some the other. The road had been sealed off and tyre-track impressions had already been taken, so it didn't much matter where anyone parked.

There was a white tent nestling under the trees. It straddled a low wall, the fabric hitched up awkwardly over the stones like a badly fitting shirt. People walked around in white overalls and boots, and each time one of them stepped into the glare of the overhead floodlight they became dazzlingly bright against the darkness of the trees behind, as though they were on stage.

For a while he stood and watched the morning sun creep in through the foliage, changing the balance of everything by slow degrees. And with each passing minute the place looked slightly less atrocious, less cold and evil.

'Joe, great, you're back!'

He'd been in touch with Rita a few times over the course of the night, as he'd worked the phones and database in Leeds, relaying info to and fro, collating material from Kirklees District. Two inquiry hubs were being kept open until there was a decision from higher up about a joint operation.

'You eaten anything?' she asked. 'There's a loaf of bread and some biscuits in the Landy. I got our curry delivered, but it all went ages ago.'

He shook his head. It occurred to him that other than a few starters in the curry place he'd eaten nothing since... since when?

'You had any sleep?' she asked.

'Grabbed an hour at my desk. You?'

'Sleep's for wusses.'

Fair enough.

'Where you at?'

'Pathologist's coming in an hour,' she said, wiggling her hips as she yanked up her jeans. 'Then Forensics'll sweep the area, once there's enough light. After that I reckon Jason'll be getting a taxi to the morgue.'

'You're on first-name terms?'

'You might say that!'

So far, the victim had been little more than a name:

cross-referencing him with Shaw, getting support staff in Leeds to crank up data searches on the two men, likely associates, points of intersection, a mass of info that might or might not be useful… Rita was definitely moving things along quickly.

'I…' he began, but wished he hadn't.

He'd spoken to a few other officers from Kirklees during the night as well. And he was detecting the same tone in Rita now.

'Come on, spit it out!' she said.

He sighed, stuck his hands in his pockets.

'I dunno, but I'm getting weird vibes from you lot.' He looked around to make sure no one else was close enough to hear. 'The kid was nineteen. Not much more than a boy. He…'

But he didn't know what to say. The case was being handled with prompt efficiency. Yet the caved-in head, the pencil right through the brain? None of it felt particularly important.

He'd been involved in quite a few murders over the years, and normally there's a quiet respect for a dead body, the natural human response to the worst crime of all. Not a respect for the victim, perhaps; more a recognition that life is itself fragile, that each of us is separated from the most chilling of deaths by the finest, most tenuous of threads.

'…I mean, don't get me wrong, but it all feels more like a robbery around here.'

She nodded with uncharacteristic patience, allowing him to go on.

'That sadness? Y'know, the way a murder scene grinds you down a bit, the fact that a life has just been taken away, docked out like a cigarette. The starkness of it.'

She let his words linger. And there was a softness to her face now, a kindness.

'Jason Beverage,' she said.

'Yeah, interesting name.'

'Scum. How much do you want us to care?'

'It's a murder, no?'

She pursed her lips. Thought about it for a second.

'Yeah, and it's being taken seriously.' She paused, glanced at the stone wall, the white tent. "I interviewed three women he raped. He used Rohypnol on two of them. There were probably a lot more. Oh, he sold prescription drugs on the side. Hobby of his.'

'Were there convictions, for the rapes?'

'We only managed to get one to court. She'd been so shit-faced he didn't need to drug her. They go back to her place, and she lets him in. So that's apparent consent, soon as she opens the door. Oh,' she added, 'he liked to rob 'em while he was at it. The one that went to trial? He does her, then he robs her, takes everything. Empties her fridge on the way out, an'all. Takes his friggin' brekkie in a carrier bag.'

'You couldn't make it stick?'

Immediately he regretted it. Proving rape in a context like that was a nightmare.

'Defence had a bloody field day. Brushes up well, our Jason. Good-looking young fella in the dock, and half the women in court thinking they wouldn't kick him out of bed. The victim gave evidence. Twenty minutes on the stand, she looked like a desperate old slapper.'

'You got a conviction for robbery, though?' he said, recalling the case summary he'd read.

'Yeah. Big whoop. Nine months, suspended, if memory serves. Truth is, I'd've stuck another pencil in his face if it would have done any good.'

157

He let that one settle.

Rita wasn't having any of it.

'One of your little pauses, eh? Bollocks, Joe. I'll be done here soon as the pathologist shows up. We can get a fry-up. I'm starving.'

With that she was off again, marching over to the crime-scene manager, who was milling around close to the tent, clipboard in hand.

Joe got his phone and searched the *Yorkshire Post* website. There were two articles on Jason Beverage. He'd already seen the victim's record, but the public account was more dramatic, more colourful. *Date rape* in both headlines. The first time he'd been found not guilty, the second time only with robbery. On both occasions his victim was a divorcee in her thirties.

He watched the sun for a couple of minutes. Breakfast with Rita? Perhaps not.

25

A fine mist hung on the air, like cigar smoke in an empty room, as if it was in no hurry to disperse. Yet Joe could see right across the valley, and onto the next, then the next. Each ridge was a deep emerald-green, criss-crossed with old walls, the odd farm building here and there. In the valleys there were modest mill towns, little more than dark smudges, hidden between the great pleats of land that rose steadily towards the Pennines. God's Own County? That might be pushing it a bit, but on a crisp, bright morning, Yorkshire could be pretty inspiring.

He leant on a stone wall that ran along the side of the road in a line just cockeyed enough to seem wilful. Both his hands were wrapped around a large paper cup of coffee that he'd got at a Starbucks in Cleckheaton, next to the junction for the M62. The wind was cold enough to make the coffee a welcome companion, although it tasted of nothing much.

He was only a handful of miles from the motorway, yet it felt like another world. He'd grown up in Leeds, close to the city centre, and he'd never got used to West Yorkshire's quick-fire transitions from the urban to the absolutely rural. The nearest his parents had come to showing their sons the glories of the Broadacres was when they'd occasionally driven up through the

Dales on their way to a gig in Darlington or Middlesbrough. Whenever they saw a field full of sheep they'd all cry, 'Mint sauce!'

His phone buzzed.

'Joe? It's Gwyn. Where are you?'

'Just going to interview someone. Did you get my message?'

'Yeah. Pencil man strikes again. Rita got me up to speed. I just had brekkie with her, as it happens.'

A pause.

'Right, right,' Joe said. 'So, we're waiting for a decision on joint operations. See you in Leeds in an hour or two?'

He ended the call, wondered what he'd missed at the breakfast meeting. He looked directly to his right. Gabriel Farm was just up ahead, standing a little way back from the road. No longer a farm, only the main house now remained, an eighteenth-century building, attractive in its way, with narrow windows along the upper floor where hand-loom weavers would have worked, taking advantage of every last bit of daylight.

As he took stock of the premises, noting the modest gentrification – a broad gravel driveway, a well-kept lawn, and a decent 4x4 outside – the dark-blue front door opened. Out came Leo Turner, carrying a rubbish bag which he took around to a bin at the side of the house.

'OK,' Joe said, reaching for his notebook and quickly finding Turner's number, 'who's betting...'

He watched as Turner stopped, searching his pockets for his phone, then stared at the screen for a second.

'Hello?'

'Hi, this is Detective Romano, Leeds CID. We met yesterday.'

'Ah, yes. You abandoned me in the library.'

'Call of duty, I'm afraid. Murders, they're unpredictable.'

'Yes, I suppose they are. Your no-show yesterday gave me pause, so I spoke to some people. The League is happy to supply you with a full list of members. I can email it over to you.'

'I'm in the area, as it happens. I can pop round. Are you at home?'

'I'm afraid not. Don't know when I'll be back either. I'm spending the day with my mother.'

'And where would that be?'

'Derbyshire. Really, I think email would be the best bet. I might be very late back tonight.'

Joe was too tired to bother replying. He ended the call and got back in the car. He was about to turn the ignition on. Then he changed his mind.

He tapped WhatsApp, while with his other hand he got his notebook and found her number.

Hello. DS Romano here. We met yesterday in Cleckheaton Library? I'm doing some background inter-views today. I wondered whether you might be available at some point in the afternoon for a chat? If not, perhaps tomorrow? Thanks in advance, Joe Romano.

He'd never been comfortable with the abbreviated language of digital messaging. He liked the flow and feel of full sentences. It was a more respectful form of language, somehow gentler.

He threw his phone onto the passenger seat and looked at Turner's country cottage.

'Right, here I come.'

The door had a brass knocker in the shape of a clenched fist. Joe made good use of it. When Turner appeared, he looked surprised, then a little embarrassed.

'Ah...'

'You got back sharpish!' Joe said, all smiles. 'Can I?'

It wasn't a question. He walked straight into the house. The door gave onto a large open-plan living room which retained the best of the building's original features, enhanced by heavy, traditional furniture and several large sofas of considerable age and quality. There was music playing in the background.

'The *Brandenburg Concertos*,' he said, noting the aroma of a log fire.

'Classic FM,' said Turner, following Joe in and closing the door. 'I had planned a day of quiet reflection, hence my small subterfuge. I do apologize. Anyway, now that you're here, let me get those lists for you.'

He disappeared without another word. Joe walked across to the old stone hearth and stood in front of it, feeling the warmth of the fire against his legs and watching the ever-changing hues of orange and yellow as they spun and twisted into one another. He'd done the same thing hundreds of times in his grandma's house, when the patterns of flames amid the glowing coals had become red dragons and swirling orange phantoms. That was before he knew what the human soul was capable of. These days he preferred not to descend too far into the Inferno.

Turner reappeared, two sheets of printed paper in his hand.

'Here you are. Full member list of the Patriot League, and the same for the discussion group. I've included all the addresses and phone numbers where I have them. Most are here.'

Joe scanned the name lists, then folded the sheets and slotted them into the inside pocket of his jacket.

'This is evidence, you know?'

'That sounds like a threat! You do know that I'm a—'

'A lawyer, yes, I know.' An hour's sleep was all he'd managed but he held back his impatience, took a breath. 'The investigation is now covering two murders. As I'm sure you'll appreciate, any failure to cooperate at this stage will be noted.'

Turner was unimpressed.

'Another drug pusher, was it?'

Joe couldn't be bothered.

'Try the Kirklees District Police Twitter feed.'

Turner made a show of searching on his phone. Joe watched, and it occurred to him how often our first response to any kind of event now involves staring at a tiny, hand-held device. We consult technology like the ancient Greeks used to seek the truth at the Deltic Oracles, as Bridgette might say. Only now the oracles sit in data warehouses and the language they speak is the aggregated squawk of a billion supplicants who already know the answer to everything.

Shaw and Beverage: were the deaths of a drug dealer and a rapist-cum-thief worth the cost of a police investigation? A majority opinion would already have emerged on social media. And let's face it, he told himself as his exhausted brain struggled to maintain any kind of rationality, it's the public who pay for the police. Perhaps they *should* decide.

'Can I offer you some tea?' Turner said, putting his phone down on the large circular table in the centre of the room. There was a breakfast setting for one, complete with a hefty brown teapot, plus several Sunday papers: the *Sunday Telegraph*, the *Yorkshire Post*.

'It might need a bit of freshening up.'

'I'm fine, thanks. Tell me, Mr Turner, where were you last night?'

Turner raised his eyebrows.

'Really? You suspect me of doing *that*?' he asked, gesturing to the phone. 'Murdering rapists is hardly my thing, officer.'

'Well, all I know at this stage is that your thing includes lying to a CID officer investigating a double murder.'

'In my defence it was only a single murder at that point.'

'Are you making light of that fact?'

'Would that be a crime?'

'Like I said, it's been noted. Last night, please?'

'I was here all evening.'

'Alone?'

'Yes. I live alone.'

'And what were you doing?'

'I was reading. In fact I was rereading this.'

He took a hardback book from the table and offered it to Joe: *12 Rules for Life*.

'A self-help book?'

'Jordan Peterson. An academic psychologist, at Harvard for many years. And quite the literary star these days. It's far more than self-help. He explains the scientific basis for many assumptions that are currently unfashionable.'

'Assumptions? Such as?'

'Being forthright, being competitive. Taking responsibility for one's actions. The profound psychological differences between men and women.'

Joe put the book down.

'Lobsters? This is the lobster guy, right?'

Turner looked mildly impressed.

'Male lobsters compete for females. The victorious male generates more serotonin for himself, which reinforces his confidence. It pushes him on, and he gets better at it, tries harder. It's the same mechanism in humans. We compete. We're supposed to.'

Joe had read a couple of things about the book in the *Guardian*. But like most things he read these days, it had seemed interesting but distant, like Nick Cave's latest album, Tarantino's latest film, anybody's latest anything... music, films and places that he would never hear, see or visit, all filed in a self-deleting part of his brain.

'What's the crossover in membership between the League and your discussion group? There's Danny Cullen and his two sidekicks. How many more?'

'None, as far as I recall.'

'Danny Cullen? Would you describe him as a man in search of the truth?'

'Aren't we all? The ones who are searching for anything, that is.'

Joe rubbed a hand across his face, forcing the tiredness away.

'The English Patriot League. I read your website, the vigilante stuff in particular. Your members actually confront people on the street?'

'Yes, the braver ones among us.'

'That's a dangerous game, wouldn't you say?'

'We try to engage them in conversation, explain what they're doing to people's lives. And, of course, we report them to the police, for what it's worth.' He smiled. 'But, yes, it's a fine line, I accept that.'

'And then there's the patriotic bit. The race button's gotta be the easiest one to push, especially now after everything that's happened over the last few years. Folk are confused, angry, constantly worried. Throw in some anti-drugs rhetoric, you've got yourself a social crusade.'

'If you've read the whole website you'll know we address all sorts of social issues.'

'When I was at the League meeting on Friday, the only thing I heard was Cullen stirring up racial hatred against Asians. What I don't really understand is what you're trying to achieve.'

'One might say we're trying to do your job. But that would be facetious. The truth is, we're trying to build a grassroots base, a response to what's going wrong in our communities. This isn't about racism. Institutional racism is a scourge, in absolutely all its forms. What concerns us is how society confronts these issues. The country is on the wrong path. Disastrously so. The assumptions that underpin our society are rotten. There's a failure even to say what the problems are. The idea of the League is to get some momentum, to bring these ideas into the public eye. To make decency mainstream again.'

'Decency?'

Turner was already moving towards the door.

'Please, let me try to explain.'

The two of them stepped outside. They stood there, looking across the valleys of West Yorkshire. The mist was lifting, and the view was remarkable.

'That long valley?' Turner said, pointing to the east. 'Do you know what it's called?'

'I'm afraid you'll have to help me with the geography.'

'It's the Calder Valley. But they call it *Happy Valley*. You may have seen the TV show. A police drama, entertainment for people who don't have to live there.'

Joe knew the reputation of the area, but not the TV show. The towns of Hebden Bridge and Todmorden had been focal points of hippy communities in the sixties and seventies, and the following generations had inherited the drug culture, which had spread along the valley and become deeply ingrained.

'Drugs,' Turner continued. 'It's no longer about well-to-do kids having a spliff at college. Or the educated middle classes enjoying the occasional line of coke. It's children from deprived homes getting addicted at eleven, twelve. Pushers hanging around outside schools. That's where the growth market is. Go and park up outside a school. You'll see them, every day. The result? Dysfunctional families, kids growing up with no role models, no one working, no stability, no normalcy. It's destroying the fabric of our communities, creating a drugged, aimless underclass.' His eyes lit up. 'You see? Underclass? One of the words we're not allowed to use anymore. Yet it exists. Like I say, go to *Happy Valley*. See how happy they really are.'

Joe looked out across the valley. It was so achingly majestic that he couldn't quite believe that he lived in the same county. He'd never appreciated what he had on his doorstep, what he'd always had. *Mint sauce!*

'You make a persuasive case,' he said. 'Perhaps you should be the one leading the Patriot League.'

Turner shook his head.

'A popular movement needs a popular leader. Populist, if you like.'

'And Danny Cullen's your man? Hand-picked?'

'You'd be surprised. It takes courage to ban drugs from a pub on a housing estate in Batley. And to enforce it.'

'He enforces it?'

'I've seen it myself. He turfs them out.'

Joe took the two lists from his pocket, confirming that Cullen and his two assistants were on both.

'Mr Rank and Mr Scholes. Ranksy and Daz, I assume?'

Turner nodded, with just the hint of a smile.

'Our trusty foot soldiers.'

'Tell me,' Joe said, 'what do you know about Craig Shaw?'

Turner's eyes widened in surprise.

'Very little. Other than he was a known drug dealer.'

Joe put the lists back in his pocket.

'Known to you?'

'Certainly not.'

'We're looking into the Patriot League's links to Shaw. It'd be helpful if you could start to think of possible points of connection. Does anything spring to mind?'

'Nothing that I can think of.'

'Nothing at all? You can think of no connection between Craig Shaw and any members of the Patriot League?'

'No. I cannot.'

Joe took a moment. Turner must have known something about Cullen's daughter and her relationship with Shaw. Not much to be gained from accusing him of lying, though, not just now.

'OK. I'll be in touch. Please be available this time.'

Turner accompanied him to his car.

'A-ha!' Joe said as he opened the door, his best Columbo impression. 'Do you own a bike? Mind if I take a quick look?'

Turner paused.

'A bicycle? I... I do have one, as it happens.'

Without another word he strode out around the side of the house, pristine gravel crunching underfoot. The garage was at the back, a small, freestanding stone building out of sight from the main road.

'Here,' he said, pulling the doors open to reveal a black bike.

'Impressive,' Joe said, running a hand gently along the crossbar. 'Twelve-speed?'

'Fifteen. It's a hybrid. Like a racer but a bit more robust. Perfect for the roads around here.'

'Do you use it a lot?' he asked as he took a couple of pictures on his phone, including a close-up of the tyre.

'Most days. I try to keep fit. Either cycling or long walks.'

Joe nodded appreciatively. Sam kept telling him to join a gym. But he worked on the assumption that if he couldn't be bothered to drag himself there to register, it was unlikely he'd ever be inspired to use the facilities.

'Last Thursday, for example? Thursday evening?'

'Thursday? Yes, I probably had a training session. Ninety minutes, thereabouts. Up and down the valley. I take the cycling quite seriously.'

'What time?'

'Mid-evening. Eight-ish, I guess.'

'Can anyone confirm that?'

Turner held up his phone.

'I think I checked my emails when I got back. I don't have the location activated, I'm afraid. Google doesn't need to know every time I pop out for a loaf of bread, does it?'

'Quite so. We'll sort all that out later.' Joe was already making his way back to his car. Turner followed. 'Would you allow us to see your internet and phone history without a warrant?'

'No problem.'

'Great. I'll be in touch.'

He got into his car, checked his WhatsApp.

Hi, Joe! Absolutely. I'm in Tong village. Any time today is fine. Early evening?

He felt a smile creep onto his face as he turned onto the road and headed back to the motorway. A main suspect and a date, and it wasn't even midday.

He called Rita as he drove. She was slowing down a bit now, the bouncy urgency in her speech replaced with a more measured tone.

'Leo Turner, eh?' she asked.

'Yep. As of now, he's my main suspect.'

'Well, let's see what you come up with. I'm off for a few hours' kip. Oh, by the way, the stuff about the pencil is all over the internet.'

'Jesus! How did that happen? Rita? Are you still there?'

'Yeah, just. I've got no idea. It wasn't me. You made the right call on that. But I'll tell you what, Joe, I dunno about Leeds, but over here we fuckin' hate rapists.'

'Especially ones you never got sent down?'

'You might have a point there, partner. But that pencil stuff was never gonna stay quiet for long. There were a lot of folk at that crime scene, and some of 'em have got big mouths.'

'OK. I'm off for a bite. We'll speak this afternoon, OK?'

'Yeah. One of us'll be busy by then. Decision on a single hub by mid-afternoon, they're saying.'

'Yes,' he told himself after he ended the call. 'And I have a main suspect.'

26

His eyelids were drooping badly now. He only noticed the arrival of his haddock and chips when the aroma of hot beef dripping made him spontaneously dribble. By the time he'd shaken himself awake, the waitress was already walking away.

'Thank you,' he called after her, fighting back the spittle.

She turned her head and gave him a smile. She might have been twenty, he thought, fresh-faced, the unmistakable look of a girl from *a good family.*

'Bloody hell, Joe,' he told himself as he grabbed the vinegar and doused his battered fish, 'you're turning into your grandma!'

He watched the girl for a second or two as she took an order at another table. She *was* nice, though. A student, perhaps? She had a mature kind of confidence, a politeness, secure in the knowledge that she wouldn't be working in a place like this forever. The kind of girl he hoped Sam would be getting to know.

He pulled out his phone. Sam had replied to his text.

Hi Dad. Cool here. Busy. Goin prague nxt week. See you xmas!

Then there was a second text from him.

Use WhatsApp, loser?!

I do use it, he thought as he grudgingly added Sam's name to his WhatsApp contact list. Old-fashioned texting felt more personal, like a private line of communication between the two of them, something that almost no one else did anymore. Now even that was deemed unacceptable.

Prague? Christmas? He counted the weeks as he checked his WhatsApp for new messages. There was one from Chris Saunders, and another from Bridgette in Forensics. Duty-bound, he chose the latter.

Joe. You might want to drop by when you've got a sec.
A little present for you from the Shaw vehicle.

He thought about giving her a call. Nah. He'd be there in forty minutes. It could wait. Meanwhile, there was the message from Chris.

Hi, Joe. It's Chris Saunders again.

He liked the way that she also announced herself unnecessarily.

Something's cropped up. But I'm still free later this
evening, if that's any use.

He replied straight away.

That sounds good. I'll send a message when I know how
things are going here. See you in Tong!

The batter around the fish was now sodden with vinegar, perfect for the adhesion of salt, which he sprinkled on liberally. It wasn't going to do his heart any good, but one of the enduring pleasures of adulthood was that there was nobody to tell you not to do it. He'd realized this when he sat down for his first meal as a student in Nottingham, a quarter of a century ago. A plate of instant noodles, and no one there to tell him off for going mad with the ketchup. He'd never lost the daft, adolescent pleasure of smothering his food in ketchup, just because he could.

But now, with Sam up in Edinburgh, he worried himself sick about what the new freedoms of his son's new life might lead to. It was ridiculous, he knew. But he'd heard all about medical students. In fact, he'd arrested a couple of them. He'd also picked one up off the pavement in Leeds, a shit-faced kid, first year away from home, so drunk that eventually some kind soul had used him as a punchbag, kicked him to the ground and taken his wallet.

What on earth could he say to Sam? Don't get too drunk? Stay out of danger? Wrap yourself in cotton wool? He put his phone down and stabbed a chip. He had it halfway to his mouth when the phone pinged.

The Greyhound pub in Tong? I'm very close, if you fancy it.

He fancied it, he told himself, grabbing the ketchup and emptying half its contents onto his chips.

27

Back at Elland Road, he didn't need to traipse all the way down to Forensics. Gwyn Merchant was in the operations room, grinning like a dog with two dicks.

'Joe! You heard?'

'Obviously not.'

'Your man Shaw? Mr Class B, eh? Or is he? Ta-*dah*!'

A bellyful of well-ketchupped cow grease did little to make Merchant's childishness any more bearable. Fortunately, Bridgette's report was already on the system.

As Joe logged on and read it, Merchant reclined in a nearby chair, feet up on the desk, hands behind his head, like a lobster dripping in serotonin.

The report was brief. Under Shaw's car, within reach of the driver, two small magnetic boxes had been found, the kind that some drivers still use to keep a spare key in. One box had contained a dozen wraps of cocaine and fentanyl, the other, ecstasy and ketamine.

'They took their bloody time finding that!' Joe said, clicking the file closed.

'Heat from the fire had kind of moulded 'em to the chassis.'

'I know, I just read it. *Shit!*'

'Yep. Shit. Doesn't get us anywhere, but shit.'

'Cheers for the input. You know what I think? If someone was warning Shaw off, if I was part of a rival drugs operation, for example, what would be the best cover? How about anti-drugs vigilantes? Ranksy and Daz? They've been seen warning drug pushers on the street. We still haven't spoken to them. Do it now?'

Merchant swung his legs off the desk.

'Ticked that box, as it happens. I chased 'em up this morning. They're off the radar.'

'What? They threatened the mother of a murder victim. Said they'd sort him out. They're right on my radar.'

'Yeah, no, no, I mean, for Beverage. I was over there early on today. Did a bit of digging. I've got 'em outside Spider's nightclub in Batley 'til two in the morning. They work the door, both of 'em. Plenty of witnesses, bar staff, manager. They started at six the previous evening. Poor bastards have to clean the bogs before the place opens! The victim was still alive at a quarter to eight.'

'Rita's got that already?'

'Yeah. Beverage phoned a mate, said he was off to meet a copper. They've already got a statement. She's a fast worker, Rita.'

'He was meeting a copper? What details do we have on that?'

'His mate said the copper were called Peters or Peterson or something.'

'Peterson? Any coppers with that name? In Kirklees?'

'Dunno. We don't have joint ops yet. No access to their system. Any road, Rita'll be looking into that.'

Joe thought about it.

'OK, so let's assume they got Beverage to the park by pretending to be a police officer. I still want to speak to Daz and Ranksy.'

Merchant shrugged.

'They're not in the frame for Beverage. Plus, they're a couple of ball-less tossers. Always have been.'

'What? You *know* 'em?'

'Yeah, I used to play rugby with Daz. And Ranksy? He's just a bell-end. Y'know, if...'

'If you come from Batley.'

Merchant met his stare.

'Aye, if you come from Batley.'

Joe turned to his screen, keen to write up the notes from his interview with Turner while it was fresh in his mind.

'What's the news on joint ops?' he asked as he typed.

'Still waiting. Gonna be a single inquiry, once the brass've finished their rounds of friggin' golf. Apart from that,' he said, shaking his phone, 'we got a lot of interest on the twattersphere.'

'Don't tell me, the general public want us to give the killer a medal. No, on better thoughts, don't tell me.'

'He's got a name now. The Graphite Assassin!'

'That information was supposed to be kept back. Who the f—'

'Kirklees, eh? You can't trust that lot.'

'Ah, hell! Better get this onto the system. I'll explain as I type. Mr Leo Turner, a.k.a. the Professor...'

By the time the report was finished and uploaded, Merchant was sitting next to Joe, and his frivolity had dissipated. They had a main suspect.

'I dunno, is it a match?' Merchant said, as Joe held his phone up next to the monitor and they compared Turner's bike with a screen shot from the footage of the bike racing away from Shaw's burning car on Thursday evening.

'Looks a decent fit to me.'

'The back light's different. You sure there was no residue?'

'From the tape? I couldn't feel any on the crossbar. I didn't want to arouse his suspicions. Forensics might say different. And the light could've been changed.'

'Or he could have another bike? He's a lawyer. He's smart enough to use a different bike.'

Joe nodded. 'Probably smart enough to get rid of it as well.'

There was only one way to find out: they had to search the Turner residence.

'Question is—' Joe began.

'Question is,' Merchant interrupted, looking at his watch, 'we only get one shot. And it's gotta be now.'

Joe's heart sank, just a touch.

'Asking for a warrant on a Sunday afternoon, on flimsy evidence? Who's the sitting magistrate?'

'Makes no difference,' Merchant said. 'We don't have enough to take it to Andy.'

Joe sat back, looked at the ceiling.

'We've got the timeframes. Tuesday, Thursday and Saturday. There might be CCTV somewhere near Turner's house. Get him coming and going at the relevant times?'

Merchant was already shaking his head.

'It's Kirklees District. We might as well just feed this into Rita's inquiry. They'll be all over him anyway, once they've seen your report.'

Joe was now staring at the ceiling so intently that his neck began to go into cramp.

'He said we could look at his internet and phone history without a warrant. How about it? We could pick Alex up, shoot over there now, see if there are any gaps in his internet use, his TV streaming, I dunno, anything that...' He stopped. 'I mean, if he's planned it, he must've read about Beverage online.'

'Dicks like that still read real papers.'

'He had the *Yorkshire Post* on his table today. But you'd want to know more. You'd do a Google search, wouldn't you?' He was already standing up, grabbing his jacket. 'Come on. Let's take a punt. I bet Alex'll find something.'

Merchant drew himself up from his seat with a lot less vigour, despite his relative youth.

'You're the boss,' he said.

Suddenly there was a subtle but perceptible shift in the atmosphere. They both stopped and looked over towards the door to see Andy Mills coming towards them, hands deep in his pockets.

'Talk of the devil,' Merchant whispered. 'On a friggin' Sunday, an'all.'

It took Joe a second or two. Then he knew.

'Gents, a word,' Mills said. 'Kirklees are taking over the investigation.'

'Both murders?' Joe asked.

'Yep. They're assuming it's the same killer.'

Merchant was already turning to leave. 'I'll get a coffee. One for you, Sir?'

Mills shook his head.

28

Joe remained at his desk. DCI Andy Mills was leaning on the adjacent one, hands still in his pockets, jangling his keys. He looked down at the floor in front of him. There were three or four other people in the room, all discreetly busying themselves, pretending not to listen: it wasn't every day you saw an officer being relieved of a double murder.

'Not much I could do, Joe. It's turned very serious very quickly.'

They'd trained together, been best man at each other's wedding, and they'd both come close to tears when Tetley's stopped brewing Bitter in Leeds. There didn't really need to be any apologies. Yet.

'Have you seen the press this is getting?'

'Doing my best not to,' Joe said.

'It's the Graphite Assassin now. *Hash-friggin'-tag*. They're already calling him a bloody serial killer.'

'Leaked before Beverage was in the morgue.'

'Aye, that's as maybe, but Kirklees reckon they can get a result. Who was I to argue?'

'The implication being that you don't think I can?'

Mills considered the question. There was no one on the Force he admired as much as Joe, and there was no one else he could really call a friend. Their families had spent summer holidays together. Even their kids liked each other. Then Joe had gone to Interpol. That had messed things up a bit. In fact, it had messed everything up.

'Kirklees wanted overall control. You stay on the Shaw case, though.'

'OK. I'm sure you argued my corner.'

'I bloody didn't. They've got a team ready to go. Whereas I've got some knobhead who's been in France translating international arrest warrants and playing pétanque. It'll save us a fair bit of money, an'all.'

'I assume I'm not getting any more men this end?'

Mills exhaled, long and hard. And he was a bulky guy; there was a lot of air to come out. It was the same when the two of them were out drinking. There'd be too much beer, then a late-night curry, washed down with more needless pints. At some point Andy would just sit back, empty his lungs, and he'd be done. Half-comatose, he'd stagger to a taxi rank, his night over. You either love a bloke for that, or you don't.

'Money's too tight to mention, pal. If you need owt, ask. But from what I've heard, they're gonna have more to go on with the second body.'

'OK, OK. Who do I report to over there?'

'Yeah, it's, y'know, who you've been working with.'

'Rita! She gets a double murder, and I get the shaft.'

Mills shrugged.

'She's local, and she's got experience of the kind of folk they're looking at. Who would you have chosen?'

Joe had to admit it, he'd've chosen Rita too.

'Thing is,' he said, 'we just got a main suspect.'

Mills nodded. 'Let them have it. You're still officially SIO on the first murder, but you'll be answering to Kirklees on the overall investigation. Sorry, mate. You want an unsolved against your name? Two? If it's black on black, let them have the bad stats.'

'It's not black on black.'

Mills raised his eyebrows.

'OK. What is it, then?'

'I dunno just yet.'

'That's the ticket. The Joe of old!' Mills said, venting his exasperation into the air above him as he made his way to the door.

An hour later, the investigation hub for the double murder was up and running at Wakefield HQ. Joe made sure all the case files on the system were copied across. Two data clerks helped him, scrupulously polite and efficient, avoiding eye contact as they worked. The last items to go were Turner's lists of the members of the Patriot League and the Lobster Pot discussion group. They were scanned and uploaded, with copies emailed directly to Rita.

He'd already told Gwyn Merchant to go home. There wasn't much more to do late on a Sunday. They'd regroup tomorrow morning, see where they were on Shaw.

Joe sat down at his desk and checked his phone. Sam had sent a WhatsApp message: **Welcome to the modern world, Dad!**

He considered a witty riposte, but couldn't think of one.

He clicked on Twitter, searched for the Kirklees District Police feed. There she was, a one-minute video of DS Scannon on the steps of HQ, all po-faced and official. The Comms Officer had even managed to find her a nice sombre jacket.

He listened without really taking it in. Her tone was different now. The victims were *young men*, and the killer was *ruthless* and *calculated*. There was nothing about rapist scum, no mention of the fact that she would have snuffed Beverage herself given half a chance. He was glad Merchant had gone home; he'd have been rolling on the floor, creased up with laughter, going on about all that one-sixty-six bullshit.

His phone buzzed.

A text, unrecognized number:

I've got something to say.

He looked at the number. It meant nothing to him. Who'd be texting him, apart from Sam? He went through his jacket pockets until he found the beer mat. Scribbled on it in Biro was the same number, plus: *Text first.*

Karen Cullen.

He replied:

Where?

McDonald's, Junction 27, off M62.

Half an hour?

OK.

Karen Cullen clearly wasn't one for full sentences. Was it nerves? Or had she needed to be quick? He checked Google Maps. There were a couple of McDonald's nearer to the Brown Cow in Batley. There must have been a dozen similar places as well. *But there's nowhere quite so anonymous as a Maccy D's at a motorway junction, eh, Karen?*

He gulped down one last mouthful of coffee and stood up. He wanted to be there when she arrived.

29

He'd driven this way enough times, especially over the last few days, but he'd never stopped here. It hit you as soon as you dropped down off the motorway: a commercial sprawl that dominated the landscape like an enormous mound of gaudily lit Americana. On one side a massive cinema complex, on the other an equally huge Ikea. Around both were litters of smaller places, block-built piglets sucking on the neon teat, loud and electric, Argos, Costa, PC World…

High street names, he told himself as he joined the slow-moving line of vehicles on the slip road. But these days you didn't see the famous names on the high street. They were in shopping centres and 'outlets', in service stations, hotel lobbies. The towns were full of charity shops, nail salons and pound stores.

Five o'clock on a bloody Sunday and the roads were packed. Since when was this prime going-out time? As he inched onto the roundabout he could see McDonald's up ahead. It was heaving.

Ten minutes later he was circling the car park and wondering whether he could stick his car in a disabled spot and use his police pass. The moral dilemma evaporated when a people carrier suddenly lit up ahead of him. A family of five arrived, piled in and were away.

As he prepared to turn into the space, the car in front of him in the queue sounded its horn and reversed towards the spot. It came close to hitting Joe's front bumper but stopped just in time, leaving it impossible for either car to park. Meanwhile, the driver was gesticulating, mouthing words into his mirror.

'Twat-face challenge!' Joe cried out, and had to stifle his laughter before the guy in front saw him.

He and Andy had started playing twat-face challenge as soon as they got into plain clothes. The rules were simple: whenever a situation of boorish arrogance or general twattery arises involving a member of the public, you earn points based on how long you can let it go on without whipping out your warrant card. Deliberate provocation is not allowed; the officer merely has to be polite, tolerant or otherwise passive, preferably until the twat in question auto-explodes in a fit of disbelief.

'Andy, where are you when I need you!'

Holding his ground and playing innocent was the obvious way to go. So that's what he did. It didn't take long. After more sounding of the horn and some aggressive revving from the car in front, the driver's door flew open and a young man in grey jogging pants came towards Joe, a jaunty spring in his step.

Joe wound down his window.

'Move the fuckin' motor, fella,' the gent said.

He was in his early twenties, no visible tattoos, clean shaven, and had that strangely perceptible aura of someone who is having a lot of sex.

What would Andy Mills say here? This was his absolute favourite kind of twat-face. Then again, Mr Mills had actually been known to cross the road just in case there was an argument worth having on the other side. He simply loved confrontation.

'Pardon?' Joe asked.

He could already imagine himself telling Andy over a pint in Whitelock's. *I just said 'pardon'!*

Grey pants tamped down his aggression. He was an edgy, jack-in-the-box type, the tasty fly-weight, the kind of guy who you could imagine working as a bouncer, the skinny one, and everybody thinks the same thing: why's he working as a bouncer? But everybody knows why.

'Just back up, will yer, mate? I've got mi kid with me, and she's fuckin' cryin' we've been here so long. Back it up, fella.'

He said it almost fraternally, the message now received and understood, the masculine order re-established. He returned to his vehicle, the same jaunty walk. Job done.

Joe watched him go. How difficult would it have been to put a fist into that face? And if a fist, why not a pencil? In the right circumstances, why the hell not?

'Right,' he said, settling down in his seat, 'maximum twat-face.'

He turned on his indicator, folded his arms and sat back to watch the scene play out in front of him.

The young man had got back into his car. But he was now twisting impatiently in his seat as he waited for Joe's car to move. It didn't. Then the door flew open again. This time he was more stompy than jaunty, and he came fast.

'What's yer problem? Back up or I'll...'

Something took Joe's attention. The entrance to the car park was just ahead. A black BMW pulled up on the corner. He pressed the button and wound the window up as he watched Karen Cullen get out of the Beemer. Meanwhile, the shouting from outside became more agitated.

He kept his eyes on her as she made her way up the short driveway. By the time Joe had got into reverse, the bloke outside was actually bawling at the window, the tendons on his neck strained, his whole body in an Incredible Hulk stance, as if he was about to lift the car up and hurl it out of the way.

Joe backed up a couple of feet, all the time watching Karen Cullen, who walked quickly, her face pale and determined. Hulk was now storming back to his car.

'The pencil is suddenly a very understandable option,' he said as he waited for the car in front of him to reverse into the available space.

By the time he'd found somewhere else to park, Karen Cullen was at a window table nursing a portion of chips and a Coke. The place was full. Mainly families, although on closer inspection most of the kids were with one parent, not two. And the parents themselves looked so disengaged with their children that it appeared that they were deliberately ignoring them. *They'll leave*, he wanted to whisper in their ears. *They'll grow up, and one day they'll just vanish from your life.*

Karen Cullen saw him as soon as he walked in. She watched as he made his way through the spontaneous kindergarten that took up much of the central area of the restaurant.

'You beat me to it,' he said, slipping into the seat opposite.

'Had a bit of aggro in the car park?' she said.

Her eyes were slightly red, and she had lost what little colour there had been in her cheeks.

'You saw that?'

'I don't miss much.'

'I'll take that as a good sign. What did you want to see me about?'

'Lisa thinks her dad got Craig killed. She's threatening to go to the, y'know, to you lot.'

'And did he?'

'No.'

'You're sure?'

'Yeah. Danny was in the pub on Tuesday night. Behind the bar.'

'Race Night?'

'Yeah, he were there till closing time. There's cameras inside and out.'

'That goes for your husband's associates too?'

She screwed up her face, thought about it.

'That posh fella came round. The Professor, they call him.'

'Leo Turner? When was this?'

'Today. I heard 'em talking. This is between you and me, right?'

'This is a double murder. There might be more to come. You need to tell me everything you know.'

'He said they're gonna use the murders for publicity.'

'Publicity?'

'Y'know, if someone from the League is arrested for it, Danny gets himself on telly, kicks up a fuss, says the League is being blamed 'cos of the anti-drugs stuff and what-'ave-yer.'

'That's plausible. But it's two murders we're talking about. So far. Kind of high risk, don't you think? All that vigilante stuff on the website? The League's definitely gonna be under suspicion.'

'Not Danny. All Tuesday he were in the pub.'

'OK, let's go back to Leo Turner. What did he say exactly?'

'Soon as someone from the League gets taken in for questioning, Danny's gonna do a press conference. Make it look like police harassment.'

'Who does he think is likely to get brought in for questioning? Let me guess. Daz and Ranksy? Do they fit the bill?'

'That's what I want to tell you. They've been threatening Craig Shaw's mum.'

He paused, forced himself to remain calm. 'Go on.'

'All that stuff about only selling spliffs? He were doing coke and ket, an'all. Owt yer wanted, the cocky twat. Used to come down our estate. Taking the fuckin' piss.'

'So?'

'I phoned him a few times.'

'How did you get his number?'

She looked at Joe as if he was stupid.

'He sells drugs. Half the bloody estate's got his number. He told me to mind my own business.'

'And your daughter?'

'I tried to talk to her. But she's an adult. I couldn't go round there and drag her out, could I?'

'So you threatened his mum?'

She looked away.

'I paid Daz and Ranksy to do it. Anonymous, no names. I thought his mum might get through to him.'

'You scared her shitless. Made it look like a rival gang. Was that the idea? Stuff through the letterbox, the nasty phone calls? Was all of that you?'

'I'm not proud. I didn't know what else to do.'

'Does Danny know?'

'No. Didn't think I needed to tell him. It worked, or I thought it had.'

'The black Beemer disappeared, right?'

She nodded.

'But,' he continued, 'all he'd done was switch to his mum's car.'

'Didn't take long to work that out. And then…'

'Then?'

'Then he's dead.'

'Meanwhile, we've got Daz and Ranksy driving over to Leeds, telling his mum that they're going to sort Craig out. And, by the way, you're the second person to confirm that.'

He looked at the parents around them, all safe in the knowledge that their kids were within easy reach. But what if one of them was in danger? Real danger? How far would they go?

'I'll just get a coffee. Why don't you tell Lisa to park that big black car and come in? I need a word with her too.'

Karen Cullen looked surprised.

'I don't miss much, either,' he said.

As he queued at the counter, he saw the guy from the car park over at a table in the far corner, watching his young daughter as she ate chips from her Happy Meal, making sure she didn't get too much ketchup on each one, a paper serviette in his hand to wipe her mouth. It was almost impossible to believe that it was the same man.

Joe gave Rita a call. She answered immediately, her voice hoarse, edged with exhaustion.

'Hi, how's it going? Saw you on the internet. Very sombre.'

'Bollocks. We're looking into Leo Turner now. Closely. We've got a big team on this. Getting' bigger, an'all.'

'I bet you are. I've got a bit more on him as it happens.' He briefly explained the situation with Karen Cullen. 'Shall I send 'em across to make statements?'

'Sweet. Tell 'em to ask for me. I'll be waiting. Cheers, Joe.'

'No problem. By the way, what's this about Beverage meeting a copper?'

'Hold on, it's here on the system. *Peters or Peterson or something.* That's what the kid said. Beverage phoned him, said he was off to see a copper. We've got a DCI called Peters. Could be name-checking him. But there's no obvious link. I've got somebody on it.'

'No. He's name-checking a Canadian psychologist.'

'Explain!'

But he'd already hung up.

He texted Rita as he made his way back across the restaurant:

Jordan Peterson. Author of 12 Rules for Life. The Lobster Book. There's a copy in Turner's house.

'Hello, Lisa,' he said, sliding back into the seat.

Her expression was blank. There was none of the former attitude. She looked younger now, and smaller, her resilience stripped away until only the child remained. And she wasn't pretending this time.

'I assume your mum's told you about what she did?'

Karen nodded, answering for her daughter.

'Lisa, you should know this. When Craig's car was found, there was coke, fentanyl, e and ket in it. That's what he was carrying when he was killed. Wrapped and ready to sell. Your mum was trying to protect you. I'd've done the same.' He took a long breath, as a wave of emotion threatened to subsume him. 'A parent'll do almost anything to protect their kid. I hope you know that. It's… it's difficult to put into words.'

Lisa looked right at him.

'What do we do now? For Daz and Ranksy?'

He wrote Rita's details on a page from his notebook, tore it out, handed it over.

'You drive over to Wakefield now, both of you. Make full statements. And I mean full. They're expecting you. Lisa? You need to tell them everything you know.'

Mother and daughter glanced at each other, and then, without a word, they got up.

'Meanwhile,' he told himself as he watched them leave, 'I have another appointment.'

He raised an arm and scratched the back of his head as he sniffed his armpit.

'Shower first.'

30

The Greyhound pub sat a little way back from the single road that ran through Tong village. Its uneven stone walls were painted white, its windows were small and leaded, and the slate roof rose and sank very slightly, like the graceful droop of an elderly gentleman's shoulders. The tarmacked car parks on either side were a little less than idyllic, yet the larger of these backed onto a cricket field, complete with a small clubhouse worthy of its own chocolate box, and a pitch roller bearing a velvety patina of rust. The addition of a hay wain might have been excessive. But only just.

'Don't talk about the case,' he told himself as he got out of the taxi. 'Don't talk about your divorce. Don't talk about how much you're missing your bloody son.'

Repeating these notes-to-self a few times, he walked towards the pub. Then it struck him: what on earth was he going to talk about?

The main bar had a stone floor, and a collection of Toby jugs hanging above the counter. There were various hand-pulled ales on offer, horse brasses on the walls, a large bell to call time... In fact, it had everything that made a pub worth drinking in.

It also had Sky Sports, high up in the far corner on a screen the size of a small bed, but even that seemed fitting, Mr Murdoch having now taken his rightful place in the most cherished of English shrines.

He stood at the bar and let his hands run along its thick polished wood edge. How many pissed Yorkshiremen had slumped against its comforting bulk? Two centuries' worth, give or take. All the arguments that had been settled here, swilled down with Best and Mild and pints of half 'n' half, the bullshit talked, opinions given, received, discarded like empty crisp packets.

He inhaled the lightly acidic smell of beer swills as if it were the lingering presence of candle wax in a church an hour after mass. He could have stayed here forever. Then he saw her. She was propped up at the bar in the corner, her back to him, watching rugby league on the TV screen. She was in black jeans and a loose white shirt. Very casual. Then again, this was technically a background interview, nothing more than that. What was she supposed to wear, a cocktail dress?

For a while he stayed where he was and looked at her. She was slim, about his height, and had the poise and angularity of someone in good physical shape. Naturally attractive, there was a kind of understated sensuality to her. Even now he could see that she had the air of a woman slightly beyond his reach. The idea of any sort of mutual attraction seemed implausible, the whole thing a joke at his expense. He'd had plenty of time to indulge in this kind of self-doubt since moving back from France. Dating had never been his thing, but now, in middle age, it felt utterly alien. So, with that huge vote of confidence in himself, he made his way over to her.

She turned on her stool as he arrived, a large glass of white wine in her hand. At the same moment, a young, heavy-set barman on the other side of the counter appeared.

'What can I get you?' the barman asked.

Joe looked at him, then at Chris.

'Hi Joe!' she said, jumping into the awkward moment. 'Let me get this!'

'Pint of Mild, please,' he asked the barman.

'Mild?'

'Mild. Tetley's Mild?'

'Never heard of it, mate.' There was just a hint of derision in his voice. 'Is it non-alchy? It'll be in a bottle if we have it.'

'No, Tetley's Mild. On draught?'

'What, here?'

'Everywhere. Used to be. Wishful thinking, I guess.'

'You're losing me now, mate.'

It was the second 'mate' that did it. The perfect twat-face challenge, a young kid trying to be clever. He even had a beard, which only made things worse. Andy would have been well into it by now, winding the lad up with a mixture of faux-naïvety and implied mockery.

'Don't worry,' Joe said. 'Just stuff from the Olden Days.'

'Penny-farthings and coal mines, eh?'

'Something like that. Let's see if you can pull me a pint of Bitter.'

As the young man wandered off down the bar, Chris was doing her best not to laugh out loud.

'Penny-farthings and coal mines!'

'You know,' he said, finding himself kissing her on both cheeks, 'I don't think I've ever felt so old!'

Her face was warm, and she smelled of perfume and wine.

'Anyway, how are things going?' she said, as if they'd known each other for years.

He stopped, thought about it, then realized that he was far too close to her.

'I'm, well—' he stuttered, taking a half-step backwards, 'in the last thirty-odd hours I've had one hour's sleep, one meal, and been kicked off a murder inquiry. Two, as good as.'

Her eyes widened.

'How did that happen?'

'A new team has taken over the inquiry, different police district. I was literally in the wrong place at the wrong time. The second murder, I don't know whether you heard?'

'Yes, it's terrible. And now you're not involved?'

'I'm still on the first one.'

'But not the whole thing? That must be frustrating. It's getting pretty high-profile,' she said, nodding to her phone, which was sitting on the bar in front of her.

'Have you been following it?'

'Not really. But I'm old enough to remember the Yorkshire Ripper. A serial killer really grabs people's attention. Can you imagine the Ripper now, with social media?'

He shook his head.

'It's gotta be three for a serial killer. This one'll be behind bars before then.'

She took a long drink from her glass, which was now almost empty.

'Shall we change the subject? You must be sick to death of the whole thing!'

Her hand sprang out, grabbing his forearm.

'God, did I just say that? Let's talk about something else.'

'Good idea. Do you want another?'

'I can wait for you.'

He considered the full pint of Bitter that had just arrived on the bar for him.

'This won't take long. Let's get another round in. I need to unwind pretty urgently.'

'I'm all for that!'

For an hour they sat at the bar and went through the script. Potted biographies woven discreetly into a loose, non-committal sort of conversation. It was supposed to be an interview, but they both forgot that quickly enough. They talked naturally, calmly, nothing strident, a lot of stepping softly around each other's opinions, feeling their way tentatively towards each other. She was modest about the classes at the library, but also rather proud, he suspected. Teaching people to do something for themselves. It was all so logical, the way she described it, so generous and practical.

As they moved gradually away from generalities, a nervousness became apparent beneath her air of easy sociability. She would jump in energetic agreement with something, then seem to withdraw, to pull back and look in on herself. It was as if she was playing a part for the first time, playing herself. Perhaps they both were. Is this how it starts? he wondered. Testing the water, seeing where the attraction might lead? Or was it the opposite, the defensiveness of people too hurt to try again? This is what it must be like, he told himself, recalling that his last taste of romance had been massively drunken farewell sex with his ex-wife over a year ago.

'This is a great pub,' he said, starting in on his third pint, or was it his fourth?

He'd begun to relax now. In her company it wasn't difficult. She was an attentive listener, lively in a way, but also coy, guarded. Plus, she was matching him drink for drink.

'I live just down the road. I come here from time to time, but not regularly.'

'Cheaper to drink at home.'

'Well, I suppose it is...'

'Sorry,' he said. 'Just something I heard the other day. A woman told me she drank on her own at home because it was cheaper.'

'Part of the investigation? No, forget that, I shouldn't ask.'

Joe took a drink. He felt the beer coursing down his throat and into his stomach. The bar had become noisier and hotter. For a moment he was overcome by a wave of dizziness.

'It doesn't really matter now,' he said, pressing his eyes closed for a moment. 'I'm not heading the inquiry anymore.'

'And the woman?'

The image of Jane Shaw came to him. The cigarettes. The vomit on the carpet. Mourning her son alone in that house behind the Brick.

'I dunno, it seemed so sad, her sitting at home drinking alone because a pub's too expensive.'

'Was she a victim? I mean, perhaps she was scared to go out.'

He looked at her, confused.

'Sorry,' she added, so close to him now that their shoulders touched. 'I really shouldn't ask.'

He leant against the bar, feeling himself sink into it. He thought about her, couldn't stop himself: Jane Shaw on her own, a can of cheap cider in her hand, cigarettes, a TV screen for company.

'Her son died,' he said. 'Now she's got nobody. She's at home getting pissed on her own.'

'Joe,' she said, reaching down and squeezing his hand, 'this is work. You don't have to talk about it.'

He let her hand remain there. It felt good. The fingers were bare, no rings. He wondered whether there ever had been. All the usual shit that goes through a bloke's mind. Yet the thought of Jane Shaw, alone in her house, tonight, every night, was impossible to forget.

He downed the rest of his pint in one, the way he used to do with Andy when they were younger, always keen to be onto the next, slamming the empty glasses down on the bar like trophies. She gestured to the barman and ordered another round.

'Son was a drug dealer,' he said. 'Gets himself killed. She feels guilty, like the whole thing's her fault. Helpless.'

'Is she?'

'He's dead. What can she do?'

'I dunno. It must be difficult. I mean, to know what to do.'

He looked at her, not quite understanding. Her eyes held his gaze. They were not cold, but part of her had disappeared from view. Whoever she was, this woman he hardly knew, something had drained from her in an instant. Or perhaps he was reading too much into things. Perhaps that was always his problem.

The barman arrived with two drinks. She waved a card above the contactless device, waited for him to leave. And still she said nothing. Joe sensed no malice. She had withdrawn, but not, it seemed, because she wanted to.

'I've got a son,' he said, just to fill the silence. 'If anything happened, I dunno what I'd do.'

Without thinking, he got out his phone and checked for messages. Nothing new from Sam.

'Let's have a look at him, then,' she said, leaning so far in to him that he could feel loose strands of her hair against his face.

'I...' he said, fumbling with his phone, 'y'know, I don't think I have any. It's a new phone. Haven't got around to...'

'How old is he?'

'Sam? He's studying Medicine in Edinburgh. First year.'

She pulled out her own phone.

'What's his number?'

'Really?'

'Come on, it'll be fun!'

She typed the number in as he recited it from memory.

'Past nine?' she said, putting the phone to her ear. 'He'll be in the student bar.'

Then she held up a hand.

'Hello? Is that Sam Romano? Hi, my name's Chris Saunders. I'm getting drunk in a pub with your dad.' She listened, laughed. 'I know! But I've got him here now, so I'm making the most of it! Anyway, here's the thing. Is there a woman there? A female friend? Right, could you pass the phone to her, just for a second?'

Joe looked on, helpless and incredulous.

'Gemma? You're a friend of Sam's? Lovely. Listen, Sam's dad is such a lame brain with tech that he doesn't even have a photo of his own son on his phone. Would you be a darling and take one, then send it to me?' She stopped, listened. 'Yes, I *know*! Men, they just can't, though!'

Even Joe could hear the hilarity that this was causing among Sam's friends.

'They're taking one now,' she explained, unnecessarily.

She held up her glass and they toasted the moment.

Her phone pinged.

'Thanks, Gemma! Ask Sam if he wants to speak to his dad.'

A moment later Joe was talking to his son. Their conversation was brief and slightly embarrassing, overheard as it was by an amused audience at both ends. He asked about the university accommodation, about how the course was going. It really felt like there was little more to say, with so many people listening.

Even as he ended the call, he could feel the tears welling up in his eyes. He slipped down from the stool and rested his forearm lightly on her shoulder as they looked at the newly arrived image of Sam on her phone: the young Romano, a sheepish grin on his face, sitting among a bunch of friends and holding up a pint of lager.

'Thank you,' he said, giving her shoulder a brief squeeze before retreating to the gents'.

When he got back, she was hunched over her phone.

'I sent you the image,' she said. 'Oh, another thing. Come here.'

She pulled him close, their heads touching, and took a photo. There was a firmness in the way she drew him to her, a resolve that he hadn't expected, something more than he would have dared to show himself.

'Gemma asked me to send her a picture of us,' she said.

She tapped her phone. Across the skies it went, to another city.

'I'll send you it, as well.'

'Please do.'

It was only a matter of decorum which led them to untangle themselves and retake their seats at the bar. Joe was entering the stage of pleasant euphoria which meant that he should stop drinking, but which he knew meant that he wouldn't. The inevitability, as usual, was as intoxicating as the alcohol.

He wanted to take her in his arms, he told himself, as he stared at the bar in front of him, the rest of his surroundings now a dull murmur. He wanted to embrace her, to make the grand, romantic gesture, Hollywood style. But he held back. It wasn't embarrassment. There was something else, and he couldn't get it out of his head: the thought of a dead son and the mother left behind, of Jane Shaw sitting alone, facing the unimaginable horror of losing her only child, the rest of her life without him, without anybody.

He sucked his beer down. Huge mouthfuls, a third of the pint, more. It was the only thing that made any sense now, the familiar sensation of a gently spinning world easing its way into his consciousness. And still Jane Shaw came to him. The thought of losing a child was unimaginable. His own sadness, by contrast, was nauseating in its triviality, the self-pity of the divorce, of coming back to England, the sense of professional failure. Add the death of Sam to that and where would he be? What would that do to him?

'Sorry,' he said, realizing he'd been staring blankly for far too long. 'I was thinking about that woman, sitting on her own, her son gone. Just gone.'

'These things, they bother you, don't they?'

'Yes, still do. Always have. You say it as if they shouldn't?'

'But it's obvious, isn't it?' she said, her mouth pulled off-centre, the beginnings of a sneer that she couldn't hide. 'The world is pathetically, horrifically cruel, Joe. It's just... I mean, isn't that your *job*?'

'My job?'

'The police. To see the evil?'

'We see it, yes.'

'But to set the world right, Joe? It's your job? Isn't it? Joe?'

'I...'

'Or do you just log it down, add it to the stats? Perhaps that's the bloody problem, the... I...' She grabbed the edge of the bar and with some difficulty got to her feet. 'I've drunk too much. I'm sorry.'

He didn't want to embrace her now. He wanted to sleep, to sober up, to see his son. He wanted to go home. And the feeling appeared to be mutual.

They stood outside the pub waiting for Joe's taxi. He squeezed his eyes shut, forcing the alcoholic fug from his mind, and did his best to stand upright. Meanwhile, the cold evening air had instantly restored her to sobriety. Her face was composed, with that same confident smile that had been so captivating yesterday in the library.

'You know,' he said, 'I've lived in Leeds most of my life, and I've never really got to know many of these old villages. They crop up everywhere. And the valleys, the rolling hills, the whole thing. It's a beautiful place. My family weren't much for the countryside.'

'Well, now you know this one.' She looked out across the cricket field, and to the open grassland that rose steadily beyond.

'There are plenty more. I'll have to show you. Oh, by the way,' she added, as a taxi pulled into the entrance, 'weren't you supposed to be interviewing me tonight?'

'It went clean out of my mind. We can do it another time.'

She kissed him lightly on the lips.

'I can take you home,' he said. 'Drop you off, I mean.'

For a second they thought about it, both of them, standing so close that he could feel the warmth of her body, his hand dithering at his side.

'I think I'd like to walk.'

So that, he told himself as he slumped into the back seat of the cab and felt it move off into the darkness, was dating in middle age.

31

As the taxi came to a stop he roused himself from a fitful, half-nauseous doze. He paid the driver and hauled himself arse-first out of the car, taking care not to slam the door.

It took him a moment or two to acclimatize: a dull suburban street bathed in watery green light so insipid that it felt like he'd stepped into some random CCTV footage.

'I chose to live here?' he asked himself, his sluggish eyes running up and down the lines of modest post-war semis in search of the particularly modest one he'd rented.

The front door stuck slightly. It needed a bit of shoulder-work to open it, just as it had when the estate agent showed him and Sam around last year. Hadn't seemed like much of a problem at the time. Still wasn't.

The central heating was on and the hall smelled of airing clothes. It wasn't the kind of smell he enjoyed coming home to, but at least it was domestic. There were a few envelopes on the mat. He stepped over them and headed for the living room.

Pale laminated wooden flooring, off-white walls, Swedish furniture in greys and creams. To mitigate the sense of living in a mid-priced furniture catalogue he'd hung a framed Kandinsky print over the fireplace, and between two Nordic armchairs by the window he'd set a small table with a glass vase containing half a dozen oversized balsa-wood tulips, hand-painted in bright colours. A moment of madness, bought in a rush, like everything else.

He let himself drop onto the bizarrely uncomfortable sofa. For a while he lay there, trying to focus on the light switch by the kitchen door, then on the door handle, any fixed point... but the room kept on spinning. Normally he would have dragged himself upstairs, forced down three or four glasses of water, and crawled into bed. But tonight was different.

Willing the effects of the beer to subside, he reached down to the floor and got his laptop. As Windows booted up with its irritatingly cheerful jingle, he tried to get comfy, letting himself slither down until he was almost lying there. Then he did what any self-respecting person would do in the circumstances: he googled her.

The school's website contained nothing about its teachers. No images. No names. He tried to imagine her in front of a class of rowdy teenagers. She'd be serene, in control, managing to keep things in order as she slowly explained some mathematical conundrum. Would she be patient? he asked himself. Yes, he thought, up to a point.

General web searches for Christine Saunders also proved ineffective: there were way too many people with the same name. Finally, he tracked her down on Facebook. In her portrait photo she was every bit as attractive as she'd been tonight, her smile bright and confident, but steely; not quite guarded, but almost. He scrolled through her timeline. The posts were mainly about activities at school, chess club, humorous references to the glories of algebra and trigonometry. There were no posts about family, and the account itself was only seven years old.

Then there were maps. Lots of them. She clearly enjoyed long walks in the West Yorkshire countryside, each one plotted on a small, in-set map courtesy of an exercise app. That explained why she'd chosen to live in a village like Tong. The simple pleasures of the outdoors. He'd been missing it all. The magnificence of the valleys, the splendour, the greenness! He'd been missing every bit of it, for his entire life. Perhaps he'd found someone to share it with.

With a pang of shame, he began exploring her list of friends, clicking here and there, hardly knowing what he was doing. He hadn't been on Facebook much since he got back from France, and there were several hundred messages and friend requests on his account. He'd forgotten how to delete them. Plus, he was pissed. The icons were tiny, and they danced about in duplicate, however much he screwed up his eyes to focus on the screen. His head was beginning to feel heavy on his shoulders, and staring at the computer was not helping.

Friend request sent.

Shit. He'd clicked it by mistake. He pulled the laptop closer to his face, tried to work out what he'd done, how to delete the request. He couldn't find anything. His finger dithered on the touchpad, hardly daring to click anything now. She'd know he'd been snooping.

'Shit!'

He needed to sober up. But getting off the sofa proved to be harder than he'd imagined. His body was a dead weight, and the best he could do was to lower himself down onto the floor, then hoist his upper body onto the coffee table. From there, with one monumental push of his arms and legs, he was able to struggle upright.

Kitchen. Coffee. He looked around as he waited for the kettle to boil. It was not unlike the kitchen in Jane Shaw's house, only this didn't feel like *his* kitchen. Didn't feel like anyone's. Its fixtures were tasteful yet bland. Even the mugs lined up on the worktop surface were cloyingly anonymous in their sameness. The bottle of fancy Italian olive oil and a half-eaten baguette hardly lifted the tone.

As he spooned instant coffee into a rented mug, he tried to calculate how many meals he'd cooked here for more than one person since Sam had gone off to Edinburgh. The answer, he told himself with a bit of a smile, was zero.

Then his phone buzzed. He pulled it from his pocket and stared, his eyes taking longer than usual to register the information on the small screen.

It was her.

'You didn't strike me as a Facebook kind of person!' she said as soon as he answered.

'Oh, I'm sorry!'

'What for?'

He wondered whether he should lie. But how could he?

'I… don't know. I was just…'

'Looking me up. I was doing the same with you. You haven't been in the news for a while, Detective Romano!'

'I haven't been on a high-profile case for a while.'

'Well, you are now. Don't forget, we still have to do that interview.'

'Tomorrow?'

'Great. Look, I better get to bed. I've got advanced Maths first thing in the morning. It was lovely to see you, Joe.'

'Yes. It was. It really was. I'll be in touch tomorrow.'

He stood there, phone in his hand, as the swirling confusion in his brain began to lift. Or rather, there was now a semblance of clarity pushing through the drunkenness, as if he had two minds working in tandem: the yin and yang of the thoughtful drunk, or the Laurel and Hardy.

He made his coffee and went back to the living room, setting the mug down on the dining table in the corner. Then, reaching all the way across the table with an arm, he swept everything else – books, old newspapers, bills, a few new CDs that he hadn't played yet – to the floor.

'Right. Where the hell is it?'

He stopped, drank some coffee, then staggered off to search the house.

Five minutes later, the few cupboards that had anything in them had been ransacked, their contents now spilling out on the carpet, but haphazardly, as if a burglar had started the job then given up in disgust.

Back at the dining table, he unrolled it and admired the fine draughtsmanship. It was an architect's plan: *Maison Romano*. The small farmhouse they'd bought in France had needed some minor structural adjustments. Jackie handled the building work, armed with a Collins French-English dictionary and only minimal French. The end result had been perfect. The conversion had even been featured in *ARA-GB!*, a magazine for British ex-pats in the Auvergne-Rhône-Alpes region.

Now all that Joe was left with was half the cash value of

the cottage, which wouldn't buy much in the UK, and a very large piece of paper.

'Right.'

He turned the metre-square plan over and flattened it down on its blank side. He got a pencil from a collection of about a dozen in an earthenware mug that sat on some bookshelves against the wall. Apart from a bottle of Courvoisier, a stack of CDs, and the pencils, the shelves were empty.

He wrote CRAIG SHAW in the centre-left of the enormous empty white space. To emphasize the point, he etched a box around the name in thick, uneven lines, snapping off the point of the pencil in the process.

Tossing it to the floor, he got another one from the mug and set to work. On the right-hand side of the paper he wrote JASON BEVERAGE. Then he stood up, took off his jacket and emptied the contents of its various pockets onto the table: his notebook, the print-outs that Leo Turner had given him, the folded Lobster Pot poster, a beermat from the Brown Cow, plus a few other bits and pieces that he'd accumulated over the last few days: a beermat from the Greyhound, a sachet of sugar from McDonald's, a greasy serviette from goodness-knew-when, all the detritus of an incurable pocket-filler.

Rolling up his shirt sleeves, he made a start. At the bottom of the paper, in tiny handwriting, he drew up a list of everywhere he'd been since Thursday and every person he'd spoken to, plus every other name that had emerged during the inquiry. Then, using his notebook for reference, he wrote up his notes about every item on the list, ticking each one off as information was entered somewhere or other onto the massive sheet of paper.

An hour later and still he wasn't done. More and more ideas were emerging, little boxes with new suggestions and ideas, most of them linked with lines and looping arrows to other names and locations… The mosaic of information around the English Patriot League became denser by the minute. Then he'd jump to somewhere else on the enormous sheet, adding a reference here, a question mark there. He made scrupulously detailed progress through his notebook, folding down the top corner of each page as its information was transferred to the plan, then doing the same with the bottom corner of each reverse page.

Cleckheaton Library came to occupy most of the upper right-hand quadrant of the plan: the snivelling, faux-radical librarian (bike? activism? current affiliations?), the pencils, the name of the retired local councillor he'd spoken to (political party? interest in crime? drugs?), the member of the group who'd attended a meeting of the Lobster Pot (Trevor; wife Elaine; stent out)… Lines went everywhere, up and down, sideways, each one sprouting boxes for further suggestions, unresolved questions, possible lines of enquiry.

The word CLECKHEATON was becoming a hub through which a great many disparate clusters of information were linked. Leo Turner had a whole section there, and Chris Saunders' name was written directly below the word LIBRARY.

On he went, dragging information up from memory: the newspapers that Leo Turner read, the spiking of drinks in a Cleckheaton pub; one-sixty-six (Gwyn Merchant); Batley (Merchant, Rita, the Patriot League); Lisa (univ. fees, father, drugs)…

Finally, three or four broken pencils later, he stood up and admired his work.

'Right, that's a start.'

He rang Elland Road, knowing the duty data clerk wouldn't be busy, not at this time of night.

'Hi, Carol? It's Joe Romano here... Yeah, working late! Listen, have you got much on over there? I need you to do a bit of digging.'

He read a list of names to her, confirmed the spellings and gave her whatever additional information he had on each one, speaking fast, tripping over his words as his confidence grew.

'General background. Anything at all that sticks out. Work, life, arrests, convictions. In fact, *anything* at all.'

He ended the call. The dregs of his coffee were cold. He went through to the kitchen to make another cup. Waves of exhaustion overcame him now, and as the kettle boiled he forced himself to stay on his feet, knowing that if he sat down he'd fall asleep. He checked his phone. There were some photos that he hadn't looked at yet. He vaguely remembered taking them, but by the time the water was boiling he still hadn't worked out where the images were on his bloody iPhone.

He spooned sugar into the steaming mug and went back through to the living room. Finally, he found the photos, a series of images of what seemed to be text on blocks of vibrant colour. It took him a while to see that they were posters, the ones at Cleckheaton Library. *Creative Writing Circle... Inviting You to a Baby Shower... Living with Bereavement.*

He stared at the screen: *Living with Bereavement.* He flicked back through the others; forwards again; then back, straining hard to focus on the words of each image. What was it, what had he missed? His mind was closing down. It was late. A sip from his mug; there was no coffee in it, just water and sugar. Leaning back, he got the brandy from the bookshelf and filled the mug to the brim.

MONDAY

32

He eased himself down behind his desk at 9.30 a.m. There was not much going on in CID, but even so it was noticeably quiet. The support staff at the back were casting not-so-furtive glances in his direction, and he got the impression that they weren't the only ones, although he kept his eyes fixed on the pile of documents in front of him, willing himself towards some kind of lucidity.

The previous hour had not been pleasant. He'd woken up, fully clothed, sprawled on the sofa in the living room. An empty mug and a bottle of Courvoisier were within easy reach on the floor. The bottle, although somewhat depleted, was not empty. Small mercies.

He'd never been one to suffer headaches or particularly severe hangovers, so he got himself up without much trouble and made his way upstairs for a shower. He was weak and shaky, but none the worse for wear. With each step, though, the events of the previous night began to take shape in his mind.

By the time he felt the blast of scalding hot water on his naked body, the full horror of what he'd done hit him. After calling the data clerk last night, he'd retired to the sofa to wait. The brandy must have gone with him. The next thing he remembered was his phone ringing. By that stage he was drunk, half-asleep, and only passably articulate. Yet he'd managed to say the name Christine Saunders. He'd said it various times, confused, rambling, repeating himself. Anything they could get on Christine Saunders.

The data clerks had done their job well. On his desk now sat an impressive pile of printed material, organized into half a dozen thin bundles, each held together with a rubber band. All the individuals he was interested in, including Chris. He was dying for a coffee, but after all the work he'd caused, he thought he better make a start.

Before anything else, though, he logged onto his terminal and updated his movements for the last twenty-four hours: places he'd been, people he'd spoken to, every detail. The investigation hub was expanding by the minute. Even the log of entries was now too long to read in full. He scrolled down to the most recent additions. And there it was. Turner. They were already at his house.

He texted Rita. **Got a moment?**

As he waited for her reply, he read the entry. A full search of Turner's home and his office premises had been ordered and approved. Turner himself was to be brought in for questioning. An 8 a.m. start.

His phone rang.

'Rita. You have a main suspect!'

'Yup. He's here now. Waiting for his lawyer.'

'Mmm. He's a lawyer, isn't he? Already phoning for back-up?'

'Lawyers always do.'

'And you really have him down for double murder?'

'Don't have anybody else. Get a main. Go in hard. What

can I do?' She paused. 'By the way, hope you don't mind, I've asked your deputy to do us a favour.'

'Gwyn? Haven't seen him today yet.'

'I asked him to start monitoring social media, see if the Patriot League lot are playing us. Like you said.'

He thought about it. About everything.

'OK. I'll check in with him. Have you made a statement about Turner?'

'Jesus Christ, Joe! Aren't you following this shit? Two down and counting. Not seen the papers today?'

'Sorry, I'm... I've just been on something.'

'Whatever. Let's speak later, if the Twittersphere doesn't get me first.'

She hung up.

He didn't need to check Twitter. A minute on Google was all it took. The Graphite Assassin was everywhere. Mugshots of Shaw and Beverage on the front page of every online newspaper, plus a video of Rita outside Kirklees HQ, announcing that a man was being questioned in connection with the murders.

The case was national news, and he'd been too drunk or hung-over to notice. He sat there, closed his eyes, forcing himself to breathe slow and steady.

'At last, you're here!'

It was Gwyn Merchant's voice. He took big, lunging steps across the floor towards Joe.

'You seen this shit?' he said, pulling up a chair. 'Mega! Trending like a bugger. Got our own friggin' hashtag, an'all. The business!' He spun a phone in his fingers like a playing card. 'You talked to the boss?'

Joe shook his head. 'Not yet.'

'We've got a team on it. That Patriot League member list? We reckon half a dozen of 'em are tweeting.'

'How do you know it's them? Don't they use fake names?'

'Some do. Some don't. We're looking at their tweet histories, matching up names, locations, stuff they've posted about in the past. Alex is on it, big time.'

'Is he? Since when?'

'Since now. Look at this shit!' Merchant said, brandishing his phone with pure adolescent delight.

Joe read a tweet:

Police shld find who killed them scumbags + SHAKE HIS
BLOODY HAND!!!! #graphiteassassin

And another:

It cost cops £££s to catch druggies + rapists, they get free
defence lawyers (more £££s), then more taxpayer £££s to keep
em in jail. #graphiteassassin done us all a favour!

'And these are from members of the Patriot League?'

'Some of 'em. It's goin' off big time about Turner. They're on about police harassment, all that bollocks. Somebody'll drop a nugget, though. Bound to. If these arseholes are involved, or if they know owt, it'll come out in the end.'

'Yeah. If.'

'If what?'

'If they had anything to do with it.'

Merchant sat back, put his phone on the desk between them, like a peace offering, or a challenge.

'Leo Turner's the main suspect, as of now. You been working on something better? That's what I heard,' he said, looking over at the data clerks.

Joe ignored it.

'What if there are two killers?' he said.

Merchant cocked his head, waited for Joe to continue.

'Second one might be a different killer. Sees his chance, takes advantage. Same MO.'

'Nah, the pencil thing wasn't made public 'til after Beverage was dead.'

Joe shrugged.

A moment.

'Bloody hell, Joe! You're getting into some friggin' choppy waters there, mate.'

'Not many people knew about the pencil, not on Saturday.'

'Like I said. Choppy waters. Your point?'

'No point.'

'Sounds like a point to me. Sounds like you reckon it might be police.'

'Someone knew.'

'You're gonna need more than that to take it to the DPS.'

The operations room was now silent.

'Who mentioned Professional Standards?'

Merchant held his gaze. Then he got up, grabbed his phone and leant in close.

'I'll tell you what, *sarge*,' he said, lowering his voice, 'the shit you pulled last night, it should be you talking to Professional Standards. I'm off for a coffee.'

As Merchant disappeared, the room remained silent. Joe didn't care. He'd got the response he wanted.

He returned to his monitor, scanned the story on the BBC website. A ninety-second video of Rita, plus a few paragraphs outlining the crimes. Below this was a summary of public opinion, citing various posts linked directly from Twitter. Modern journalism at its very best. He clicked over to the *Yorkshire Post*. At least they were actually reporting events in detail, he noted, as he began reading a long description of the background to the case.

Then his phone rang.

33

DCI Andy Mills looked up, saw Joe, waved at a chair in front of his desk.

'Now then!' he said, heaving in his seat.

'Andy.'

'Prepare for a bollocking, *mes amis*.'

'*Mon ami*.'

'Fuck off.'

It wasn't said in anger. He looked tired and disappointed, like a parent who was about to reprimand a teenager but couldn't really be bothered.

'Right. We have a double murder on our hands. Serial killer if another body turns up. Did that slip your mind, y'know, while you were out wining and dining a witness?'

'How did...'

Andy held up a hand, palm outwards.

'Then you're back home, off yer tits, middle of the night, asking Her Majesty's Constabulary to use its considerable powers to dig up information on her.'

'That...'

'Shut it, you knobhead!' He stared at his friend, eyes glazed. A pause. 'Jesus Christ, you don't know, do you?'

'The database stuff? Yes, I do. It's not what it looks like.'

Andy shook his head until his flabby cheeks threatened to work themselves clean off his face. He grabbed a mobile phone from the desk and held it up.

'Know what this is?'

Joe said nothing.

'It's our worst enemy. Look.'

He handed it over. There on the screen was the photo of Chris and Joe in the pub, heads touching, both of them grinning in an alcoholic semi-embrace, his eyes just a touch red.

'Where did this come from?' Joe asked as he read the Twitter post that accompanied it:

Detective Romano of #LeedsCID enjoying a drink tonight with unknown lady friend. He's more handsome than you @SamRomanoLS12!!!!

'Now look at the number of retweets, Joe.'

There were over a hundred. Joe passed the phone back, and tried to think. He couldn't work it out.

'Some girl called Gemma, ring any bells?' Andy asked.

'Oh God, she's a friend of Sam's.'

'Is she now! Well, unless you'd forgotten, you're the SIO on the Shaw murder. Your name's been on the press releases, it's public knowledge. Meanwhile, you're out getting pissed a day after the *second* murder.'

'But how did you see this?'

''Cos she's bloody hashtagged us! The whole world's seen it. I've just been on to the *Yorkshire Post*. Once it's on their website, every bloody newsroom in the country'll see it. *Leeds*

detective investigates Graphite Assassin from a barstool.
You dick!'

They both let the aggression disperse. From outside came the distant hammering of construction work. There was always building work going on at HQ, or nearby, a constant repetitive noise for all those with the luxury of an outside office.

'This woman? Chris Saunders, right? She's in the case file. Just tell me you've eliminated her. She's not a witness, is she, Joe?'

'I got pissed, but it was work. This is all...'

'Sorry, Joe. Can't listen to you. Not if she's a witness.'

Andy waited until it had sunk in.

'DPS?' Joe asked.

'Nah, internal. Just say you were doing background interviews. It'll be OK.'

'But I...'

'Save it, Joe. I'll be on the panel. Can't hear it 'til then. Meanwhile, keep out of the news for a few days, and get your story straight, all right? Gwyn's taking over. He's all I've got. And he's already working with Kirklees. It makes sense.'

'Gwyn? No, no, Andy. Look...'

'No more.'

'Andy, you've got to...'

'No, you've gotta shut your mouth. Now.'

Joe sighed.

'I can't believe what just happened.'

'Believe it.'

'Am I suspended?'

'As soon as we get round to ordering the investigation. It might not come to that. Just keep a low profile. I'll see what I can do.'

Joe waited, expecting more.

There was nothing more.

Back in the operation room, the chatter fell away immediately, discretion having lost out to schadenfreude.

Sod 'em. Sod 'em all. He grabbed the pile of documents on his desk, plus duplicate case files for both murders, and headed for the doors, pointedly returning the stare of anyone who dared to look at him.

34

He spent most of the time it took to drive up the A46 to York switching from one radio station to another. Rock, jazz, pop, classical... couldn't quite find what he wanted. He knew it would only take one piece of music to sort him out, not so much a matter of soothing the savage breast as restoring the balance of his sanity. It had been out of kilter for a while, and the threat of an internal investigation wasn't helping.

By the time he pulled into the first car park on York University's sprawling campus, he still hadn't found the magical song. Perhaps the right music for his current predicament simply hadn't been written. If that were the case, he really was in trouble.

The car park was protected by a barrier.

'Detective Sergeant Joe Romano, Leeds CID,' he said into the intercom.

'Who is it concerning, please?'

'Crime.'

'Do you have an appointment, Sir?'

'I have a warrant card. The last time I checked the statutes, that was enough.'

Having pointlessly annoyed a random member of the security

staff, it crossed his mind that she might have seen the tweet, and name-checked him: boozy cop Romano out carousing with a witness. It was probably all over the internet by now.

'I'm here to see Dr Megan Vicary, Department of Psychology,' he added.

'I will just check that, Sir.'

He bit his tongue and waited, knowing that however long he was kept waiting, it was his rightful punishment for thoughtless arrogance. As he sat there, he considered calling Rita. But over in Kirklees they'd be getting stuck into Turner by now, which was as good an excuse as any for not having to offer her a grovelling apology. He checked his messages. Nothing from her. Perhaps best if it stayed that way for a while.

Finally, the barrier lifted and he was spared further humiliation.

Megan was in their usual meeting spot, sitting on a bench under a willow tree, a cloud of cigarette smoke hanging around her. She wasn't far off, almost close enough to shout, but there was a lot of water in the way.

The university campus was built around a large artificial lake that meandered across several acres of sculptured grassland, decorated by covered walkways and bridges, and populated by a large community of geese and ducks. Dotted along the lake's edge were low-rise residence blocks and faculty buildings, all prefab concrete and wooden panels. It was the same functional sixties architecture as the Brown Cow in Batley, only here, surrounded by trees, grass, and with the gentle flutter of the breeze on the water's surface, the effect was charming, almost dream-like.

Definitely not charming was the quantity of goose shit. By the time he'd found a footbridge to cross, then made his way over the lawns towards Megan, his shoes were caked in the stuff.

'Are all these wild fowl strictly necessary in a seat of learning?'

'You're joking,' she said, getting up and kissing him lightly on both cheeks. 'The geese are smarter than most of my students. How're you doing, Joe?'

Megan's accent was part American drawl, part English temptress. It was the kind of voice a well-aged fairy godmother might have after three continents, two divorces and a life-long penchant for late nights and single malts. Born on the plains of Alberta, Canada, she'd moved to Santa Barbara, to Mexico City, to Sydney, and finally to York, hopping from university to university, where she taught psychology and dabbled in criminal profiling as a hobby.

'I'm doing...' he said, as they sat down, 'I'm doing, ehm, I don't know whether you...'

'Oh, I've seen the tweet. Nice-looking woman. I assume it's got you in trouble?'

'Follow your own road, and let the people talk!'

She raised her eyebrows, but left it at that.

'You've got something for me, then?'

He handed her the files on Shaw and Beverage.

'Just the murders, plus background on the victims. Is that OK?'

She held the files in one hand, weighing them.

'Give me half an hour. There's a coffee shop through that archway.'

He bummed a cigarette and left her to it, ignoring her

suggestion of coffee and walking around the edge of the lake as he smoked. He wondered how much more stress it would take before he found himself with a packet of Marlboro permanently in his pocket. He puffed on the cigarette, not really enjoying the taste, but knowing that it gave him an excuse to put off the inevitable call to Rita.

He got his phone out, googled himself. He was already national news. The *Sun*:

BANGED TO RIGHTS!

The detective heading the hunt for the Graphite Assassin was snapped boozing the night away less than twenty-four hours after the killer claimed his second victim. West Yorkshire Police has so far made no comment on Sergeant Joe Romano's unusual investigation techniques…

He didn't bother with any of the other papers. Twitter was far more illuminating; #graphiteassassin was still trending, with inappropriate police behaviour adding new zest to the stream of opinions on offer. Gemma's original post now had close to five hundred retweets, and many of them, strangely, were in support of him:

Good work, Det. Romano. Best way to deal with #graphiteassassin. Lay back an think of england!!!

DS bags MILF as #graphiteassassin gets away. streets a bit safer. go joe!

And then, amid the stream of predictable nonsense, something new:

#graphiteassassin going after the 1%? Raises a fair question, doesn't it? #OneSixtySix

He searched the hashtag #OneSixtySix. It was gaining momentum, and not all the tweets were the brainless squawks of the angry masses. The case was generating serious discussion. Some of the posts were even written in full sentences.

He found a bench and slumped down. His legs and back had started to ache. He stubbed out the cigarette in a tissue and dropped it into his pocket. There was a message from Sam.

Dad, Gemma says she's really sorry. Didn't know you were on the Graphite murder thing. Hope we didn't cause you any problems. Sam.

The ache in his back began to creep higher. He dug his fingers into the muscles at the base of his neck, pushing the pain around. Two young women walked past, deep in conversation. Not so long ago he would have avoided looking directly at them. These days it didn't matter; the age-gap was such that they didn't seem to notice that he was there at all.

He wondered what Gemma was like. Considerate? Selfish? Had she really been sorry when she saw the photo splashed all over the national press? Or were she and Sam laughing about it now, giggling over their phones, oblivious to the damage they'd done?

New friends, new romances, a new life. *What bliss it was in that dawn to be alive...* Sam was a young man, and Joe desperately wanted his son's time in Edinburgh to be bliss, the kind spent in the company of caring people. Wholesome, decent people. He repeated the words to himself. They sounded inadequate, yet he could think of none better. Jason Beverage and Craig Shaw? He doubted that their youths had been blissful.

He sat there and watched the ducks, knowing that he had to ring Rita. *Follow your own road, and let the people talk!* Where was that from? Dante. Were there any ducks in the *Divine Comedy*? Dante, ducks? Where would ducks go? Down in the 'Inferno', or up with the innocents? He looked at the traces of slimy green shit on the edges of his shoes, and hoped the ones in York would be going all the way down. A quick search online didn't help: *Dante the Duck*, apparently, was a video game.

Finally, having run out of excuses, he gave her a call.

'Rita? Hi, how's it going?'

'We've done Turner's house, office. Nothing yet. He's getting the full treatment, though.'

She let out a long, audible sigh.

'Any luck on the bike?' he asked.

'The tyre print matches. But so do half the bloody tyres in the world. They're analysing the mud traces now.'

He gave it a second.

'Sorry about the stuff with Twitter,' he said. 'It's not what it looks like.'

'Ah, screw that. Keep going, Joe. My super's just talked to Andy Mills. He's holding off on an internal, apparently.'

'For how long? Did he say?'

'We told him all that stuff in the pub was part of the case. He was politely asked to leave you alone. I mean, you were working, weren't you, give or take a few drinks?'

He watched a family of ducks wander past on the path in front of him.

'I'm on the case now. I'll be on it 'til they chuck me off.'

'Bollocks to the lot of 'em, Joe. Keep digging. I'll ring you later.'

'I'm digging. Speak soon.'

'Oh, just one thing. Will you run everything past Gwyn from now on? I mean, while you're keeping your head down? He's in charge at your end, right?'

He was already back on his feet, striding out across the grass, as he ended the call. The backache had gone, and he kicked coils of dried goose shit into the air as he went. Not quite digging, but it would do as a metaphor.

'You've read them?'

'Yup,' Megan said, the files already sitting next to her, closed. 'I was familiar with the case anyway.'

'Really? Why's that?'

She squinted, head back.

'Because I'm interested in Forensic Psychology. Because I know you. Because…' She stopped. 'Joe, everybody's talking about this. Hadn't you noticed?'

'I've been a bit too busy trying to solve it.'

'Oh, by the way, you got lucky. There's just been an explosion at an oil refinery in Wales. No one hurt, but, y'know, a bit Jerry Lee Lewis.'

'What?'

'Great balls of fire. God, you're really not on form today!'

'Could be a slight hangover.'

'Oh, I see. Anyway, you're not the top story on the lunchtime bulletins.'

'Relegated to old news almost before I knew I was new news.'

'Welcome to the digital age!'

He sat down.

'So, what do you think?'

'The first murder's unusual, intriguing. The car more or less disappears, which presents us with an interesting state of mind.'

'How?'

'Well, the killer's definitely lucid as he drives off. Thinking straight. That's not easy, right after you've murdered someone. Plus, it suggests he knows the roads, the traffic cameras, the lie of the land.'

'Local knowledge.'

'*Obvs*, as my daughters would say. How's Sam doing in Edinburgh, by the way?'

'Fine. Can't thank you enough for the reference.'

'Smart lad. He got in on merit.'

'Smart, but he never rings. The twins?'

She snorted.

'Private schools around here, you know how much they cost? They've got posh boyfriends called Giles, Jake, I dunno. The money? It just goes.'

She paused, the very thought of school fees enough to crush her soul.

'Also,' she said, 'there's zero forensics, apart from the pencil. Even with the fire, it's meticulous. And the timeframe? Looks like the car and body were hidden somewhere for, what, two whole days? Then it's left burnt out in a car park, where it'll definitely be found. Somebody who knows what they're doing. It's all very thoughtful, efficient. But...' She shook her head. 'They leave him in the passenger footwell. He must have been put there post mortem, yet there's no clear signs of a struggle before that. A drug dealer who doesn't put up a fight?'

'Body in that state it's difficult to know for sure.'

'Still, someone puts a pencil into your eye socket and it goes all the way in? You don't try to fight 'em off?'

'He was taken by surprise?'

'Must have been, I guess. No substances in his blood either, no sedation? Jesus, Joe, you know how to pick 'em!'

'It's opportunistic, right?'

'Yes, it looks that way. But the pencil? That's the strange part. The killer must have known the victim, or was comfortable in his presence. At the very least they must have been close up, talking. It's the only way. Even then, it's a stretch to incapacitate someone with a well-sharpened HB. But, y'know, the first kill? The unplanned ones can be weird. They can come from nowhere.'

'Spontaneous?'

'You wouldn't *choose* a pencil, would you?'

'The second kill? That was a choice.'

'Yes. Different kind of thing altogether.'

'Could it be two killers?'

She shifted on the bench.

'It's possible. But, I dunno, there's something about both murders, apart from the pencils, something that connects them. They're mad, but there's an element of control. Manic but calm. I can't put my finger on it... The second one, he gets the victim there by posing as a police officer. Forensics still pretty minimal. Meticulous. But it's so completely different. Everything about it.'

'I know, I know...'

'Classic escalation, though. That's my instinct. The first

one: we don't really know. But then he goes out, gets another victim, simple, planned, wallop. But you see the difference with the pencil?'

Joe nodded. 'He only leaves it the second time.'

'A calling card. But only he knows for certain that it leads back to the first kill.'

'For his own satisfaction?'

'Gotta be. Strengthens the case for the first one being opportunistic.'

'If so, what's the second? A campaign, a *cause*?'

'I dunno, but it's personal. It's not for our benefit. This is all about the killer. Something about that first kill in particular, and the transition to the second. Kill number one *becomes* important. It overpowers him, compels him.'

'A crusade?'

'Drug dealers, social detritus? Could be. Get low-lifes off the street. The victims were known criminals, their names in the papers. If the second one's been selected, it was an easy pick.'

'Who are we looking for?'

'Best guess, the first kill's a trigger. We've got no idea how, or why. Nothing. But it sets off a rage in the killer's mind, something that's been sublimated. It's made him want to do it again, given him a *raison d'être*. The second kill is very clean and calculated, but it's also odd, unhinged. And it feels a bit too quick. Too soon. Then, of course, there's the ages.'

'Ages?'

She looked at Joe as if he was dim.

'First victim, twenty-five. Second, nineteen. Barely a man. I might be wrong, but the second victim was chosen. And he was six years younger. If there's a plan to get low-lifes off the street, age might be another criterion.'

'Age?'

'Get 'em while they're young. Or younger.'

'Shit.'

'Shit indeed. You want me to put a few quid on it?'

'The next one? You mean…'

'Oh, there'll be a next one. And soon.'

'Younger still?'

'Fifty quid says yes. Let me know. I need the money.'

She handed him the files.

'So, Mr Romano, apart from the murders, how're you doing? Anything of significance going on with you?'

'Not really. Why do you ask?'

'Let me see. There's a slight swagger in the way you walk. It's very subtle, but it's oh-so-new. You're tense, out of sorts, but you're carrying it well. A bit too well for the old Joe. Plus, *vis-à-vis* the lady in the pub, there's Occam.'

'You can apply Occam's Razor to a single photo taken in a pub?'

'A photo with your arms round each other, heads together? And the eyes! Oh, the eyes, Joe!'

'It was nothing! It's… nothing!'

'You sure?'

'I'm on a bloody murder inquiry!'

'Not forever, you're not.'

35

There were several calls on the way back from York. He ignored them, having finally found a radio station playing a string of Bruce Springsteen favourites, which came closer to hitting the spot than anything else so far. Curiosity got the better of him in the end. Up ahead he saw a familiar layby, and an even more familiar building. He pulled over to see who'd been ringing.

The calls were all from the District Communications Officer, who had also left a voicemail and an email. Joe had seen the Comms bloke around HQ. Early thirties, poached from the Merseyside Force for his social media savvy. He'd done a few presentations for CID, which had been pretty interesting, although the *durability of news cycles* and the *predictability of trending peaks* had been of little interest to Joe, with his usual workload of break-ins and low-level missing persons. It was interesting now, though. Pity he'd not bothered to take any notes.

The voicemail was brief, the tone clipped and efficient. A press statement had been released stating that DS Joe Romano was no longer Senior Investigating Officer on the current investigation, but that he would remain on the team until all details of the situation were known.

The message ended with a number of suggestions, which were repeated in the email, in the inevitable bullet-point form:

- do not use Twitter or any other social media
- do not frequent any licenced premises
- do not speak to the press (under ANY circumstances)
- electronic correspondence with unknown parties should only be entered into after clearance from Corporate Communications (District Officer).

Up ahead Kathy's Hot Butties was open for business. Running a hand briefly down his midriff, he decided a bit of bacon might perk him up. As he got out of the car, a lorry swept past, a great whoosh of wind knocking him back against the door. The air was cold and bitter with diesel fumes, and suddenly the world felt heavy with thoughtless cruelty. Heavy enough to drown out the small things, the insignificant deaths, a couple of low-lifes. They meant nothing at all.

Shaw's killer had driven down a road just like this. It was the last sighting of the Toyota. He tried to imagine the sequence of events. Was Shaw already dead at that stage? Either way, it took some guts, driving the car of your recently murdered victim, his body right beside you, still warm, or still dying. What kind of person can handle a situation like that without making some sort of mistake? For one thing, you'd need a pretty good idea of where the CCTV cameras were, and more importantly, where they weren't.

A man in a charcoal suit was standing at the counter of the small, brick-built café waiting to be served. The suit was slightly too small for him, and he wore it badly, as if he should never have been wearing a suit in the first place. Inside, a woman talked over her shoulder as she worked at the hot plate.

'Bacon's coming. You after a butty, love?'

'Please,' Joe said.

There was a copy of the *Yorkshire Post* on the counter. The Graphite Assassin took up the top half of the front page. He felt a strange flicker of disappointment to discover that his picture wasn't on it; the Twitter revelations had come too late for the morning edition. On his phone, though, the *Post*'s website was full of him:

Yorks detective drinks as Graphite Assassin strikes for second time.

He decided to take a quick sounding of the vox populi. Holding his phone up close to his face, he squinted at the small picture of him and Chris smiling into the camera.

'Crikey, it does look like me!'

The man next to him appeared to be only marginally interested.

'The detective in this Assassin business,' Joe explained. 'People have been telling me all morning. I'm a dead-ringer.'

'Coffee, is it?' the woman asked Joe as she handed a large bread roll filled with bacon to the man in the suit.

'Yes, black, please.'

The guy opened up his sandwich and squeezed so much ketchup onto it that the bacon disappeared from view.

'He does it with a pencil!' he said, grinning.

'I think the second one was also bludgeoned with a hammer,' Joe said, pretending to consult his phone to confirm the fact.

'Leave him to it. Let's have a couple more!'

'You reckon?'

He shrugged, holding the sandwich up to his mouth.

'Who gives a shit about scum like that? Good on him!'

There was a TV on the wall at the back of the café. The sound was muted, but Joe could see someone giving the weather forecast.

He looked at his watch. Good timing.

'Would you mind turning that up for a minute, please?'

She glanced at the screen.

'It's gonna rain, love,' she said, as she turned up the sound, then piled three large, grease-dripping rashers into a white tea cake and handed it to him.

The national news had just finished, and the BBC now switched to its regional bulletins. *Look North*'s lead story was the Graphite Assassin. A double image of Shaw and Beverage flashed onto the screen as the case was summarized in half a dozen sentences.

The sound of traffic made it difficult to hear what was being said, but all three of them watched footage of Rita speaking to the press. Then another face: Danny Cullen. He was exactly where Rita had stood, on the steps outside Kirklees HQ. He was wearing a dark blue blazer and an open-neck white shirt. And he was surrounded by supporters, all of them male.

'Right according to plan,' Joe muttered to himself.

He didn't even bother listening to what the leader of the English Patriot League had to say. It didn't matter. They'd got their publicity. And what was the phrase? *The camera loved him.* There was no denying it. Cullen looked the part: respectable, authoritative, intellectual even.

'They've got him, then?' the woman asked, casting a suspicious glance at Joe.

'Got someone, by the looks of things.'

'Should've bloody let him go,' the man in the suit said.

With that he nodded to the woman behind the counter, turned, and made his way back to his Vauxhall Mokka.

They both watched him go.

'You all right, Sergeant?'

'Yeah. How's it going, Kath?'

'Same old. Nice photo, by the way,' she said with the beginnings of a smile that never quite materialized.

About nine months ago, Joe had investigated a fire that had gutted Kathy's Hot Butties. There hadn't been any evidence of arson, and the fact that she'd spent the insurance money on a refit with identical equipment hardly suggested criminal conspiracy on a grand scale.

Since then he'd kept on good terms with her, not least because the bacon was so good. She was about his age, thin and pale-faced, with heavy make-up around her eyes.

'What next, friggin' death squads?' she said, still watching as the bloke got into his car. 'Any kids that've been in a bit of bother, their mums'll be shittin' the'sens.'

He nodded as he handed over a fiver, noting that her face was more pinched than normal, that the thin hint of irony which normally ran through her voice was missing.

'The murders are getting absolute priority.'

'They've got him, have they?'

'Dunno. We'll see.'

He wanted to say more, to convince her that everything was being done to catch the killer. He wanted to convince the mothers of all wayward sons that this would stop, that a death is a death, whatever people took it upon themselves to say as they tapped away at their bloody mobile phones, that no one has the right to kill. He couldn't think of anything more worthwhile, more sacred, than honouring a commitment to that.

As he walked back to his car, she watched him, then reached for her phone and found the picture on Twitter: DS Joe Romano and an unknown woman, both of them smiling, their heads touching, their eyes wide open and happy.

'Lucky bitch.'

He sat in his car and made a start on his butty. He glanced at his phone. A WhatsApp from Chris. His hands were greasy, and the phone fell to the floor. But when he picked it up, his thumb swiped the 'call' button by mistake.

'Shit!'

He looked for the stop button, but it was too late.

'Hello? Joe? Is that you?'

'Sorry,' he said, swallowing a mouthful of bacon as fast as he could. 'Wrong button.'

'Oh. I'm just about to start a class.'

'Right, yes. Sorry. Have you seen the news?'

'The photo on Twitter? I just told everybody at work that it was a joke in bad taste, and that the photo was from months ago.'

'And did they believe it?'

'I don't know. I guess.'

She sounded confused, distracted.

'We need to do that follow-up interview,' he said. 'Are you free after school?'

'I have to call in at the library on my way home. We could meet there?'

'Fine. I'll ring.'

'OK. Goodbye, Joe.'

He put down his grease-streaked phone and tucked into the bacon.

36

There wasn't any point going back to Elland Road, so he drove to Cleckheaton, taking a circuitous route, as many country lanes as he could find, doubling back on himself, noting how few cameras there were, and wondering how far you might get untracked in this part of the world.

It was already mid-afternoon when he parked in the centre of the town, just across the road from the Bull's Head. He'd met Rita there, when was it, Friday? Jesus, it seemed like weeks ago.

He walked up the main street, stopping to look in the window of Pet's Corner, attracted more by the rogue apostrophe than the animals. Further along was a hairdresser's, several charity shops, a florist and two bakeries, including the inevitable Greggs. Not a bad assortment of places. But very few people. He thought about how Leeds city centre would be right now, with its constant hordes of shoppers, food stands, buskers and beggars.

Then he saw it up ahead. Metcalf's Beef & Pork. The famous pie shop. He'd been here before, years ago, on the way to a gig with the Romanos. He couldn't have been more than fourteen. They'd stuffed themselves on pork pies, washed down with cans of 7 Up, then played at a wedding reception in a hotel near the motorway junction. He didn't remember much about the music, but the evening's food had been pretty good.

Apart from the Greggs on the corner, Metcalf's was the only shop doing any business. As he picked up his step, he felt his hand wavering lightly over his stomach once more. Then he stopped. The warm, fatty smell of pork pies was already in his nostrils, but something familiar caught his eye: the word *Lobster*. There it was again, Turner's poster, pasted to a lamp-post:

The Lobster Pot
Modern society: A fresh view

How many things are you not allowed to do or say anymore?

He asked himself, but couldn't think of anything obvious.

We're becoming an endangered species: the Great White Male (GWM)…

He imagined Turner at home, looking out across the majestic valleys of Yorkshire, as he penned his paean to conservative outrage.

…Let's build an alternative view of society, one based on decency, honesty and common sense.

Turner was being questioned now. Had he manufactured the whole thing? The first kill might have been opportunistic, but the second one chimed pretty well with Turner and his half-arsed vigilantes. Or a more sinister version of them. Could Turner have provoked it, or somehow encouraged it? Was it the kind of murder a lawyer might devise, a lawyer motivated by rage? Rage or indignation? Hatred? Loathing?

His mind slipped a gear. Two killers? The thought had been dancing around at the back of his mind all day. He hadn't allowed himself to think about it too much. But now it felt right, and Rita was sure to have considered the possibility as well. Where did that leave Megan's suggestion that there'd be a third kill, and soon?

He looked up the street at the butcher's window, perhaps hoping that the neat rows of pies would give him a clue. The siren call of hog-soaked piecrust was strong, but the knowledge that he was so close to the site of Craig Shaw's murder took the edge off his appetite.

'Great White Male?' he said, turning on his heels. 'Perhaps it's a not-so-great white male I need to talk to.'

The light was just beginning to fade when he got up to the library. He was about to drive into the car park when he saw two youngish men in suits coming out of the building. He pulled up at the side of the road and watched them. The main doors were about twenty yards away, but even at that distance he could tell they were coppers.

They walked as far as the corner of the building, then stopped. Joe got out of the car and leant on the wall, phone pressed to his ear, shielding his face as best he could, pretending to talk. There was a bicycle against the side of the library building. The officers were giving it a pretty good going-over, taking pictures, heads nodding as they spoke. They examined the crossbar in detail, bending down until their noses almost touched it.

Then his attention was taken by a subtle shift in the light reflected off the main doors. The young librarian poked his head out of the entrance. Joe couldn't make out whether there was a scowl on his face or something more troubled. Whichever it was, he dithered in the doorway, not sure what to do, before eventually disappearing back inside.

'Mark Sugden,' he whispered.

He shifted position, edging halfway behind a bush in case the Kirklees men happened to look in his direction. He considered his options. He couldn't very well go and give the librarian a poke now. But Sugden was most definitely a person of interest. He was one of the individuals that Joe had ordered background material on last night. Now Rita's men also had him in their sights. Perhaps whatever they were looking for was in that file, which was now on the back seat of the car with the others, where they'd been all day.

Last night. Something about the library. It had been niggling him. What was it? The librarian? No, something else, something he hadn't worked out, but which he knew was there, waiting for him, staring at him. He looked across at the building. It was where he'd met Chris. She'd been putting up a poster for Job Club. He got out his phone, found the photos of the posters. Last night? Just before his brain stopped working, he'd flicked through the photos. *Job Club... Living with Bereavement... Building with Lego...*

Living with Bereavement. What was it? There was something familiar about the poster, its layout, the unfussiness, so different from most of the others, with their jazzy fonts and excessive use of exclamation marks. It reminded him of her. Of Chris Saunders. He zoomed in, found the contact number, then grabbed his notebook, flicking through it clumsily with one hand until he came to the right page. It was her. The same number. Chris Saunders ran that group too: *Living with Bereavement.*

He leant on the wall, crushed by the sense of someone else's suffering, and by the thought of his own weakness. To life's setbacks his response had always been to wallow in self-pity. Yet here was a woman who gave her time to others, that they might suffer less. She'd lost someone, she must have done. And her response had been to help those who were suffering through their own grief.

'Jesus, you poor woman.'

A frenzy of competing ideas raced through his mind, colliding with one another, refusing to let him form a cogent line of thought. Then the library's doors opened again. Instinctively he pulled back, until he was further out of view. And there she was. He looked at his watch. Shit, he was supposed to ring her. What time did teachers knock off these days?

She emerged, stopped and took a couple of breaths, as if to steady herself. Her eyes were wide open, and there was an angularity to her body, her senses sharpened. She was guarded, on edge.

Joe stood dead still and watched. After a brief pause, she turned to her right and made her way to the corner of the building. As she went, she got out a phone and pressed it to her ear. Her movements were careful, alert. She ignored the two besuited men crouched over a bike. Up the drive she came, towards him, moving fast now, her strides long and deliberate. She'd seen him.

'Joe? Are you skulking in the shadows?'

Her tone was friendly but forced. Her smile was painfully unconvincing, anxious, her eyes just a touch red, he thought.

'No,' he said. 'I'm... working.'

As he spoke, he realized that he was also tense. When they'd met in the pub yesterday, they'd kissed each other spontaneously. Now it felt like one of those ghastly social niceties you'd do anything to avoid.

Meanwhile, the two detectives disappeared into a car a little way beyond the bike and drove off.

'Could you wait just a minute? I need to check something.'

He left her there, unkissed, and walked down the drive, taking photos of the bike as he went, the flash from his phone lighting up the near side of the library building, turning it a sickly, anaemic yellow.

The bike was similar to the one he'd seen on Saturday morning, chained up in exactly the same place. The same bike? He couldn't be sure, but it certainly looked similar, a racer, but slightly sturdier than a speed bike, more of a general-purpose model.

He took a few close-ups, as many angles of the back view as he could.

'Do you mind? That's private property.'

He didn't need to look up. He carried on, took one final shot, then slipped his phone into his jacket pocket.

'You mean this,' he said, pointing to the bike.

He ran his finger very lightly over the crossbar, failing to find any tell-tale signs of where plastic tape might have been stuck.

'Keen cyclist, Mr Sugden?'

'Don't you lot ever leave folk alone?'

'I'm sure my colleagues have already asked you, but last Tuesday evening, were you here when the Lobster Pot group met? Were you the one who locked up after they finished?'

'Am I being questioned again?'

'Well, it is a question. And as you can see I'm waiting for an answer.'

'I was here on Tuesday 'til about nine. We open late on Tuesdays.'

'And you came by bike?'

Sugden shifted on his feet. Joe could imagine the clichés that were now swirling about in the young man's mind: the police state, the repressive forces of power, smash the status quo with a big bowl of hummus.

'Do you really need to ask? *Again?* I thought you'd got CCTV cameras everywhere.'

'Yep. It's impossible to go anywhere without being spotted these days. But, y'know, it's sometimes better just to ask a person where they've been. Call me old-fashioned.'

He waited patiently, relishing the thick shroud of awkwardness that hung between them.

'I told them, and I'll tell you. The bike's not mine.'

Joe waited. He didn't believe it. Or, perhaps, he didn't want to believe it. Sugden fit the bill so perfectly. It was no surprise that Rita's men were sniffing around. The Shaw killing? Perhaps it had been a mistake, a moment of madness when he was buying something, or an argument that got out of hand. Whatever, the key was Craig Shaw.

'You know whose it is, then?'

He shook his head.

'Seen it before?'

Again, no.

'OK, thanks for your time, Mr Sugden.'

37

They dropped down into Cleckheaton town centre. Her eyes were still wide, but they were slightly glazed, not a hint of sympathy in them. It was as if she was a different person.

'You really don't need to interview me again, right?'

'No. I assume you've already spoken to someone else on the case?'

'Yes. They came to school today. Has there been an arrest? There was something on the news about it.'

'Still questioning, last I heard.'

She closed her eyes and exhaled, long and hard.

A pause.

'Do you know why I like Maths?'

'Why?' he asked slowly, keeping his eyes on the road as they drove.

'Because you get an answer. The perfect answer. In life, things don't always resolve themselves neatly. Maths generally does. There's clarity, a sense of getting things exactly right.'

'What's brought this on?'

'Pardon? You think you *know* me?'

'No, I mean...'

'Life doesn't always turn out well, Joe. There isn't always a neat answer.'

They turned right and drove past the old mill building that dominated the town. On the other side of the road was what looked like the remains of a railway line, minus the tracks.

'It's a Greenway,' she said. 'Railway's long gone.'

'It was pure Industrial Revolution around here, wasn't it?' he said, just to make conversation, sensing that she was tense, and that she regretted having accepted a lift from him. 'But the village where you live? It's only a handful of miles away, but could be in the Dales. Never touched by industry. Incredible.'

'Ah, Tong! Scene of the infamous photograph! Front-page stuff!'

'You know the weird thing about social media? If you don't pay any attention, it all seems so distant, like it's got absolutely nothing to do with you. I did get suspended, though.'

'Really?'

'Well, perhaps. I'm officially keeping a low profile while they decide what to do with me. Not allowed in pubs, though.'

'Shame. There's another nice one just up the road in Gomersal. The Wheatsheaf. I go there from time to time.'

'Well, as long as it's somewhere discreet. Rules are always open to interpretation, aren't they?'

'You know what? Would you mind dropping me at Tesco's instead? I need to get a few things. And I don't think this is a good time, is it? Look, we can go down here.'

They turned left, the road taking them beneath the course of the old railway, down along an old underpass, the very spot where Craig Shaw used to park to do business, where it was assumed he'd been murdered.

Joe came to a brief stop at the darkest point, the grey light of the early evening sky visible in odd snatches between the massive iron girders of the structure above them, caked in decades of paint and rust.

'The bereavement group, up at the library?' he asked.

She attempted a smile. But it looked painful, all her teeth on show. There were tears in the corner of her eyes.

'How on earth did you know?' she asked, reaching into her bag and pulling out a ball of screwed up paper. 'Anyway, I've just taken the poster down. I've made a decision.'

'And what was that?'

'I've run that group for five years. But I've decided to pack it in. Nothing really works, Joe. You can't talk your way through it. I realized that last night in the pub.'

'I'm sure it does help. And the other people in the group, I'm sure they are helped by it. By you.'

'I've done all I can. It's too late.'

She wound down the window and tossed it out.

'Apologies for littering. The supermarket's just up here, sharp left. I hope we don't get photographed!'

She laughed, but it didn't sound like a joke.

They parked up near the back. Before them was a large expanse of tarmac, nine or ten long rows marked out for vehicles, about half of them filled. Tesco was doing brisk trade even now, before the rush hour.

'I had a son,' she said, watching him as she spoke. 'He died.'

'I'm so sorry.'

She forced the tiniest of smiles.

'The woman you mentioned yesterday, with the dead son? She'll live with it forever. It doesn't go away.'

'I can imagine.'

'No, you can't. You can't imagine it.'

'I...'

'You don't have to say anything, Joe. It happens. Life. It just happens. Then you get on with it.'

'How the hell do you cope with something like that?'

'In practical terms? I became a teacher. Tried to help people. The other stuff, too. Job club, bereavement group. In the end, though, it doesn't work.'

'You sure about that?'

She paused, considered what he'd said. And it wasn't with fondness.

'Thomas would have been sixteen tomorrow.'

'Jesus, I'm so sorry.'

She paused, looking out through the side window.

'Sixteen. My little man! I wonder what he would have grown up to be?'

Joe counted his breaths, unsure what to say.

'A soldier, I reckon,' she said, turning to look straight ahead, across the rows of parked cars. 'Something outdoors, anyway. We used to take him to a park near his school. There was a little café, a shack really. It served ice cream. He'd play there for hours, whatever the weather. The cold never bothered him. When he fell he never complained. Never cried. Tough little bugger. He loved ice cream.'

As she spoke, she was watching two young lads, a couple of rows down. One was a lot taller than the other, but it was the short, scrawny one that caught Joe's attention.

'Who knows,' she said, 'he might've turned out like that!'

There was a heightened casualness in the way the smaller boy moved, a presumption. His face was angelic yet threatening, the skin around his eyes pulled tight, as if his humanity was a mask, something far older than his years.

They sat and watched as the boys made their way through the rows of cars, taking what appeared to be a deliberately indirect route.

'They're not...' Joe said, intrigued. 'They're not gonna steal one, are they?'

The smaller of the two walked down the side of a black Subaru, dragging something along it as he went.

'He's keying it!'

Then, as he got to the side mirror, his young body swung into the car with a well-practiced jerk. A second later the mirror was hanging from the door, and the boys were walking away.

'Shall I nick him?' He watched as the kids wandered off, not a hint of haste in their movements. 'I mean, why would he even do that?'

''Cos he's no good,' she whispered.

'You know him?'

'Yep. *A wrong 'un*, as they say. It's the evil gene, Joe.'

'That's a bit strong, don't you think? What is he, eleven?'

'Thirteen. Go chase after him. You'll see.'

'Will I?'

'You'll see it immediately. A flicker of badness. It'll make you shudder.'

He watched as the boys disappeared into the supermarket, shoving each other, messing about, the Subaru's broken side mirror already forgotten.

Meanwhile, Chris was looking at Joe. She was smiling, and it was a patronizing smile, as though she pitied his ignorance. There was a tear hanging on one of her eyelids, just waiting to fall.

'It's like the clever ones, y'know? The really bright kids at school?'

'I don't follow.'

'Clever kids get bored, because it's all so easy. They're just waiting for university, for the rest of their lives. They know it's gonna get better. It's the same with the truly nasty ones. They're waiting to be old enough, biding their time until they can launch themselves onto the world. They already know what's waiting for them.'

'Isn't a school's job to steer them away from that kind of future?'

She laughed out loud. The tear began its slow progress down her cheek.

'The ones who are gonna end up in jail, who are going to do really bad things? I can spot 'em a mile off. There's not many, but they're easy to recognize. And they're not all from bad homes.'

'What are you saying, then? It's genetic?'

She shrugged.

'They have an aura. You can feel it. It's unnerving. I mean,' she said, pausing for thought, 'you must know this?'

'I don't. Not the way you put it.' He was still looking at the entrance to the supermarket. 'Have you been following the Graphite Assassin case?'

She nodded.

'Did you read about Jason Beverage?'

'I did,' she said. 'Do you need more proof? Really?'

'The evil gene, eh?'

'OK.' She bit her lip, took a moment to think. 'I'll tell you what. Go after him. Kieron Burnett, that's his name. He's thirteen and he's got a juvenile record as long as your arm. Go on, take him under your wing. Shower him with social workers. Be his surrogate dad. His mentor. Take him bowling, hiking, give him books to read, whatever. But you know what? None of it will make any difference. He won't change.'

'A wrong 'un?'

That shrug again. She wasn't arguing with him. She was simply stating the truth, a truth that seemed to crush her. She was crying now, silent tears as she looked out through the window.

'And that's why you became a teacher?' he asked.

She unbuckled her seat belt.

'I became a teacher for the good kids, the huge majority. The odd rotten one just comes with the territory.'

She opened the door and got a leg out.

'Do you need a lift home?' he asked. 'Anything? Someone to talk to?'

'I'm fine. I might take a walk up the hill to Gomersal, have a quiet drink in that pub. I think I need to be alone tonight.'

'In a day or two, perhaps?'

'Yes, perhaps.'

She leant back into the car and kissed him on the cheek.

'See you, Joe.'

38

He got settled down on his uncomfortable, mid-priced sofa, a dish of microwaved tagliatelle on his lap, and switched on *Look North*. The Graphite Assassin was still the lead story. There'd been a bit of a media scrimmage outside Kirklees HQ sometime in the afternoon when Rita emerged to deliver the news that they were still questioning a man. A sizeable crowd had gathered by then, blocking the steps of the building, several banners of the Patriot League held up for the cameras. She didn't add anything new, but managed to hint that they were near a breakthrough.

The item was about a minute long, and the drunken photo of Joe and Chris was only shown right at the end, the image only on screen for a couple of seconds. He saw himself: the face of an older man, of someone else, eyes tinged with red and held unnaturally open for the camera, the sense of being relaxed yet unsure of himself. Cautious in pleasure. Is that what he was? A man unsure of himself?

He put his pasta to one side and poured a glass of wine as the news moved on. For a moment he considered searching for the photo on the internet, just to see how many websites and blogs now featured his face. He had a web browser on the TV. Once, after a long evening alone with too much wine, he'd used it to search the internet for porn, only to find that when he tried to turn it off again, he couldn't. He'd managed to press the wrong button, and the frozen image of a gurning sex actress was left on screen until he got up and switched the whole TV off. And she was still there when he turned it back on. The longest fake orgasm in history.

He sat there and savoured his wine for a while. Then he let out a long, dog-tired sigh, turned the news off and made a start on all the background reports he'd ordered the previous night.

He began with Mark Sugden, the cocky twat who'd sounded a good deal less cocky today. Sugden had grown up in Todmorden, the epicentre of *Happy Valley*. One arrest for breach of the peace at a fracking demonstration. Jobs in various libraries, interspersed with periods as registered unemployed. Previous and current addresses all in and around Halifax and Brighouse.

'Sticks close to the Valley,' he said, getting up and moving across to the table, where his metre-square plan of the case was laid out.

An hour later he was still there, a half-empty bottle of wine by his side. There were now papers everywhere on the floor in what might once have been some sort of order but was now simply a mess. The enormous sheet of paper on the dining table was heavy with thickly etched lines, names circled again and again, many of them linked to others in irregular triangles and squares, and everything overlaid with bursts of unsteady handwriting that flew out at all angles, like the mind-map of a madman.

Data support had trawled up some interesting stuff on

Dave Bannister, the retired local councillor, who had been investigated twice (and absolved twice) by his local party for corruption, and had stood down from politics halfway through his last term of office. Just a few inches away from Bannister's name on the plan there was now a patch of heavy scrawling around the names of Danny Cullen and his Patriot League associates, so dense that it was difficult to see whether there was any sort of design to it, or if Jackson Pollock had lost his shit with a pencil.

Each time he stopped reading the reports and looked down at the huge sheet of paper, his eyes were drawn to the name of Craig Shaw. He considered giving Jane Shaw a ring, just to see how she was. He wished he had news for her, a lead, a line of enquiry, anything promising he could refer to with honesty, rather than the upbeat bullshit Rita was obliged to churn out for the media. He also wished he had a cigarette.

In fact, Rita was the next best thing to a smoke. He pulled out his phone.

'Hi, it's me. Any news?'

He listened to a brief summary of a wasted day. She was tired, but still she managed to sound in command of the facts. Turner was still being interviewed, but it didn't sound promising.

'What about Mark Sugden?' he asked. 'You checked the CCTV to see if that bike fits? I saw your lot sniffing around there today.'

'He says the bike's not his. They're looking at the footage now.'

'And Turner's bike?'

'Nothing yet. Forensics are still trying to place it at the

scene. Ditto Turner. And by the way, what were you doing up at the library?'

'Digging away. Give me an hour or two. I'll ring again. Something's gonna turn up.'

'Who are you looking at? 'Cos I've got nowt here.'

'Give me an hour.'

He returned to the table, found the word *Bike*, and scored a thick line to a name that so far had been circled and linked to less than most. He'd been putting it off, perhaps hoping that something else would surface from all the information. But it hadn't. Armed with a fresh glass of wine, he moved across to the sofa and opened the final bundle of printed documents: *Christine Saunders.*

It didn't take an hour. But by the time he'd read the report a couple of times the wine was gone and his face was shiny with tears, his lips quivering like a baby's.

He set the papers down and concentrated on his breathing, willing it to slow down, to become smooth and regular. He tried not to think, just gather up the loose ends of his emotions and wait for them to settle.

Then he phoned her.

'Rita, I need to see you.'

'I'm ready for bed. I'm friggin' exhausted. Gwyn's still at HQ if...'

'Tomorrow, then. First thing.'

TUESDAY

39

They met at Broadyards Country Park. It was eight in the morning and it was cold. There was a picnic bench close to some trees, a fair distance from where Shaw's burnt-out Toyota had been found. But they could see the ghostly shadow of the car on the ground, the four scorch marks of the tyres, a patch of darkened earth where the engine had dripped its molten oil.

'OK,' she said, settling down on the bench and zipping up her leather jacket against the wind. 'Turner was released last night. We just didn't have enough to hold him. And he knew it. Him and his bloody lawyer.'

Joe nodded.

'What about the rest?' she asked. 'Are you managing to keep up with it all?'

'Just popped into Elland Road. Saw all the stuff on the system. How many officers you got on it?'

'Loads.'

They looked out across the car park. There were a few vehicles, a handful of dog-walkers, one of whom stopped as he got to the darkened earth, peered down at the ground for a moment, then took a couple of shots on his phone.

'Popular spot,' he said.

'It is now. Makes you think, eh? Two bodies in four days.' She watched Joe, noting the strain in his eyes, the way in which his face seemed to have lost all colour and animation. This is a weird one, Joe.'

Still she watched.

'Yeah,' he said, finally. 'I reckon it is.'

She gave him more time. It wasn't a Romano pause, silence as a means of cajoling the truth from someone. She sensed that now he needed time just to breathe. His whole body seemed to be heavy with a deep, unremitting lethargy.

'Joe, there doesn't need to be another kill. We can stop this now.'

He tried to smile. 'I'm off to the Greyhound in Tong this evening. The pub. You know, the one in the Twitter photo?'

'I know it.'

A pause.

'Tell me,' he said, 'what kind of copper do you think I am?'

She blew out an exasperated sigh.

'No,' he added. 'Put it another way. What kind of copper do you think *I* think *you* are?'

'Jesus!'

'Go on. What do I think about you? Tell me.'

He watched as an uncharacteristic nervousness spread across her kind, round face. A motherly face, he reckoned, though she claimed to hate kids.

'We've been working together for next to no time,' she said, 'but for what it's worth, I reckon you know that I've got your back. I mean, you trust me, right?'

He nodded.

'What have you got in that folder, Rita?'

'Folder?'

'It's a metaphor. It's all on pen drives now. Servers, clouds, whatever.'

'Your point?'

'You know my point. What have you got for me? 'Cos I bet it's the same as I've got for you.'

'You show me yours, I'll...'

'Christine Saunders.'

She relaxed a little.

'You met her in the library on Saturday, Joe. You logged it on the system. Then you met her on Sunday, and you logged that as well, including notes, despite all the shit on social media. Then you met her again yesterday, outside the library in Cleckheaton. You logged that an hour ago, for Christ's sake. Gwyn's pretty sharp, y'know?'

'Gwyn?'

'He's handling things at your end, if you hadn't noticed. He'd been going over the investigation. Doesn't miss much, our Gwyn. Apparently, you ordered a load of background stuff on her when you were pissed. So, he's thinking, either you're a meticulous pervert, or...'

'He's been looking at the file?'

'On Saunders? Yes. We both have. Thought we should, y'know, since you're otherwise involved with her...'

'I'm not, as it happens. But I have been looking into her.'

'Ironically,' she said, 'I do have all this in a folder. Print-outs. I read them all last night, late on, in bed.'

She began a story that Joe didn't need to hear, because he'd read the same story, assembled by data support at Elland Road and copied across to the investigation hub by Gwyn Merchant.

Christine Saunders had been a senior accountant at Asda's head offices in Leeds. At thirty-three she was earning more than a Deputy Chief Constable, she was married to a management consultant at Accenture and they were living in a leafy north Leeds suburb with their young son. Within a matter of months she had none of those things.

'The accident report?' Rita said.

'I almost couldn't.'

'I know. I cried. I just cried when I read it.'

Thomas Saunders, six years old, came out of school and was met by his young Portuguese nanny. The afternoon was fine, if a little cold and windy, but he was in a thick duffle coat that was slightly too large for him.

Holding hands, they walked to the top of the road, turned left and continued as far as a pedestrian crossing. They waited for the green man then began to cross. As they reached the middle of the road a silver Jeep Cherokee appeared. Its speed was later estimated to have been in excess of seventy miles per hour.

It never slowed down. When it hit them it was in the very middle of the road. So were they. Neil Barden, the driver, had seen neither them nor the red lights. He hadn't seen them because, as he raced down the road, he was bending forwards, trying to snort cocaine from a small mound on his jeans, just above the knee.

The impact sent the car careering onto the kerb. It glanced off a bus stop before rebounding back into the road. At which point Barden accelerated, as if the massive physical jolt to his system had been an amazing coke rush. He accelerated. Accelerated. Right into the back of a parked Ocado delivery truck. The impact wrecked the Jeep. But the airbag saved his life.

The young nanny would need three separate operations before they moved her out of intensive care. Yet as she lay there in the road, her hand still held onto the smaller one of Thomas Saunders.

His head bore the discernible tread marks of a car tyre. The back half of his skull had been flattened so absolutely that it appeared to have been hewn from him by the swift, effective blow of a sword.

The Saunders' marriage ended soon after, although Chris kept her ex-husband's surname. She resigned her position as a corporate accountant, a decision which had been 'by mutual consent'. The family home was sold. She attended the trial of the driver, then disappeared. Two years after the accident she enrolled on a teacher training course at Leeds Metropolitan University.

'Did you read about the Barden trial, the sentencing?' Rita asked, pressing her hands into her face.

Joe managed a sneer, the nearest he could get to an ironic smile as he felt the visceral disgust that he sometimes harboured for the whole criminal process, somewhere between loathing and a futile scream for help.

'The report of the defence's closing statement?' she said. 'I read that twice. Couldn't believe it. Five years.'

'Out in two.'

'I know. I bloody read it! I *know*!' A pause. 'Sorry.'

'Did you read the follow-up on him?'

She nodded.

After leaving prison, Neil Barden had returned to his previous profession as a self-employed provider of Class A and B drugs. He'd had several arrests over the years, including one charge. But his lawyers got the charges dropped before it went to court. He now drove a Mercedes C-class and lived in a leafy suburb of Leeds.

'She retrained as a teacher, worked in a couple of schools before taking up her current position in Cleckheaton five years ago. Where Jason Beverage was a student. He got expelled for sexual aggression towards a teacher.'

Joe looked at her.

'It's her son's birthday today.'

'Jesus, I missed that.'

'He'd have been sixteen.'

'Diminished responsibility? Come on, let's bring her in.'

Joe shook his head.

'Any forensics on that bike at the library?'

'Nothing definite, as of yet. Still, we've gotta bring her in, Joe.'

'Can we do this my way?'

40

The last remnants of light were disappearing from the sky as the Land Rover entered the car park fast, gunning straight for the cricket field before lurching to a halt next to Joe's car.

'Is she here?' Rita said as she jumped out.

'Yup. Inside. She just WhatsApp'd me.'

'Jesus Christ, Joe! No one saw her leave work this afternoon. And her car's not at home. We've been going fuckin' ape.'

'I know. You phoned me. A lot. She's *here*.'

Rita shook her head.

'I've had someone outside the school all day. Saw her go in this morning. No one saw her leave, and that bike's still chained to the library drainpipe. She hasn't been home all day, either. We've had her house staked out. What the hell's going on?'

'She's in here. Relax.'

Two unmarked cars arrived and parked close to the entrance. Rita rolled a cigarette as Joe went to speak to the four officers that got out, sending one of them on a quick recce of the pub's perimeter.

'Can I have one of those?' he asked her as he returned to the Land Rover.

She chuckled, in that annoying way that smokers have with almost-non-smokers.

'All that's going on,' he said, accepting the one she'd just rolled and waiting as she rummaged in her jeans for a lighter, 'is that I'm going to have a nice meal with a lady friend. Who you are then going to arrest for two murders.'

'Textbook, eh?'

'Chapter one.'

'Yeah, Don Juan meets the Criminal Evidence Act.' She held out the lighter. 'And you're supposed to have the fag after the sex.'

He drew hard. The smoke hit him at the back of the throat, then somewhere behind the eyes, a nasty, visceral pain, fleeting but intense, like the thinnest of blades passing through his brain. Smoking suddenly felt like the most ridiculous thing one could imagine doing. Which it wasn't, obviously: the most ridiculous thing was having dinner with a murderer.

The other officers were now in a huddle, whispering to each other. Then the fourth of them came back around the other side of the pub.

'No sign of her car, guv.'

'She's not friggin' here!' Rita said.

Joe ignored her.

'She's inside the pub now.'

'Who says? WhatsApp? Jesus Christ!'

He watched Rita as she lit her own roll-up and inhaled so hard that a quarter of it turned to ash.

He took another long draw on his own, shuddering at the taste.

'Gather round, gents.' He dropped the barely smoked

274

cigarette and ground it into the tarmac with his shoe. 'Right. You all have a recent image of her. Get it fixed in your mind. At some point she'll come out. Just stop her, nice and gentle. Rita'll make the arrest.'

'Why not now, guv?' someone asked.

'We already have enough to bring her in. But I want her to admit it, the whole narrative, stuff we can use, details she'll find it difficult to retract later. We're taking down a double murderer. Forget who the victims were. They were killed in cold blood. Let's just get as much as we can from her now. You all have my number? Good.'

With that he was gone, marching up to the pub as if it were his first date, like a teenager out to impress, nervous, the confidence half fake and half bare optimism. Pure Joe Romano.

'Right,' Rita said, 'there's a door out the back. We need one of you there. And there's another door from the kitchen a bit further round. Another body there. Two of you stay close to the front entrance with me. We OK?'

They were OK. They would've perched on the steeple of the parish church if it meant they could tell their kids that they'd taken down a multiple killer.

41

Inside the pub nothing had changed. Rugby League highlights on the muted TV up in the corner, Toby jugs still smiling, beer pumps standing to attention along the bar, waiting to go into battle in the cause of all that was good and wholesome in England.

He ordered a pint of Tetley's. He knew she was here. But he didn't look for her. He waited for the beer to arrive, then stood and admired it. A drink, tonight? Not a chance. This pint, which he could see was utter perfection, would remain untouched. Apart from, well, just an inch or two. To remind himself what he was missing.

Even as he brought it to his lips, she was there beside him, a glass of white wine in her hand. A large glass, and not much left in it.

'Evenin' officer,' she said, then tipped her head back and took a drink.

Her face was pale, almost grey, her eyes sunken and puffy. She was buoyant, a spikiness of anticipation in her movements, but it was forced, awkward. They stood there in the silence for a moment or two. She moved from foot to foot, looking around the pub, which wasn't busy.

'Well,' she said in the end, 'not often I get invited out via a text message at seven in the morning!'

He took a tiny sip of his beer. It was a couple of shades warmer than cool. The head was creamy, and it had that strangely minty aftertaste of Tetley's.

'I think we can call this a working dinner. I am working, you know.'

'I'm fully aware of the situation, officer,' she said, as if his seriousness was endearing. 'Why don't we grab a table, get down to work?'

They made their way into the dining area and chose a quiet spot in the corner. They went through the motions of getting seated.

'Right,' he said, as they squinted at the menu board on the wall.

'Right.'

They waited.

'Right,' he said again. 'I get the impression that you know what I'm going to say.'

'Best just say it then, no?'

He glanced around. Several tables were occupied, but nobody close enough to hear.

'Did you think the pencil was enough?'

'Enough?'

'To blame everything on those nutters in the Patriot League, or someone from the library?'

She looked puzzled, turning the wine glass in her hands.

'I didn't think that at all. It never occurred to me.'

'What did you think?'

'That it was the right thing to do.'

'Right? The pencil?'

'Everything.'

'Care to explain?'

She drank the last of her wine, then set the glass on the table, frowning slightly.

'I was coming down from the library. I sometimes walk into town, take the bus home. Don't always drive. I noticed the car, saw him sitting there in the dark. He wound the window down, and I asked if anything was wrong. He told me to go fuck myself.'

'OK...'

'I knew what kind of person he was. It's like I said yesterday. You can pick 'em out when they're ten years old.'

'And that's why you did it? Because you could see what kind of person he was?'

'Something changed. It only took a second. I didn't know where I was. Still don't, really. It was that quick. A pencil was the only thing I had.'

A young waiter came over. He might have been seventeen, mousy-blond hair in a fashionable mess, his face soft and gentle.

'Are you...?'

'Ready, yes,' Joe said. 'I think so. Shall we order?'

'I'll have the steak and ale pie. With chips,' she said, smiling up at the young man.

Joe ordered the gnocchi.

'Any starters?' the soft-skinned angel asked.

'Some onion rings? For the table?' she said. 'And another large white wine for me, please.'

The waiter nodded, raising his eyebrows as he left.

'A *Sopranos* fan?' she said, watching him as he disappeared into the kitchen. 'Endearing in one so young.'

'No pencil for him, then?'

She paused, took her napkin, refolded it. Her eyes were wide open, imploring. But they were unsteady, edged with a calm desperation.

'You told me that the bereavement group didn't do you any good,' Joe said. 'Was this the alternative?'

She reached out and squeezed his hand. He left it there for a second, then pulled it away.

'I never chose to do this, Joe. None of it. Do you blame me? Really?'

He kept his mouth shut. The digital recorder in his pocket was running. Just let her talk.

'Under the railway bridge? I stood there and I thought, this isn't me, is it? Or is it? After all the time, year after year, suddenly everything was clear. There I was, in the present. This can't be right, I told myself, but it was.'

'No. Not murder.'

Her face lit up. She threw herself back in her seat, giddy, as though he'd suddenly hit on the truth.

'You see? It's exactly that! This can't be right, can it? But it is. It *was*. It just happened. Like a lot of things. A lot of things just happen. Horrible things. They happen to people who do not deserve to die.'

'Jason Beverage didn't just happen. You meant that to happen. Can I ask you something? Have you been hearing voices? Voices that were telling you to do this?'

'Yes. No! I mean, no, no.'

She looked around, flapping her hands a little, trying to find the words to express herself.

'Society? What is it, in the end? It's just a ledger of good things and bad things. A simple account. I'd never realized it before, never been able to understand. That's what Craig Shaw gave me.'

'*Gave* you?'

'Down there, under the old railway. Something happened to me. I was taken somewhere, because of him. He showed me, he drove me there. And I'm still there. I see things differently now.'

'What do you see?'

'That I did something good, Joe. I adjusted the ledger. They robbed, raped, sold drugs to the poor and the hopeless. The world's a better place without them. Do the maths. Getting rid of just one of them means, I dunno, fifty, a hundred, two hundred crimes will not be committed.'

'And you know that for a fact?'

'Joe, you know I'm right!'

'Do I?'

'We let people die all the time. Bullshit wars whenever the price of oil demands it. Tobacco. Processed sugar. Air pollution. Pandemics. Death is a measure of how we live. It's part of the equation. It's maths. That's why I was chosen, don't you see? Because I understand the significance of it.'

'Not murder. We draw the line at...'

'Sending young men and women to Iraq and Afghanistan is murder.'

'I'm with you on...'

'Stop trying to be the liberal male, you chump!' she said, laughing, but on the verge of tears.

He relaxed, just a little, and tried his best to look crestfallen. He had her now, although he wasn't sure how long she was going to last in this state.

Arrest her now? No. One last push. Get some details.

'What kind of solution is yours? Killing Jason Beverage? How did that come about?'

She clasped her empty wine glass with both hands, until it seemed that it might shatter.

'You know what's trending on Twitter? *One-sixty-six*.'

He nodded.

'When all the police stuff is over with, have I not saved the world from a modicum of future pain?'

'Beverage was younger than my son. Little more than a kid.'

'Rapist-cum-thief and drug dealer. He even managed to do all three together: drug 'em, rape 'em, rob 'em! What are the chances he would have reformed, become a model citizen? It's maths, see?'

'Tell me what happened with Jason.'

'The whole thing was out of my control. It was as if I was watching. And I felt nothing. Ruthless, that's the word: without sorrow, without compassion. I felt no sorrow for his death. Or the other one. Craig.'

'I understand what you must have been through.'

'No, no. Really you don't. It's the *rightness* of feeling no compassion that's the strange thing. You can't possibly know. It's weird. It can't be right. But it is. It *is* right.'

'Chris, we know what happened to you.'

She shook her head, harder and harder, until she looked like a young girl desperate to convince you of her innocence.

'You're a good man. I could see that the moment we met. But a good man can't understand this.'

He wondered how long he should wait before mentioning it. A double murderer, but he felt deeply ashamed for the pain he was about to cause her. Meanwhile, she looked around the dining room, watching as another couple wandered in and got settled at a table.

'I read the report on your son's death.'

She sat forward, rested her chin on her hands.

'Did it make you cry?'

He nodded. He felt like crying now, for her, for everything.

But she wasn't crying. Her eyes were wide open, unwavering, unhinged. He could see that now. Mad and desperate, yet defiant.

He decided to wait, let her speak. Pity? He no longer knew what he felt.

She swallowed hard.

'You thought I'd crumble when you mentioned Thomas, right?'

Before he could answer, the onion rings arrived, along with her wine.

'I'm in a new place, Joe!' she whispered as the dish was placed between them in the middle of the table. 'Beyond your justice.'

The waiter turned and left without a word.

'So,' she said, 'are we doing the whole act? I mean, I quite fancy that steak and ale pie.'

'Whatever you want. I'm not hungry.'

The beginnings of a smile tugged at the edges of her mouth as she considered the onion rings, eyeing them up from various angles. A deranged mind? *Diminished responsibility*? This couldn't go on.

'Did you see *The Sopranos*?' she asked as she stared at the dish between them. 'The last episode, how it just stopped? It's the same here. This is gonna stop. It's over.'

'Just like that?'

'I'll stop. Never do anything again. I promise.'

He took a long breath, watching her as she sat back and drank some wine. Promise? He had no idea what she meant.

'That's not how this ends. You must know that.'

'You, your partner outside in the car park, and whoever else there is waiting for me? You should all know.'

He tried to stay absolutely still, maintained eye contact.

She took an onion ring as though it was a trinket that had caught her attention.

'I'm going to walk out of this pub and get on my bike, as if the whole evening had gone completely according to plan.'

'How could you even begin to think I'd let that happen? Anyway, your bike's still up at the library. Why don't we...'

'I've done something, Joe.'

'I think we need to...'

'Something else. Something terrible.'

She took her glass and drank the whole of it down in one draught. He watched her neck flex as she strained with the effort of it. Then she set the glass down and wiped the back of a hand across her mouth. She was shaking visibly, and her words came out unsteadily.

'Kieron Burnett. I didn't know what... what else...'

'Who?'

'Kieron. Yesterday in Tesco's car park? The kid who damaged that car?'

He felt his body go rigid.

'You don't need to do this, Chris.'

Her hands shook even more. The onion ring dropped from her fingers, glanced off the edge of the table and fell to the floor.

What little colour there had been in her cheeks was gone. She looked scared, but still quick-witted, like an animal. Her chest rose and fell as her breathing became faster.

'Kieron Burnett?' he said. 'You don't have to play games. Chris? Chris? Where is he?'

'*Who*, Joe. That's the issue.'

'Where? Please, tell me what you've done.'

'I took him after school today. He's at a secure location. I wish I hadn't...'

'Took him? Is he conscious?'

'Now? Perhaps.'

'Tell me where.'

'I can't. This is how it's going to be. I didn't want to do it.' Her lips were glistening, and her eyes were streaming with tears. 'It was all I could... Oh God!'

He grabbed his phone.

'I'm going to throw up,' she said, pulling herself unsteadily to her feet. 'Don't make me do it here, Joe, please. I need to...'

He sprang up, panicking, fingers prodding the screen of his phone.

'OK.'

With the phone pressed to his ear he grabbed her by the arm and dragged her to a passageway that ran down the side of the pub. With every diner in the place watching them, he pushed her towards the toilets and positioned himself on the corner, just a few strides away.

'Rita? Rita! Kieron Burnett. He's a kid from her school. Thirteen years old. She's got him locked up somewhere. Repeat: Kieron Burnett. Kieron Burnett.'

42

I've got no choice now.

A woman about my age has just gone to the ladies'. She's in a bright-red jacket and cream trousers. Her hair is dark, a bit like mine. The trousers? Mine are black. I've got no choice.

As I follow her in, Joe's standing at the beginning of the passageway, a couple of paces behind me, shouting into his phone, telling them about Kieron.

The woman is going into one of the cubicles when I get there. I slam my foot into the door before she locks it. The door batters into her. She topples forward, hugging the toilet basin as she falls. There's a little gasp, shock more than anything. I stand over her, punch her in the temple. Twice. Three times. Not very hard. It doesn't need to be.

I drag the jacket from her as she whimpers. She's already peeing herself, arms above her head in self-defence, but her body's loose, and she's only semi-conscious. I ditch my jacket, swap it for hers. Her glasses are on the floor. I grab them, put them on. I look in her handbag. I take a phone in a white wallet, a cigarette from an open packet and a lighter. I get my car keys ready.

I pause at the door for one deep breath. Red jacket and

glasses; white phone up to my face; cigarette between my lips, lighter and keys in the other hand, the lighter also held up to my face. It's the best I can do. Plus, the car's right outside.

As I emerge into the passageway I'm nodding into the phone, flicking the lighter, my back to Joe. Just past the toilets, at the end of the passageway, there's a fire door that leads outside to a gazebo for smokers. The push bar on the door is a bit stiff, but it opens OK. I tried it earlier.

Outside there's a copper in the car park, about fifteen feet away, just beyond the gazebo. He looks at me. I stop, nod, light up and start talking into the phone, nice and loud, animated. He watches me for a second. I take one hard draw on the cigarette and exhale, blowing smoke between us.

He's not sure. He starts to move in my direction. I walk around the other side of the gazebo. He's looking at his phone as he comes towards me, getting faster. I have the key ready. The car's right there. It's not locked.

He's running now.

'Excuse me…'

I pull open the car door.

'Hey…'

Key in.

'Hey…'

The motor screams into action.

He's got his arms in the air. He's shouting.

I'm away.

43

Joe was listening to his phone as Rita barked orders at one of her officers, who was already relaying the info about Kieron Burnett to HQ.

A woman in a red jacket came out of the toilets. He was thinking: Kieron Burnett? The little kid from yesterday? Is she bluffing? The woman in red was speaking into a mobile. Glasses. Cigarette.

'Joe?' he heard on his phone.

The woman went out through the fire door to smoke.

'Joe?'

Something wasn't right.

'Joe, are you still...'

'It's her,' he said.

'She's coming. Stop! Stop her!'

The revving of a car engine rang out from behind the building. He spun around, ran towards the front entrance. As he pushed the doors open, Rita's Land Rover was already jerking into reverse, arcing across the car park to block the exit.

At the same moment a black Renault Clio appeared from behind the pub, going at a staggering speed, whining in second gear as it flew across the tarmac. The gap between the Land

Rover and the hawthorn hedge that bordered the exit had narrowed almost to nothing.

The Renault drove straight at the Land Rover, which was now at an acute angle, blocking the way out. At the last moment the Clio swerved to its right, ploughing into the hedge but also smashing into the side of the Landy, shunting it several feet to the side, the shriek of metal on metal drowning out even the noise of the engine.

The angle of impact, plus the car's momentum, was enough for it to push its way through. Coming to a brief halt, the Clio's engine whined yet louder as it was thrown into first gear. Within seconds it was gone, careering down the dimly lit road and out of the village.

'Now!' Joe was bawling as he looked around for officers in vehicles, pointing at the exit. 'Now!'

He was grappling with his phone as he shouted, watching the little black car disappear into the night, and knowing that it was heading into a patchwork of rural hamlets criss-crossed with tiny, winding lanes.

Phone it in. Get a helicopter. Killer on the loose. Half the Force'd be out. What a bloody disaster.

Again he looked around. There was a car gunning for the exit, swerving around the Landy, clattering into the bushes as it went. Another one was right behind it, nearly losing its back end as it was thrown out onto the road.

And Rita?

Both the officers stationed behind the building came running. Joe raised an arm, pointing at them.

'The registration. Did you get the...'

They were shouting it out as they ran.

288

'Radio it in as you go.' He pointed to the Land Rover as he ran towards it. 'Get in!'

Both unmarked cars had now disappeared into the rural darkness, the sound of their motors receding to nothing in a matter of seconds.

'Rita? Rita?'

Nothing was moving inside. She was there, head down on the steering wheel.

He yanked the door open and clambered in, trying to see the extent of her injuries.

'Rita? Are you...'

'Get after her, dickhead!' came a croaky voice from the driver's seat. 'It's just a bump.'

He saw her eyes close. One of the other officers was phoning for an ambulance. Joe called in the incident.

'This is DS Joe Romano,' he said, loud and clear. 'Urgent back-up requested...'

Yet even as he spoke, he knew that none of this would be worth it. Her route would have been planned in advance. Twenty, perhaps thirty seconds' advantage in these parts was enough, especially at night. She'd be snaking her way down a network of tiny lanes by now, headlights off, in her dark, anonymous hire-car or whatever it was; the same car she'd used to come out of the school, the reason that no one had seen her leave this afternoon.

Would another car be waiting somewhere close? Just for a second he imagined himself back at Elland Road, poring over her credit card bills, identifying the entries for car rentals: strategically placed vehicles that she'd used to dupe that sucker Joe Romano.

This would be the story: a multiple killer and kidnapper had escaped from a six-man security cordon outside a pub. A pub in which she was being wined and dined for the second time by...

No. Not that. Not now.

'Rita?'

'I'm fine,' she growled. 'Get her.'

44

The car park at the Greyhound was rapidly filling up. There were two ambulances, an array of patrol cars, plus several unmarked cars, with more arriving constantly. The Land Rover was being photographed, and both Rita and the woman from the toilets were in the ambulances.

It was only a matter of minutes since Chris Saunders had sped away, but the West Yorkshire Police helicopter was already making noisy circuits overhead, its silvery beam criss-crossing the night sky. Kieron Burnett had been confirmed as missing. Half a mile down the road, Chris's house was being taken apart, and a few miles further off, in Cleckheaton, Whitcliffe Mount School was overrun with police search teams.

Meanwhile, the car park was alive to the constant chatter of radios, as officers arrived from Leeds and from various points in Kirklees. There was also a healthy presence of bystanders, many of them holding up their phones as they videoed events. A couple of uniformed officers were having trouble keeping the public back, especially those whose cars were now trapped in the car park. It was chaos, and it would already be on Twitter and dozens of live-streaming sites.

Joe watched as a small, red Audi arrived, came to a momentary stop, then drove slowly in his direction. Gwyn Merchant flashed his headlights as he pulled up next to Joe.

'How's Rita?' he said as Joe got into the passenger seat, glad to be out of the circus.

'She's OK. Mild concussion.'

'What about the kid? How's that going?'

'Kirklees are dealing with—'

'Fuck Kirklees. We'll find him.' He grabbed a small laptop from the back seat and fired it up. 'What do we know about this woman, Joe? Social media? Where's her presence?'

Joe paused. But only for a second.

'Facebook.'

'Right. We're looking for somewhere to hide a kid. Christine Saunders. Tell me about her,' Gwyn said as he searched for her Facebook account.

'She's ordered. In control. Neat dresser, stylish but not fancy.'

'Right. Character? Habits?'

'Runs courses on finance at the local library. One on bereavement too. Believes in helping folk, or she used to.'

'OK,' he said as his fingers moved with practiced speed across the keyboard. 'Right! I've got her. Carry on.'

'She's a Maths teacher, background in accountancy. I dunno...'

'She's about your age, right? Is she fit?'

'What?'

'Is she fit? Seriously? I mean, fit, ripped, skinny? What's your relationship with her?'

'No, nothing like that. But she is fit. She goes on long walks in the country... Oh, Jesus! Look back through her Facebook posts. It's an app.'

292

Gwyn's face was about an inch away from the screen.

'What app? Speak to me, Joe.'

'Maps. She posts the routes. Likes long walks.'

'Maps, maps...'

'Y'know, maps of where you've been.'

A massive breath from Gwyn.

'Oh, I know!'

He scrolled down the page. Ten seconds. Twenty.

'These aren't walks, mate. Too long. They're cycling stats.' His phone was already in his hand. 'She sees somewhere when she's out on her bike in the countryside, somewhere to lock up the kid. It's gotta be this, Joe. Gotta be.'

He phoned Elland Road, read out the Facebook details, telling them to go look at all the routes she'd taken.

'Remote spots, abandoned buildings, places to hide some-one...' he told them, his voice fast but clear, no emotion. 'Get everybody on it. Soon as, eh?'

Gwyn ended the call and sat back. He looked out onto the busy car park.

'Shit round here, innit? Pokey back lanes and fields and what-not? Where d'you get a friggin' pint of milk? There's nowt here.' He glanced at the cricket field with mild disgust. 'It's how she got Shaw's Toyota to her house without it showing up on any CCTV. I didn't see a single camera coming up here from the Ring Road. As for escaping from you lot, I already called you a twat, right?'

There was something boyish about the way he said it, as if it was the kindest thing he could think of in the circumstances.

'I was trying to get a confession on tape, all the details, the lot, pretty much wrap it up before the arrest.'

'Whereas in fact you got the shaft. Six of you. Six! Jesus Christ!'

Joe found himself cradling his face in his hands. There'd be senior officers here soon enough. And they'd have Comms officers in tow, one from each district, making sure he was kept well away from the cameras. Not that it mattered. The whole thing would already be on the internet, live action of police incompetence, late-night TV bulletins. The media escalation would be horrendous, and if they didn't get her quickly, or if the little lad...

He squeezed his eyes shut, finding a small space within himself, enough to force the screams from his mind.

They remained there for a while in silence. Then he felt a slight pressure on his shoulder.

'Joe? We get the kid, then we get her, right? You'll have yourself a double murder. OK, bud?'

He gave Joe's shoulder a shove.

'One-sixty-six, eh?' Joe said, blinking himself awake. 'Isn't that your motto?'

'Aye, well I'm a fuckin' gobshite, if you hadn't noticed. A murder's a murder, my friend.'

Merchant's phone rang.

'This better be good news.'

He listened, nodding, already firing up the motor.

'Right,' he said, swivelling in his seat as he backed the Audi up. 'Two possibles. There's what looks like an abandoned farm building in a place called Gomersal, about three miles from here. Then there's an old air raid shelter near Cleckheaton, same deal. Both secluded, and she's ridden past 'em both loads of times.' He revved the car. 'Come on, Joe. Which one is it?

Think. You've got ten seconds. Choose. Them tossers from Kirklees get the other one.'

'She mentioned Gomersal village yesterday. Said she was going to walk there. A pub.'

Merchant got on his phone, made sure that the other possible location was communicated to the Kirklees team. He drove slowly as far the ambulances, then came to a stop. Wound down his window.

'Rita! Rita?'

A subdued DS Scannon poked her head out.

'What?'

'We're off! Come on!'

She paused for a split second, then hobbled down from the back of the ambulance and joined them.

The Audi topped out at ninety, lighting up the hedgerows of Tong village as they sped towards Gomersal.

'Google Maps!' Merchant screamed as he drove, the light from his mobile phone turning his face blue. 'Fuckin' love it!'

45

They were on a road in Gomersal, houses to one side, to the other a large village green that sloped off into the darkness.

'Made a few arrests in there,' Rita said, peering out of the window. 'You want Class B, you've come to the right...'

'It's not far,' said Gwyn, still holding his phone up as he drove.

They got to a junction of three narrow roads. There were old houses, and some new ones, stone-built in a similar, old-world style. A nice spot.

No time. They spun to the left, took a lane that ran down past a pub. It was almost as picturesque as the one in Tong.

'That's the place she mentioned,' Joe said.

'It's around here,' said Gwyn, still staring at his phone.

The car slowed as they all looked into the darkness ahead.

Gwyn pulled up on a verge and they piled out. There were fields running from the road all the way down to the valley bottom. In the far distance was the faint glow of street lighting, but in between it was pitch black.

'Where the friggin' hell is it?' Gwyn said, phone in one hand, a torch now in the other.

'I can't see a bloody thing, never mind a building,' Rita said as they climbed the low stone wall, scrambling over the single line of barbed wire, hardly noticing it was there.

Joe looked back the way they'd come. The lights of the Wheatsheaf glowed, warm and welcoming.

'It was on her mind yesterday. She mentioned the pub. It's gotta be here.'

He took out his phone. There was a torch on it. He'd never used it before. The grass in front of him lit up, a nasty blue-grey colour.

'Good thinking, Batman,' Rita said, as she did the same. 'Come on, it can't be far. She must have seen it from the road.'

The three of them spread out and walked down the slope, the expanse of black now animated by dancing pools of hard metallic light. In the sky behind them the sound of a helicopter could be heard in waves that came and went on the wind.

'There!' Joe said.

He was already running, phone held out in front of him. In the corner of the field was a small, rectangular building, no bigger than a garage, and a little lower.

They sprinted towards to it, shouting Kieron's name. The sound filled the valley, massive blasts of human urgency echoing in the darkness.

Joe got there first. It was an old building, no windows on the side that faced him, but neatly maintained. The door was old, but the Yale lock, though tarnished, was clearly not as old. He yanked at the handle, screaming Kieron's name. The door was locked.

'Kieron!' Rita cried as she and Gwyn arrived. 'We're here! Police!'

They pulled at the door, all three of them now bawling as loud as they could, but it hardly moved at all.

'Stand back,' Gwyn said.

He took a short run and rammed into it with his shoulder. The door and frame seemed to move. But not enough.

'Take it in turns,' he said, as he gave it another go.

Joe followed, crashing into it so hard that the pain of the impact shot across his back and down his spine. Then Rita began slamming her foot into the middle of the door. It shifted a little more with each kick, dust and bits of darkened, hundred-year-old mortar dropping to the ground.

'The whole frame,' Joe said. 'Pull the whole frame out.'

He dug his fingers into the old mortar around the bricks, scraping at it with his nails, breathing in the dust until he almost choked, as if he was inhaling clouds of pepper. Finally he managed to get his hand around a whole brick. He worked it loose and pulled it out.

Still shouting Kieron's name, Rita and Gwyn were now dislodging more bricks, the three of them crowding around the door, shoulder to shoulder, their faces covered in dark-grey mortar dust as they all tried desperately to get a hand around the frame.

'Come on,' Gwyn shouted, 'we're nearly there. We're getting it.'

Then there was a noise. They stopped, stood back, as the door opened slowly from the inside.

Two boys were there, each one with an ice-cream cone in his hand.

Rita exploded, grabbing the smaller one, hugging him, repeating his name. He let her hug him. But he was passive, his body loose, like a stuffed toy for which she'd suddenly discovered a deep and inexpressible love. Meanwhile, the taller of the two looked on with mild contempt.

'It's over, Kieron,' she continued, oblivious to everything. 'It's sorted. Your mum's on her way. You hear me? You're safe.'

It took about twenty seconds, Joe reckoned. But he couldn't be sure, because he was busy trying to work out what the bloody hell was going on.

Rita finally loosened her grip on Kieron and looked around. 'What?' she asked Joe and Gwyn as she pulled herself together. Then, turning back to the two boys: 'Who gave you them friggin' Cornettos?'

'I thought you didn't like kids?' Joe said as they watched Kieron and his friend being escorted to a patrol car.

They were back on the road, which was now closed off and was bustling with police officers. Her face was slightly puffed up.

'Kieron? Known him since 'e were seven. Every copper round here does. A right little bugger.'

'I know the type,' Joe said. 'You can see it in their eyes.'

'The pizza? Ice creams? Jesus Christ!'

Inside the building where the boys had been found there were two empty pizza boxes, a cooler bag full of ice creams, plus a couple of Gameboys. All of this, they explained, had been left for them by that nice Maths teacher. She'd told them to stay out of the police's way for few hours; something to do with damage to a Subaru yesterday, about how she could fix it with the police if Kieron and his mate laid low for a while.

'And they believed her?' Joe said.

'Seems like it. Whatever she said, she got 'em here, and she took us for mugs.'

Joe's WhatsApp pinged. He studied the screen, took his time, ignoring everything around him.

'She just sent me the location,' he said, holding up his phone so Rita could see it.

Rita snorted. 'Think that'll make a difference, after what she's done? She's going down for kidnapping, an'all.'

Gwyn Merchant bounded up to them.

'Are you coming? There's a friggin' man-hunt going on! I'm off now if you want a lift.'

'We better go,' Joe said.

She smiled at him, didn't move.

'We'll give you a lift back to Tong. You can get your car. But you're being stood down, Joe.'

He closed his eyes.

'OK. But why did they get you to tell me?'

She waited until he'd opened them again.

''Cos it was my decision. Go home, Joe.'

WEDNESDAY

46

He drove past the school gates, going as slow as he dared without drawing attention to himself. It was just gone nine. A few parents were hanging around, chatting, looking tired but relieved. Six hours without bloody SpongeBob. Six hours to be an adult.

She wasn't there.

At the top of the road he turned left, found the pedestrian crossing where Thomas Saunders had died. No sign of his mother.

He'd spent the night driving around, up through Cleckheaton, past the library, then across to north Leeds, trawling the area where she'd lived when she was married. Gwyn was keeping him up to date on the search. The black Renault had been found abandoned a few miles from Tong. Her own car was still missing, but it hadn't been tracked over the course of the night. So they had no idea how she was travelling. If she was travelling.

As dawn stretched into morning, his tiredness had gradually been replaced by something more penetrating; a sense of escalating dread, a nausea at the thought of himself, his own existence. Of how things had come to this.

He turned and came back, parking just short of the school

building then walking as far as the gates. They'd know by now. It was on every news bulletin. A former parent. Tragic accident ten years ago. *That* parent. There'd be a police team here soon enough, just to check that she hadn't been back, to see if she still had any contacts in the area. No stone left unturned. Press too. They'd be here in no time.

Better not show up at the school. Not now. His face would be on the news too. It was a toss-up as to who was a bigger hate figure: a two-time murderer or the dickhead copper who let her get away. Ex-copper? Perhaps. Even Andy had rung to tell him to stay out of sight.

He gave her another call. He'd been calling her all night. It always went straight to voicemail. Meanwhile, an unmarked car pulled up. A young man and woman got out and made their way purposefully into the school building. They were coppers. Had to be.

He drove back up towards the site of the accident, going over the report in his head. The nanny had collected him from school. They'd walked up the road, turned left. Halfway down they crossed the road... She'd picked up the child from school, and they were going home... They crossed halfway down.

He pulled into the kerb and googled the old family address. He zoomed out, located the school and ran a finger along the route they'd taken. He double-checked. Zoomed in and out again. This wasn't the way home, not exactly. They should have carried on at the junction, not gone left. It was one street out of their way. And it was a long street. On a blustery day? Why make the trip longer? He looked harder. And there it was: a patch of green on the map. Thomas and his nanny had been going to the park.

He came to a stop on the outer perimeter. There was a cold wind, just as there had been ten years ago. But Thomas had loved the ice cream here, whatever the weather. That's what she'd said. Tough little bugger.

From his car he could see the old café, just a wooden shack really, but a nicely maintained one, with large doors that opened outwards, a handful of small tables and a serving counter within. And there she was. The colour was unmistakable. She was still in the red jacket.

He got out and began to walk towards her, past a duck pond, its edges strewn with bird shit, massive splodges of the stuff. Was it goose shit that stank bad? Or chicken? He couldn't remember. After the kind of night he'd had, he couldn't even be bothered to avoid stepping in the stuff. Or perhaps it was deliberate. Another metaphor? He wasn't thinking straight. He was walking in shit.

She was at a table against the wall at the back. There wasn't much light. But it was her, in the jacket she'd stolen. The dark hair, the outline of her face, taut and angular, not a scrap of fat on her.

A thought. He retraced his steps, sat on a bench so that he was partially concealed behind a large holly bush, and phoned her. Why would she answer now?

'Turn the bloody thing on!'

He let it click to voicemail.

Then he waited, watching a fragmented version of her through the spiky leaves as she sat there, hardly moving. Didn't look like she was in a rush.

After a while he phoned for local back-up. A patrol car arrived within minutes. He flagged it down a little way along the road, told them to stay close but out of sight of the café.

Then it was time.

'Chris?'

She looked up.

Nothing.

'You knew I'd find you here, didn't you?'

'You're the detective!'

Was it defiance? Not really. She sounded like a child. He wanted to hold her. It was ridiculous, he knew.

'This way's best.'

Still she said nothing. Her shoulders dropped fractionally, but otherwise she was motionless.

He took a seat.

'Suspect was waiting in a place known to the investigating officer.'

She smiled. 'Gets me a brownie point, does it?'

'It's best like this.'

'And it'll make a difference?'

He read a couple of the handwritten signs on the wall. Brunch rolls and carrot cake, plus a few breakfast items. This was the kind of area where people could afford to have breakfast out. It reminded him of Lyon. Breakfast out? What kind of home do you have, that you want to eat breakfast somewhere else?

Then again, what kind of home did he have?

No time for that, not now.

A woman came over.

'I'm good,' he said with all the curtness of someone who's had a sleepless night and lost a double murderer.

She moved away without a word.

For a while they sat there without speaking.

In front of her was an empty coffee cup, plus a small stainless-steel dish with the remains of a serving of white ice cream, now melted. She stirred it with the spoon. There was a deliberateness in the way she did so, a deeply feminine charm that made it seem incomprehensible that she'd killed two fit, able-bodied, young men.

Yet she had.

'I thought I'd go on the run. I've been living off the adrenalin for a week. High as a kite! The getaway was good, you'll give me that, no?'

'Planned to precision.'

'Not that much planning, to be honest.'

'But why? Why escape like that?'

'I don't know. To show you I could? To show you how random it all is, everything?'

'You really thought you'd become a fugitive from justice?'

'I haven't been thinking at all. Not really. But I have been remembering things. The man who killed Thomas? I can remember his barrister in court. He was wearing a little wig. The *terrible odds*, he said. *One in a million*. This *awful tragedy*. The sound of his words was like being punched in the face, again and again, until it no longer hurt, until you didn't care if it stopped or not.'

Joe recalled the report of the trial. The very thought of reading it made him feel sick. One-sixty-six? Depends who the *one* is... All night long he'd tried to convince himself that a kind of madness had compelled her to commit murder, something from the unfathomable depths of human despair. Yet over the course of the night he'd come to understand her actions more and more clearly.

'Why now?' he said. 'After all these years?'

She shifted in her seat, raised her eyebrows a little.

'Do it, he was saying. Make it right.'

'Who was saying it?'

'I didn't know. Not at the time. It wasn't until last night, when it was all over, that I realized. It was Thomas, his voice, telling me that something needed to be done. For everybody. Everybody else. Make it right.'

'Voices in your head, Chris. Save that thought, eh? For later?'

She seemed flattered.

'You don't have to do this.'

'I want to understand.'

'A rightness. The feeling that it was absolutely right.'

'Like maths?'

She nodded.

'Do you understand? As a parent, perhaps? It felt like the end point of everything, the culmination of all those years...'

As he listened, he tried to assess her state of mind. She was lucid, but her eyes were wandering, untethered, as if she was searching for something.

'...Damian, my ex-husband, he went to the States. Threw himself into his work. Did well. Very well. He's in private consulting now, lives in Cayman. Every six months or so he rings me, late at night for him, evening for me, so it's all right. He's always so drunk he can hardly speak. He asks how I'm doing, y'know. Then he cries. Says he's scared, that he wants to go out and kill Neil Barden. Or someone like him. One of the evil ones.'

She stopped. Pursed her lips, staring at him in that quizzical way she had, as though weighing up some trivial but intriguing conundrum.

'Do you want anything to eat?'

'No, I'm fine, thanks.'

'I'll just finish this,' she said, taking a spoonful of her melted ice cream, then another. 'The last chance I'll get!'

'For a while.'

'*For a while!*' She liked that. 'It took me a few years to work Damian out. He wasn't scared that he might kill someone. He was ashamed, because he knew that he'd *never* kill anyone. What he couldn't bear was the shame.'

'And you? How did you bear it, any of it?'

'By doing the best I could. New career, trying to help people, to make a difference.'

'So what changed?'

'Someone took me.'

'Took?'

'Took me out of the fiction I'd created. I felt myself being carried along that road, the road where Thomas died. Have you...?'

'Yes, I was there just now.'

'I was transported there. To that very spot. And I saw the truth. The truth of the world. It's simpler than you could imagine, Joe. Opposite angles. You remember trigonometry? When you show kids that, their eyes light up. It's so obvious! So perfect!'

He closed his eyes. Found no explanation here, no way of resolving this.

'No,' he said, placing his hand firmly onto the table. 'That only explains Craig Shaw. I can understand that. You were there. The strangeness of the moment. After all those years of suffering. But Jason Beverage?'

Her eyes widened.

'Joe, are you coaching me for a trial?'

'Please. I want to know.'

He sat there, hardly daring to look at her, and waited to hear if she had anything else to say. One long, long Romano pause.

'I was terrified, but compelled.'

'Excited?'

'No. But I knew I would go on. I'll go down as a calculated killer. That's fine.'

'You were driven by something out of your control. Voices in your head? Like I said, keep that thought.'

'Stop trying to save me, Joe! I'm not blaming this on anything. That would be cowardly.'

'And you're no coward, are you?'

'No, I'm not. I did what I did, and I stand by it. I'll take it to my grave and I won't be ashamed. I did what I thought was right. My boy is still dead, and I did what I did. He's still dead.'

She ate several spoonfuls of liquid ice cream, until there was almost none left. With each one she shuddered as she swallowed, but forced herself to smile.

'Can I ask you something?'

'Yes,' he said.

'When did you know?'

'That it was you? When you walked out of the library. The bike was yours. You saw the police there, so you ignored it.'

'You knew then?'

'I didn't want to believe it.'

She nodded.

Her movements were slow and deliberate now. The elegance

of her expression was gone, replaced by a pastiness, a sudden stiffness, a sense of discomfort. Reality had finally hit.

'Joe, I felt no compassion. I'm sorry, but I didn't. Please know that.'

He looked at her, and felt a loathing for the world, for his job and everything it represented.

'I understand,' he said.

But he didn't.

Then his bloody phone pinged.

'I know it's insensitive, but I have to check this.'

'Don't worry,' she began, her voice trailing off.

He thumbed through the messages that had accumulated since he'd last checked fifteen minutes ago. Messages from Rita, Gwyn Merchant and Andy. Nothing new to report.

When he looked up at her, there was the slightest droop in her torso. Her eyelids began to flutter, and she struggled to keep them fully open. She was still smiling, though.

'Don't worry,' she said again. 'Justice has been done!' Her eyes were full of fondness for him, but were not quite focusing now. 'Go on, officer, make the arrest. You should. You should do it now.'

He studied her face, tried to assess the bare malevolence that must surely be there. But he could find none. He wanted to touch her, to… to what? He had no idea. He wanted the world to be different. And for that he felt weak, pathetic.

'We can do that later.'

'You're the boss.' Her words were slightly out of kilter. 'It's when the smell goes, y'know? From his clothes. You keep them all, but in the end you lose the smell of him… It fades until you don't know whether you're just imagining it. You can't even remember what he smelled like, and it's... just...' She was struggling to keep looking at him, her eyes imploring, but fading. 'There's nothing left.'

Her head was moving, one way then the other.

He shifted in his seat. Saw something inside the dish. What was it? A light brown sludge in the bottom.

'Ambulance!' he shouted as he sprung up. 'Ambulance now!'

He grabbed her under the arms and pulled her to her feet, bawling in her ear.

'What was it, Chris?'

'Doesn't matter,' she said, suddenly frail and vulnerable.

'Tell me!'

He looked at the woman behind the counter, who was on already on the phone.

'Overdose,' he shouted. 'Tell 'em we don't know what she's taken.'

He sat Chris on the edge of the table and got his wallet out. Ramming the corner of it into her mouth, he managed to prise her teeth apart enough to shove it further in.

'No! No!' she was trying to say, her body squirming in his grasp, too weak to resist.

He stuck his fingers into her mouth, waggling the wallet to one side so he could get the width of his hand inside. She tried to bite down, her eyes filling with tears and terror. The wallet was slipping out.

He had one arm around her body to keep her upright. He forced his other hand further in, ignoring the pain, knowing that her teeth had broken the skin of his fingers. She was biting hard. If the wallet slipped out, she'd be down to the bone.

A low scream came from somewhere deep within her, but it was breathless and desperate, as her body flayed beneath her.

'What was it?' he shouted, knowing that she couldn't tell him, not now.

She was resourceful, determined. It would have been enough. Plenty enough to kill her.

He wouldn't allow that to happen.

When her body began to jerk, he knew he was there. Years ago, Andy had taught him how to make himself vomit, the *squaddie's nightcap*. Eight pints and a morning shift looming, it was the best way to finish off a session. Just tickle the back of the throat 'til it spasms, then again, forcing yourself to go on, wiggling your fingers in until your stomach is empty.

'Come on!' he said, feeling the sweat on his face as he fought to keep his hand deep in her mouth.

One little spurt of bile. He pressed on. Her body went into spasm. He was losing her, but his fingers went further in, feeling the muscles of her throat contract around them like a soft embrace.

Then it came. A massive convulsion. Immediately another. Huge, hawking coughs from the guts. Her body was losing the last of its resistance. He struggled to keep her stable as sweet-smelling vomit covered him.

By the time it was over, she was hardly conscious. Joe's face was streaming with sweat, and he was soaked in watery puke.

The woman in the café, not knowing else what to do, had gone outside to wait for the ambulance. The two uniforms from the patrol car saw her and came running.

'Grab her,' Joe shouted. 'Overdose. She's thrown it up. Keep her walking. Ambulance on its way?'

The woman nodded. She didn't need to. They could hear the siren in the distance.

'Right. Keep her awake. Keep her on her feet.'

He reached for his phone and dialled. His hands were shaking, and there was blood on his fingers, mixed with the slime of her vomit. He looked down at his Burton's two-piece. It shone in the morning light, as if a monster slug had crawled across it. And to be honest, he told himself, it didn't look much worse than normal.

'Rita? I've got her.'

EPILOGUE

47

He stood with his hands in his pockets and looked across the street. The old red brickwork was a rich, dusky brown, as though the house had been sitting on a beach for the last twelve decades and had now reached the point at which it couldn't get any more sunburnt. The lintels, though, were a little lighter than he'd expected. Someone had been having at 'em with a scrubbing brush, just like his grandma used to do.

To his right, out across the main road, was the Brick pub. He checked his watch: still plenty of time. So he stayed where he was, turning to look again at the terraced houses in front of him, craning his neck to admire their black slate roofs, neat and symmetrical after all the years. His grandparents used to boast that the builder had gone bankrupt after building these. He'd used high-quality materials, too high, put himself out of business.

The front door opened and a woman appeared. She had long auburn hair and pale skin. With the door ajar she hovered there, neither in nor out. She was looking at Joe, but standing at an angle, trying to make it appear that she wasn't. For a second he considered walking briskly away. Yet he paused. And as that second of indecision became two, then three, he realized how unnerving it would be for her if he were to leave now; that some weirdo had been staring at her home, only to disappear with no explanation.

He raised an arm as he crossed the road.

'Sorry!' he said, noting that the tiny patches of lawn in the front yard were well-maintained, and dotted with plastic toys.

He repeated his apologies as he got to the gate, speaking across the four or five yards that separated them, his voice raised against the niggling wind. Meanwhile, she regarded him with a strange combination of trepidation and amusement.

'I'm a police officer.'

The words worked some sort of magic. Her face relaxed, and the door swung open.

'DS Joe Romano,' he added, holding up his card as he walked up the narrow path for the first time in twenty-odd years.

She nodded, looking at the bandage on his right hand as he approached.

'I thought I recognized you.'

'Really?'

'Detective Romano. Your photo's been in the papers. Those murders? Congratulations, by the way. You got her.'

'Yes, we did. Thanks.'

'I assume you're here to see the house?'

She might have been thirty, with the casual air of a Pre-Raphaelite heroine, one wearing baggy jeans and a shirt of a wilfully dull green colour.

'The old deeds have your name on them,' she added, as they stepped through the door and found themselves in the front room. 'I mean, your family's name. Gustavo, wasn't it?'

'Yes. My granddad,' he said, shocked to find that he had

almost no recollection of how the place had been all those years ago, when he'd played there as a kid.

It now looked like something from a magazine, the home of an aging rock star or a venerable actor: book-lined walls, a mixture of old and new furniture, nothing even vaguely Scandinavian, framed paintings and a vintage hearth so utterly original that it took him a while to work out that, of course, it wasn't original at all.

'My grandparents saw him once.'

'Him?'

'Gustavo Romano. They saw him perform.'

'Jesus, that makes me feel old!'

'Charlie Cairoli, too.'

'I bet. Good old Charlie! My granddad became his agent, you know? Grandma hated him!'

'Cairoli or granddad?'

'Just Cairoli, I think!'

She smiled, nodded.

They stood for a while in silence.

'Everything seems so... different!' he said.

'Oh, it's mainly a lick of paint and some new curtains.'

The walls were a dark grey-green, the matte paint so sombre and unforgiving that it added a kind of gravitas, perfectly setting off the paintings, which were in various styles, but mainly modern.

She seemed to enjoy watching him as he spun very slowly around, taking it all in.

'My partner teaches at the university,' she said, indicating the bookshelves that had been built into the recesses on either side of the hearth, crammed full of books, until not an inch of the wall behind could be seen. 'There's mine as well. I mean, you just accumulate books, don't you? I hate to get rid of them. There's tons more upstairs.'

'Yes, it's hard to know where to put them all,' he lied.

His entire collection amounted to four removal boxes, none of which had been opened since they arrived back in the UK. They were still in the space under the stairs in his rented semi, the boxes neatly labelled: *uni, fiction, non-fiction, work/misc.* Several times he'd considered throwing them out, only to find himself unable to do it.

'So,' she said, 'is there anywhere in particular you'd like to see?'

'Actually, there are a couple of things, if it's not too much trouble. You know, it might seem strange, but I've always wondered whether the old mangle is still in the cellar.'

'Ha! Follow me!'

She led him into the kitchen. It was the same tiny space that he remembered, although completely refitted, so tightly crowded with new cupboards and shelving that there hardly seemed enough space to move, let alone cook. Yet there was a comforting kind of coldness to it, and a familiar smell of flour and butter, like there had been all those years ago. A deep yearning for the past hit him in the stomach, a desire to be transplanted there, back with his grandma, as if everything in the world might be resolved if only the verities of former times were within reach.

'Here it is,' she said, standing back to reveal an old sink, the kind that one might expect to find in the scullery of a far larger old house.

And above it was his grandma's old mangle. It had been taken off its frame and mounted on the wall, so that it could be swung out over the sink, then back against the wall when not in use.

'It was still in the cellar when we moved in. There's nothing much down there now. We can't afford to seal it against the damp, not yet. Something for the future. Here, have a go.'

She stood back and let him crank the mangle, ignoring the pain from his bandaged fingers. It was just the same, the wooden handle was still loose, and the mechanism still turned with a surprising stiffness. A little too hard for a young kid. His grandma had always had to stand behind and help him.

'It means we don't have to have the dryer on all the time.'

'Yes. Yes.'

'We did a bit of research into your family after we moved here. Quite a fascinating story.'

'Sicily to Leeds!'

'And Blackpool.'

'Yes, the summer seasons. But mainly here. Upstairs, I mean.'

'Here?'

So he told her the story. His granddad had been drinking at the White Swan in Leeds, down behind the City Varieties theatre. It was February the fourteenth, 1957, the day that Bill Haley arrived. The whole city came to a stop as people flocked into City Square to catch a glimpse of the American star emerging from the station. Gustavo couldn't get a tram home, and had to walk most of the way. Later that evening he switched on the television set in the front parlour, and Bill Haley's arrival was on the local news. 'I don't want to be Charlie Cairoli's sidekick forever!' he announced. 'I'm in the wrong game!' With no one able to persuade him otherwise, he penned a letter of resignation to Blackpool Tower Circus, where he still had a contract for the following season. With that, the Romano Theatrical Agency was born.

'And,' Joe said, hoping his story hadn't bored her, 'for the rest of his life, the agency was based right here, up in the attics.'

'Would you like to see them?'

The narrow stairs creaked a little, but they were carpeted now. It hardly seemed like the same house. The chilly bareness of the disused top floor had gone, replaced by the smell of someone else's children, like cheese rinds and warm flowers.

In the first of the little rooms there was Lego everywhere, and amid it, tucked under the sloping ceiling, a low-slung bed with a *Thomas the Tank Engine* duvet.

The aura of happiness was striking. He tried to imagine what it must be like for a young kid to come up here every night, to climb the steep, narrow path to their own little sanctuary at the very top of the house. His granddad had died before he really knew him, and after that his dad moved the agency to offices on Town Street, just up the road. So, he'd never known the attics as anything other than cold, bare rooms. His grandma refused to let them be used for anything else.

'We stopped trying to get them to tidy up,' she said. 'And to be honest, we prefer Lego to them being glued to screens all day.'

'I'm with you on that.'

He tried to imagine the plastic flowers in the hearth, the old floorboards, the cold, damp air. But he couldn't. It had gone. All of it

'You got kids?'

'One. He's at university. Funny thing, but I can never get him to use a screen. Not to contact me, at least!'

'Well, I'm sure he's very proud of you, I mean, about the Graphite Assassin and everything.'

He thought about it.

'She's in custody now. It was a sad case, in many ways. Did you follow it?'

'Yes. I think most people did.'

He wondered whether she'd be amused to know that Sam and his girlfriend were the main reason why the case had generated so much press interest. He decided no. Other people's stories? They're never quite the same; they don't mean that much. And now it was over. It was all over. Clowns, the agency, the Romanos.

It had been over for years.

'Thanks for showing me this,' he said. 'I should be going.'

Rita was waiting for him in the Brick, thumbs busy on her phone, an untouched pint of lager in front of her. She saw him come in, watched as he got himself a drink and came over to join her.

'The hero returns! Commendation in the offing, I hear.'

He grunted a reply and got his head down into his pint.

There'd been a reception at Elland Road earlier in the afternoon, just a plastic cup of white wine and a round of applause. But his self-sacrifice had been noted, and there was a new air of cautious reverence in the way his colleagues spoke to him. He'd ignored accusations of *socialising with a suspect* not once but twice, the second time whilst suspended. That took some guts. They were impressed by his commitment, but also wary of it, knowing that they would never have risked their careers like that, dating a suspected murderer.

'And you took all that flak!' she said. 'Budding romance with a witness... in the national papers, social media... kicked off the case... And to think it was all part of the investigation!'

'Extra mile, Rita. Extra mile.'

It had been more than that. She knew it, and so did he.

She let his words hang there between them, her lips pursed in a bad attempt to hide a smile.

'Those long, thoughtful pauses?' he said. 'They don't work with me. You know that, right?'

'You got her, Joe. That's the main thing,' she said, looking up to see Jane Shaw appear at the door. 'Whatever else you had in mind.'

'I...' he began.

But Rita was grinning, irritatingly self-righteous. It was too late. He'd never be able to explain.

'Hi, Jane,' he said, jumping to his feet. 'Good to see you.'

He introduced the two women, then dashed off to get Jane a drink.

Since the arrest of Saunders, he'd spent quite a bit of time with Jane Shaw. There'd been odds and ends to clear up with her statements, and she'd been grateful for someone to talk to. He'd even helped her to sort out the insurance claim on the car and to make a start on the paperwork to settle her son's estate, which wasn't going to be straightforward.

'Did you manage to finish all those forms?' he asked as he set Jane's drink down in front of her and retook his seat.

She nodded, but without much interest.

'Rita says they're giving you a medal.'

'A commendation. It's not even a certificate.'

'Not many folk would've done all that for Craig, not the way you did. I still don't know how to thank you.'

'I did my job. Like everybody else.'

'But you got all the stick. And *that*!'

He smiled, flexing his bandaged hand a little.

'You know, most of my family were in show business, one way or another. But I was the first one to make it onto the front pages!'

'Trending on Twitter!' Rita said, before launching herself into her pint.

'I wish Granddad could've seen it.'

His phone rang. He frowned as he looked at the number.

'Hello?... *Oui?... Ah, oui! Claudette, ça va?*'

He stood and moved away from the table, talking fast.

'He speaks French,' Rita explained, as they watched him move across the room, animated, nodding and waving his arm as he spoke. 'How's it going with victim support?'

'Y'know, what you'd expect.'

'It helps.'

'Does it? How would you know, love? Lost a son, have you?

'Brother.'

'Right... You wanna talk about it?'

Rita studied her pint for a moment.

'Yeah. Do you like curry?'

'As it goes. Know a place?'

'Yeah. It's not in friggin' Leeds, though.'

'What about him?'

They looked across the room. Joe was still deep in conversation.

'I think he's gonna be busy.'

Acknowledgements

For assorted advice and expert information, thanks to Dr Chris Burke, Naz Afrin Waseem, Adrian Tudor, Amalendu Misra, Nicolas Beord and Fernando Domènech. Also, I am indebted to the real Joe Romano for lending me his name, although in fact I didn't ask first. A huge thanks to everyone at HQ, particularly Dominic Wakeford for his enthusiasm and encouragement, to Jon Appleton for valued help and suggestions along the way, and above all to Cicely Aspinall for editing the book with such precision, style and commitment in very difficult circumstances. To my agent Nicola Barr equally large amounts of gratitude for her patience, her unflinching honesty, and for being a fabulous guiding hand. Finally, to Susana, Nico and Stef; as always, without you three there wouldn't be much point.

ONE PLACE. MANY STORIES

Bold, Innovative and
empowering publishing.

FOLLOW US ON:

@HQStories